"I want my wife...and I want Ken Slattery."

Gordon's voice pierced the still night.

"Let me go to him," Nora whispered to Ken. "I know how to handle him."

"No!" Ken retorted. Then, his thumbs hooked into the front of his belt, he stepped outside. "You got a problem, Gordon?" he asked in a quiet voice.

"You're the problem, Slattery. You're after my wife."

"She's not your wife anymore, Gordon," Ken said in the same quiet voice. "She hasn't been for two years."

"She made her vows to me forever, Slattery. She'll always be mine."

Nora held her breath. *Dear God, he's going to kill us all.*

Special thanks and acknowledgment to Bethany Campbell
for her contribution to the Crystal Creek series.

Special thanks and acknowledgment to Sutton Press Inc.
for its contribution to the concept for the Crystal Creek series.

Published October 1993

ISBN 0-373-82520-X

THE THUNDER ROLLS

The Thunder Rolls

Bethany Campbell

Harlequin Books

TORONTO • NEW YORK • LONDON
AMSTERDAM • PARIS • SYDNEY • HAMBURG
STOCKHOLM • ATHENS • TOKYO • MILAN
MADRID • WARSAW • BUDAPEST • AUCKLAND

Dear Reader,

"Harlequin's new special series called Crystal Creek wonderfully evokes the hot days and steamy nights of a small Texas community... impossible to put down until the last page is turned."

—*Romantic Times*

If this is your first visit to Crystal Creek, come meet the Joneses—and the McKinneys, the Randolphs and the Harrises... just a few of the folks who live, love and ranch in the small Texas Hill Country community of Crystal Creek. And if you're returning for more of the linked stories you love, you won't be disappointed with the romances some of your favorite authors still have in store for you!

You can never tell about Gordon Jones. He's been away from Crystal Creek for a while now, and though Dottie loves her son, she has to admit it's a relief he's not around. Suddenly, that elusive peace disappears in *The Thunder Rolls*, when Gordon's threats endanger the delicately blossoming romance between Nora, Dottie's beloved ex-daughter-in-law, and Ken Slattery, ranch foreman at the Double C. Not only that, but good ol' Bubba Gibson finds himself on the receiving end of violent phone messages that make no sense, and serve only to enflame his precarious footing with Billie Jo Dumont!

The bigger they are, the harder they fall, and Wayne Jackson, who is The Law in Crystal Creek, is clearly smitten with Jessica Reynolds, the up-and-coming country singer who frequently entertains at Zack's. In *Guitars, Cadillacs*, Wayne has his work cut out for him. His gut tells him Zack is up to something not quite legal, and he's determined to get to the heart of it. And while he's at it, he finds he's got to capture Jessie's heart, too, and make it his own. Watch for Cara West's intriguing contribution to the Crystal Creek series in November, wherever Harlequin books are sold.

C'mon down to Crystal Creek—home of sultry Texas drawls, smooth Texas charm and tall, sexy Texans!

Marsha Zinberg
Coordinator, Crystal Creek

A Note from the Author

Since I so enjoyed writing about the irrepressible and irreverent Cal McKinney in *Amarillo by Morning,* I thought that nobody would make a more compatible hero for my next book in the series than Cal's best friend, Ken Slattery.

Cal and Ken at first seem opposites, but beneath their many superficial differences, they are similar. They are independent, strong and generous of spirit. Ken, the foreman of the Double C, has much of the character that Gary Cooper used to convey in his Westerns: a loner, a man of few words, but of powerful ideals. He has a certain modest shyness, but when he's challenged, he can look danger square in the eye and not blink.

The heroine, Nora, too, had a strong claim on my emotions. Like Ken, she's pulled herself up by her bootstraps, and she's struggling to create a new and better life for herself. A divorcée with a seven-year-old son, she waits tables and is working hard to put herself through school. Her dream is to be a teacher—and never to be dependent on a man again.

Ken wants Nora, Nora doesn't want any man in her life other than her son, and Nora's ex-husband, Gordon, threatens to come between her and anyone who tries to stake a claim on her. The more strongly Ken and Nora are drawn together, the more violently Gordon reacts. His most frightening trait is his complete unpredictability.

I foresaw *The Thunder Rolls* as a special love story, one that demands all the hero's considerable integrity and all of the heroine's courage. But I also saw it as a book of mounting tension, for as Gordon's life slips more wildly out of control, day by day, confrontation with him becomes more inevitable—and more dangerous.

Bethany Campbell

Cast of Characters

AT THE DOUBLE C RANCH

John Travis (J.T.) McKinney	Rancher, owner of the Double C, his family's ranch. A man who knows his own mind.
Cynthia Page McKinney	J.T.'s wife. An ex-Bostonian bank executive learning to do things the Texas way.
Tyler McKinney	J.T.'s eldest son, a graduate of Rice University. Now he wants to grow grapes in his daddy's pasture.
Cal McKinney	J.T.'s second son, an irresistible and irrepressible rodeo cowboy.
Serena Davis	The boot maker who turned Cal's head.
Lynn McKinney	J.T.'s only daughter. She bucks the trend by raising Thoroughbreds in quarter horse country.
Hank Travis	J.T.'s ancient grandfather. Old Hank has seen and done it all.
Ruth Holden	Tyler's fiancée.
Ken Slattery	Ranch foreman.

AT THE CIRCLE T RANCH

Carolyn Randolph Townsend	J.T.'s sister-in-law and neighbor.
Beverly Townsend	Carolyn's daughter and a former Miss Texas.
Vernon Trent	Real-estate agent. A childhood friend of Carolyn's.

AT THE LONGHORN

Dottie Jones	Owner of the Longhorn Motel and Coffee Shop.
Gordon Jones	Dottie's son.
Nora Jones	Gordon's ex-wife.
Rory Jones	Nora and Gordon's son.
Bubba Gibson	A good ol' boy, owner of the Flying Horse ranch.

AT THE HOLE IN THE WALL

Scott Harris	He's exchanged his pinstripes for chaps and a Stetson, to create his dream, the Hole in the Wall Dude Ranch.
Valerie Drayton	Scott's new wife and partner in the ranch.
Jeff Harris	Scott's brother. Once the Hole in the Wall puts a few bucks in his pocket, he's heading for his true love: the Texas oil fields.

To my Dan—my Ken, my everything

CHAPTER ONE

"THE DEVIL'S BEATIN' his wife."

Nora Jones's fingers tightened so hard around the coffeepot's handle that her knuckles paled. But she kept on pouring, she kept on smiling, and she commanded her hand to stay steady.

Bubba Gibson glanced up at her and winked. "Thank you, sweetheart, thank you, pretty thing," he said. Then, because neither his wife nor his girlfriend was around, he reached to pat Nora's bottom.

Nora dodged him nimbly and moved on to the next table, but she could still hear the conversation.

Outside, the thunder rolled ominously.

"Yessir, the devil's beatin' his wife," Bubba said again.

"Say what?" Brock Munroe's voice was puzzled.

Bubba smirked. Munroe had recently come to Crystal Creek from Wyoming, a farmer trying to turn rancher. He didn't speak fluent Texan. Bubba did, and it apparently pleased him to make Munroe feel like an outsider.

I do believe Bubba's a little drunk, Nora thought, watching him out of the corner of her eye. *He must have had a fight with that trashy Billie Jo Dumont again. How can his poor wife stand it?*

Bubba ran a hand over his graying hair. He was fiftyish and portly, with a belly that loomed over his hand-tooled belt. The lower part of his face was sunbaked to a weathered brown, but the color stopped abruptly at his hat line. The upper half of his forehead was as pale as if someone had whitewashed a stripe across it.

He nodded toward the door and the outside world. "I mean," he said, "it's thunder out of a clear sky. We say it's the devil, a-beatin' on his wife. What you call it where you come from?"

By the set of Munroe's mouth, he was not amused. "We call it thunder out of a clear sky."

"Well, hell," Bubba almost crowed, "where's the poetry in that?"

Munroe still didn't smile. "Don't hold with poetry. Rather have truth. Or rain. One more dry week, and my windmills be pumpin' dust."

"Then, boy, you need yourself a windmill man," Bubba said. He put his hand familiarly on Ken Slattery's shoulder. Slattery was the third man at the table. "This here's the best windmill man in seventeen counties. Ain't you, Ken?"

Slattery, the foreman of the Double C Ranch, said nothing. He merely shrugged off Bubba's touch, as if the man's hand had been a fly.

Nora stole a furtive glance at the men. Munroe and Ken Slattery had been deep in talk about bull prepotency and high gainer calves—typical cattleman talk— when Bubba had joined them, uninvited. They both looked disgusted with him.

Bubba didn't seem to notice. He looked up to see if Nora was in sight. When he caught her eye, he winked at her again. "Say, boys, did I tell you my joke about the gal from Fort Worth?" he said to the other two men.

Nora gritted her teeth. The joke was nasty, and Bubba had told it in her hearing at least four times that week.

Thank God Dottie was in the kitchen, Nora thought. Dottie was the owner of the coffee shop. She'd said if she heard Bubba tell that awful joke once more, she would hit him spang in the face with a banana cream pie. Let him see how funny he thought *that* was.

Bubba reached the punch line of his joke and chortled. Brock Munroe glanced at Nora, then looked away, shifting in his chair in embarrassment. Although he was in his thirties, he struck Nora as somehow unseasoned, as if he were an awkward boy trapped in a man's body. She could have sworn he blushed.

In contrast, Ken Slattery, who was in his early forties, was anything but boyish. A long, lean man, he had blue eyes that could go as cold as polar ice. They were arctic cold now, as he trained them on Bubba. "That's no joke for mixed company," Slattery said. "There's a lady here."

Bubba laughed. "Hell, Nora, she's growed up. Had a baby, been through a D-I-V-O-R-C-E and ever'-thing." He held out his coffee cup to her. "Come here and fill me up again, buttercup. We're pals, ain't we?"

Nora nodded noncommittally and went to him, refilling his half-empty cup. She hoped another jolt of black coffee would sober him up. He should go home to his wife, not sit here in public making a fool of himself.

"How old are you now, sweet thing?" he asked her. "Twenty-one? Twenty-two?"

"Twenty-four," Nora said from between her teeth.

"Twenty-four," Bubba said, feigning amazement. "Then how old's that little baby of yours? Seems you had him when you wasn't no more'n a baby yourself."

"Seven. My son is seven."

Bubba smiled suggestively, and Nora's face grew hot. She had been a bride at sixteen, a mother at seventeen, a divorcée at twenty-three. Somebody like Bubba might think she was hungry for another man. He couldn't be more wrong.

"Now, don't a pretty little thing like you need—" he started to say.

"No," she said, cutting him off coldly. She turned her back and left with as much dignity as possible. She wanted no truck with Bubba Gibson. Or any other man for that matter.

"What's *she* in such a huff about?" Bubba demanded.

Nobody answered.

"Some people," he said pompously, "think too much of themselves—considerin'."

"Some people talk too much—considerin'," Ken Slattery said in his flat voice.

Nora ignored both men and went behind the counter, glad to have a barrier between herself and Bubba. She pushed back a strand of brown hair from her eyes and wished for the thousandth time that day that the shop's air-conditioning hadn't gone out.

Today was the third of July, and so hot outside that heat waves simmered up from the sidewalks, making the very air shimmer. Dottie had opened every window that could be opened, but no breeze moved through the screens. She'd turned on the ancient overhead fan, too, but it only stirred the air sluggishly. To make things worse, no repairman could come until the middle of next week.

Nora's light blue uniform was limp, and her hair, damp with sweat, was beginning to curl rebelliously. She was a small, slender woman who was pretty in a quiet way, but she had never in her life thought of herself as pretty. She had deepset eyes of dark blue and a full, vulnerable-looking mouth. Her jaw was delicately carved, and her brown hair, when not bound up in a twist for work, hung to her shoulders, wavy and streaked with blond.

It never occurred to her that Bubba might eye her because she was attractive. She supposed she looked interesting to him because he was mad at Billie Jo, had drunk too much and thought that any divorcée was desperate for a man.

Once more she smoothed back her unruly hair and sighed at the heat. Bubba was talking about the weather again. About that, at least, he was accurate.

The eerie rumble of thunder was interspersed with the popping of firecrackers, which would punctuate the long Fourth of July weekend. The crack of their explosions made the day seem even more charged.

Dottie came out of the kitchen, carrying a fresh lemon meringue pie. "I swear," she said, blowing a graying strand of hair from her forehead, "it's too hot to live." She set the pie in the glass display case.

She put one hand on her hip and examined Nora with a critical eye. Then she reached out and patted Nora's cheek. "Honey, I don't know why both of us are here. There's not enough business to sneeze at. Why don't you go home, take a nice cool bubble bath? Treat yourself good for a change."

Nora caught Dottie's hand and squeezed it. "You go home," she said fondly. "You're the one who never rests."

Dottie laughed. Her face was both wrinkled and freckled, so when she smiled, a complicated shifting of lines and spots took place, but her smile was lovely. Nora thought Dottie had the best smile in Crystal Creek.

"Restin' makes me restless," Dottie said, retying her apron strings more tightly. "I like to work." She cast a glance at the men at the table and lowered her voice. "What's Bubba up to? I swear he looks jug-bitten."

"He *is* jug-bitten," Nora said. "He and Billie Jo must have had a fight."

"Humph," Dottie said. "It's because it's a holiday. He should be home with his family. Sara's supposed to be coming home from Connecticut with the kids. He should be with them. Billie Jo's nose is out of joint, sure enough."

Dottie clucked in indignant sympathy for Bubba's wife, the long-suffering Mary. Shaking her head, she picked up a perfectly clean ashtray and began to polish it with the corner of her apron.

"Oh, my," breathed Nora, looking out the front window. A car had squealed to a stop outside the coffee shop. It was a sporty red convertible that needed washing. She recognized it as her ex-husband's car. Her ex-husband, Dottie's son, Gordon.

"What?" Dottie said, catching Nora's wave of nervousness. "What is it? Lord love a duck—is that Gordon? What's he doing? He was supposed to take Rory fishing—he *promised*."

Nora took a deep, shaky breath. Gordon had picked up Rory early this morning. What was he doing back so soon? She watched as he got out of the car and swung open the back door. He reached inside and jerked the little boy from the back seat.

"Rory." She breathed her son's name as if it were a prayer.

"Nora," said Bubba Gibson, "bring me a piece of that handsome lemon pie, would you? I do believe I'm wastin' away to nothin'."

The women ignored Bubba and focused instead on the tense interplay between father and son. "What *is* he doing?" Dottie demanded in a whisper. Gordon looked angry, and Rory stared up at his father with stormy sullenness.

Dottie's tone grew more worried. "Gordon's supposed to have that boy at Lake Travis—has Rory been crying? He looks like he's been *crying*—"

Gordon seized the boy by the hand and yanked him toward the coffee shop. Nora bit her lip. She could see another person sitting in Gordon's car—a woman. The woman had yellow hair and bare, tanned arms.

Nora looked away, not wanting to see more. She stepped to the door so that she was there for Rory as soon as his father pulled him inside.

Instinctively she reached for the boy. Gordon almost pushed him to her. Gordon was a short, powerful man with a bodybuilder's thick chest and bulging biceps, and he was every bit as strong as he looked. "Take him," Gordon snapped. "I've had it."

Dottie put her hands on her hips and scowled as Nora held out her hand to the boy. Rory went to her, but kept glaring at his father. Gordon glowered back, his dark eyes narrowed.

"Gordon Albert Jones," Dottie said in irritation, "just what do you think you're doing?"

"Mom, butt out," Gordon said. "This is between me and Nora. Nora, you let this kid be a spoiled brat. He thinks he's going to make my whole day living hell—but he ain't."

"Gordon," Dottie said, anger trembling in her voice, "you know I never interfere. It's not my style. But this time I can't help it—you're out of line. You're supposed to be fishing with that child—you promised. He looked forward to it all week."

Rory rebelliously tried to wriggle away from Nora, but she gripped his shoulders protectively. The boy looked like her, small and slim, with a sensitive mouth and wary blue eyes. He didn't look in the least like his father, and Nora knew that in the complicated way that Gordon's mind worked, he blamed both her and the boy for the lack of resemblance. It was as if he suspected they had plotted against him.

"Nora," Gordon said, shaking his finger at her, "you keep my mother out of this. I'm sick of that, too. It's one thing to come between me and my son. It's another to come between me and my own mother."

"Gordon, this is purely an embarrassment," Dottie said. "Rory, honey, come into the kitchen. Get yourself an ice-cold RC cola, darlin'. And Grandma made ginger cookies. I'm going to sit you down and give you the biggest one.''

Dottie stretched her freckled hand to Rory. He took it, but not before shooting his father a final resentful look.

"Wipe that look off your face," Gordon warned the child. "Or I'll wipe it off for you."

Dottie paled, drew herself up in indignation and bustled Rory into the kitchen.

"Leave him alone," Nora ordered Gordon. "Don't talk to him like that." She settled herself squarely between him and the door to the kitchen.

"I won't take him for the day," Gordon said angrily. "You keep him. You're his mother. It's your job. You want to palm him off on me, so you can spend your day makin' money—makin' money off *my* mother. While I'm bustin' my chops all week, drivin' that big rig. I got a right to my own life."

Nora hated scenes, but Gordon was forcing her into one. "Gordon," she said, clenching her fists, "you wanted to take Rory fishing. You *insisted.*"

"Don't sass me. I got a change of plans, is what."

"Yes." Nora nodded toward the car parked outside, the blond woman sitting in the passenger seat, examining her nails. "I see your plans."

"Nora, sweetheart." Bubba Gibson's voice was louder now. "Work out your problems in private, honey. I asked you for a piece of pie—about five minutes ago. Bring it, sweet thing. *I'll* treat you right."

"You stay out of this," Gordon ordered Bubba, whose face immediately flushed an angry red.

"I'll get your pie," Nora said. "Gordon, if you've got plans, get on with them. I've got work to do. Somebody in this family has to work regularly."

Even though what she said was true—Gordon never stayed in one place or at any job for long, and he had what Dottie euphemistically called "a little gambling problem"—Nora regretted the gibe as soon as she made it. Gordon's look grew truly dangerous.

Nora reached into the display case and cut a slice of pie. Her hand shook slightly, and she prayed that Gordon would just leave, go away.

Dottie stepped back into the room, alone, her face so pale now that it frightened Nora. She looked almost faint.

Gordon was too angry to notice Dottie's presence. "Nora, I'm *talkin'* to you," he almost snarled.

Nora ignored him. She moved toward the table of men, carrying the plate with Bubba's slice of pie.

"I said I'm talking to you," Gordon repeated. He reached for her, wrenching her arm so hard that she dropped the plate. With a crash it hit the floor, shattering. The pie lay, ruined, in the broken glass.

Bubba Gibson rose heavily to his feet. "Ain't nobody gonna treat a lady like that—and waste my pie on top of it. I'm gonna whip you, boy. I'm gonna whip you like you was a pint of cream."

Oh, no, Nora thought. Bubba looked fat and unsteady, and she could sense Gordon's rage starting to refocus on the older man. He took a step toward Bubba, his fist clenched, his biceps flexing.

Then suddenly Ken Slattery was on his feet, between the two men. He was leaner than either, but far taller, and his eyes were so cold they frosted the hot room. "Nobody's whipping anybody. Bubba, go home. Brock, get him out of here. He's one sorry piece of work today. Don't let him drive."

"Who you callin' a sorry piece of work?" Bubba demanded, turning on Ken. But now Brock Munroe was on his feet, too, and he looped his arm companionably around Bubba's shoulder. "Come on," he said. "Nora doesn't need more trouble. Nobody does. Come on. I'm taking you home."

"Don't want to go home," Bubba protested. "I want pie. He dropped my pie on the floor. I want pie, dammit. Then I want to pound that little sumbitch through the floor like he was a carpet tack. Then I want to kiss on Nora till she's a happy woman—knows what a real man's like."

"No, you don't," Brock countered, hustling him out the door. "A walk is what you want."

That left Ken Slattery staring down Gordon, who suddenly looked small, mean and foolish. Slattery was a rangy man, wide in the shoulders, and although his blond hair was graying at the temples, he was so incontestably powerful that Gordon, muscled as he was, stepped back.

"You said you got plans," Slattery said in his quiet way. "Get on with them."

Slattery nodded toward the door. Gordon's face turned redder, and Nora could see a vein throbbing in his neck. His mood was volatile, but not so volatile that he would take a chance on getting hurt himself.

"I got better things to waste my time on than you," Gordon said.

"Good," said Slattery. "Go waste it."

Gordon swore, but he turned toward the door.

"Gordon!" Dottie called after him, her voice so taut it shook.

Her son stopped briefly, turning his head to look at her, rebellion in his eyes.

Dottie stood behind the counter, her chin quivering. Her hand clutched the collar of her blue uniform and her eyes swam with unshed tears.

"Gordon," she said, "don't you ever come in here again if that's how you're going to act. I'm sick of it. I mean it. I—am—*ashamed*—of you."

Gordon thrust out his lower lip and turned his back on his mother. He swore again. He pushed the door so hard with his big shoulder that it crashed shut behind him.

"Ooh," breathed Dottie and fled back into the kitchen. Nora knew better than to follow her. Dottie willingly gave sympathy to anyone who needed it, but she hated receiving it.

Nora herself felt weak. She sank to her knees and tried to clean up the mess of broken plate and spilled pie.

"No," Ken Slattery said. He put his hands on her shoulders and drew her to her feet. "You don't get on your knees. Not because of him."

She stared up at him in surprise. He was such a quiet, contained man, and she'd known him forever, ever since she was a child and he was a young man. But she had a sudden frisson of awareness that perhaps until this moment she'd never known him at all.

He'd never touched her before, and she was startled by the hardness and sureness of his hands. She sucked in her breath and started to clench her own hands together in front of her, hiding them in her apron.

But Ken Slattery took her right hand and held it, looking down at it. A bruise darkened her wrist where Gordon had seized her, and his thumbnail had scratched her deeply, leaving an ugly crescent like a bloody new moon.

"It's nothing," she said, embarrassed. She drew her hand away and tried to hide it behind her. Her wrist throbbed, but she tried to pretend it didn't.

She started to bend down to clear away the jumble of ruined pie and broken glass, but once again he touched her, stopping her. "No," he repeated with calm finality.

She didn't understand, and could only watch in amazement as he knelt before her, gathering the broken pieces of the plate. He took a handful of napkins from the table and wiped up the pie.

Then he stood, setting the napkins on the counter. Nora watched him, unable to look away. *Why,* she thought, *he knelt at my feet like a knight.*

And, although he dressed like many a cowman in town—blue work shirt, faded low-slung jeans and scuffed boots, the image would not leave her mind. She'd never even noticed before today that he was handsome, in a lean, ascetic way.

Dottie came out of the kitchen, carrying a broom and dustpan. She seemed in control of herself again, probably more for Rory's sake than anything else. Rory followed, his expression worried. "Hey, Grandma," he said, tugging nervously at the edge of her apron. "It's okay. It's over."

Dottie set down the dustpan, seized his hand and patted it distractedly. "Oh, Nora," she said, shaking her head, "you've already cleaned it up—you shouldn't have."

Nora and Ken Slattery exchanged a look. Nora wanted to say that Ken, not she, had repaired the damage, but for some reason she couldn't find the words.

"I never in my life saw Gordon that bad in public," Dottie said. "Never. I—I'm speechless. Did he—did he hurt you?"

"Not at all," Nora lied, then stared at the floor, unwilling to meet Dottie's eyes. She loved Dottie deeply, far too deeply to let the older woman know the truth. And she wanted to shield Rory as well.

"Hey, Grandma," Rory said, squeezing Dottie's hand, his expression grave. "Everything's fine. I'd rather be here. I didn't want to go anyhow—not with *her* along—that yellow-haired lady. She didn't want to do anything he'd promised. She didn't even want me to have fireworks. Not even when it's nearly Fourth of July."

He threw an eloquent glance at the door through which his father had left. Nora had no idea who the woman with Gordon had been, but she felt no jealousy. She had few feelings of any kind left for Gordon.

"Thank you, Ken, for stepping in," Dottie said, wiping the back of her hand across her eyes. "I'm just sorry you had to see it."

She ran her hand across her face again and closed her eyes. "I think I'll close down for the rest of the day. It's too hot, and I'm too upset. It's the heat, that's what it is. The heat's made everybody crazy. Nora, you run on home. I'll stay here and clean up. I always feel better when I'm cleaning...you know that, honey. Take the car."

"No, ma'am," Ken Slattery said, and Nora blinked in surprise. "I'll take her home. It's too hot for you to be a-walkin'. You look a bit peaked, if you'll excuse me sayin' so."

He turned to Nora, fixing his pale blue gaze on her. "Can I run you and the boy on home, Miz Jones?"

Instinctively Nora reached for Rory's hand. Then her heart contracted with pain, and she wished she hadn't made the gesture. The boy frowned at the bruise and scratch on her hand, his face growing hard. Then he looked up at Ken Slattery with cool, businesslike interest. "Could you beat up my dad if you had to?" he asked.

Dottie gasped. "Rory!" But, she, too, had seen Nora's wrist more clearly, and her eyes filled with sadness.

Ken gave the boy a cool, level look. "Hittin' doesn't solve problems. It just makes more."

Rory said nothing, but gave a shrug that suggested he thought otherwise. He drew his hand from Nora's, clenched it into a small fist and smacked it against the palm of his other hand. Dottie turned abruptly and went back to the kitchen.

Nora wanted to follow her, to comfort her, but didn't know how. Dottie would only say, "No, no, nothing's wrong—just let me be." So Nora could only grab Rory's hand again, and this time with her other hand, she held him so tightly he began to fidget.

Ken looked after Dottie, then back at Nora. His unwavering gaze sent her a message that went shivering through her. *You're afraid, aren't you? But you don't need to be afraid of me.*

It was as if somehow Ken knew the terrible secrets that Nora kept from the world, secrets about her life with Gordon. But how could he know?

"He wouldn't let me have no firecrackers," Rory said. The matter of fireworks seemed particularly to rankle him. "They make his old *girlfriend* nervous."

"Any firecrackers," Nora corrected nervously. "He didn't let you have *any* firecrackers."

"Same old difference," Rory said.

"You mind what your mama says about talkin' right," Ken said. "She's smart about such things." He picked his white straw Stetson from the hat rack and settled it on his head. "Come on. You mind ridin' in a pickup truck?"

"A ranch pickup? Are you kidding?" Rory asked. Nora knew he had a small boy's love of machines, and he was, in truth, far too impressed with cowboys for her taste. She tried to discourage it. She wanted a better life for him than that of a common ranch hand.

But she smiled politely, and let Ken usher them out the door toward the white pickup truck parked by the curb. His name and the emblem of the Double C were emblazoned in gold on its side.

"How come you don't have a gun or a gun rack?" Rory asked, staring at the truck's empty back window.

"Don't much believe in guns," Ken said, and Rory frowned.

Nora heard the persistent sound of firecrackers coming from down the street. Rory looked toward the sound with yearning.

Ken touched his hand to the brim of his hat, a gesture of politeness. "If you wouldn't mind, ma'am," he said, "I could buy the boy some fireworks. And if he has a mind to fish, I could take you and him to a place I know. At the ranch. I've got some tackle in the back of the truck, along with all those windmill parts. I'd planned to wet a hook myself. I'd be obliged if you'd join me."

Nora looked up at him in fresh surprise. "Fishing?"

"Yes, ma'am." He didn't look at her. He seemed to be staring at something a long way off, and his jaw was set.

"Fishing?" Rory asked. "At the ranch? And big firecrackers? Not just those little old ladyfingers?"

"Yessir," Ken said, still staring into the distance. "If it'd please your mother."

"I—think I might like that," Nora said, this time surprising herself.

An afternoon with Ken Slattery? She had never imagined such a thing. She quickly told herself the only reason she was doing it was for Rory—because once more Gordon had failed him. But now excitement was back in her son's voice. He sounded happy, eager, enthusiastic, the way a child was supposed to sound.

Ken Slattery had always been a courteous man, if an aloof one, and it would be ungracious to refuse his kindness; his offer was made, after all, for Rory. She would accept for Rory's sake, but his sake alone.

BACK IN THE Longhorn Coffee Shop, Dottie had emerged from the kitchen. She locked the door and set the Closed sign in place in the window. Momentarily she paused to stare down the street. Nora and Rory were getting into the truck, and the tall figure of Ken Slattery stood on the curb, holding the door for them.

A fresh wave of foreboding swept over her. She loved Nora as much as if she were her own daughter. Nora loved her, too. Their relationship had stayed strong in spite of Nora and Gordon's divorce.

Dottie knew Gordon was a difficult man, insecure and volatile. He had been too immature to marry, and he had a dangerous temper. He grew steadily less dependable, and his gambling was so out of control that she didn't dare loan him money these days; it would only allow him to gamble more.

Today, before taking Rory, he'd drawn her aside and asked for three thousand dollars. Three thousand dollars! She'd steeled herself and told him *no*. His mood had soured immediately. He must have taken it out on Rory. Oh, why Rory, poor Rory?

Gordon saddened Dottie deeply. She could not understand why he was the way he was. What had she done wrong?

She sat at the counter, bent her head and ran her hands through her hair in despair. She still loved Gordon, because he was her son, but she refused to fool herself about him.

Gordon had never given his wife and child anything except grief. The only thing Dottie could do was try to offer them the love and support that Gordon had not. Above all else, Dottie wanted Nora and Rory to be happy.

But now, since the set-to with Bubba, a thought kept her mind whirling with painful dizziness. Today the Slattery man had made his move. What would Nora do? How would Rory feel? What would Gordon do when he found out? It was all too much for Dottie, and it was coming at her too fast.

Oh, for months Dottie had guessed what her daughter-in-law never suspected. Ken Slattery, in his quiet way, had been *watching* Nora.

He wanted Nora; Dottie was sure of it, and the knowledge tore her in two.

Nora should find a good man and remarry. Dottie would rest easier if she did. Sometimes Dottie felt weak and old beyond her years, and secretly she feared that she might be like her mother and die before her time. Who would look after Nora and Rory then?

But Nora never spoke of marrying again; if any man showed interest in her, she never returned it. Gordon had hurt her too badly.

And there was another fear, one neither she nor Nora ever dared say aloud. What would Gordon do if Nora took up with someone else? Gordon's self-esteem was so tender, his emotions so hair-trigger and unpredictable, that he might be jealous of another man, even though he didn't want her himself.

Any man who came after Nora would have to be braver than most. And more determined, too. Dottie bowed her head a little lower and prayed that Ken Slattery was.

Outside, out of the clear, hot sky, the thunder rumbled.

CHAPTER TWO

KEN SLATTERY HAD INSISTED, in his soft-spoken way, that Nora go home so she could change out of her uniform. She'd put on jeans, a plain blouse, a pair of old cowboy boots she'd owned since high school.

She didn't dress up in the least; she didn't redo her hair; she barely freshened her makeup. She didn't want to act as if this afternoon was anything more than it was. A man was being kind to her and her son for the boy's sake.

Ken had insisted, too, on stopping at Crystal Creek's biggest grocery store, the one with the new delicatessen, where he had a cooler filled with sandwiches and drinks.

Then, at the outskirts of town, he stopped again at one of the fireworks stands and bought Rory a big sack of firecrackers and cherry bombs, bottle rockets and sparklers.

He'd driven to a lovely little pond in one of the farthest-flung sections of the Double C. He'd fed them; he'd shot off fireworks with Rory until Nora's ears rang. Then Ken had shown the boy how to bait a hook and fish for the feisty little perch that overpopulated the pond.

At last Ken took a break from fishing and sat beside Nora on a big limestone slab beneath a mesquite tree. She stared at the still green pond with nostalgia. She'd played beside it herself, years ago.

"I'd all but forgotten this pond," she said softly.

He nodded, not looking at her. "I figured you had. It's been a long time. Since you lived here, I mean."

"It has," she agreed. Both she and Ken kept watching Rory and did not so much as glance at each other. She found herself shy with Ken Slattery.

"Thirteen years ago," he said. He plucked a spear of Johnson grass and chewed it meditatively. "That's when you first moved here."

She was amazed he would remember such a trivial fact. Although polite, he'd always stayed somewhat remote from most people. He had worked at the Double C ever since Nora came there as a little girl.

Briefly his eyes met hers, but he looked away immediately, and, confused, so did she.

She thought back to her childhood and how exotic he had seemed to her then: a lanky, hard-muscled young man with ice-blue eyes. He'd moved in a natural aura of control and isolation.

Nora's older brother, Herv, had gone to work for the Double C when she was nine. She'd come to live with him and his wife, Marlene, in one of the small clapboard houses that the McKinneys provided for their tenant ranch hands.

She was with Herv and Marlene because her mother had died. Her father, a cowhand like Herv, said Nora needed a settled home with a woman in it. His woman was gone, and without her he felt too restless and lonely to stay put.

Herv accepted the situation cheerlessly, and Marlene grumbled. But Nora had had no choice but to move in with them, and her father went drifting on his way. He promised to write and send for her when he settled down and found a suitable place. He never wrote, and he didn't send for her.

She missed her mother terribly, and she felt unwanted in Marlene's house and out of place.

She'd never seen a ranch so large and prosperous as the Double C. To Nora's childish eyes, the McKinneys' main house had seemed like a palace and the McKinneys themselves glamorous creatures out of a fairy tale.

Ken Slattery had not seemed an ordinary person either, like the other cowhands and their wives and children who lived in the tenant houses. No, Slattery was a mysterious link between the two worlds, her drab one and the impossibly privileged one of the McKinneys.

He seemed to have no family of his own. But she remembered he had been surprisingly kind to the rabble of children who came and went with the cowboys who worked the ranch. To their wives he was quietly courteous. With the hands themselves he was stern, but fair.

Nora was surprised he remembered her at all; she had always felt like a nobody. Her single distinction had been that she got excellent grades. Nora's high school English teacher, Miss McDuff, said that Nora should go on to the university and become an English teacher herself.

Nora had meant to do exactly that. She'd wanted, in fact, to be like Miss McDuff in every way. She would know all about books, she would be brisk and independent and confident, and she would wear pretty suits with high-heeled shoes that matched them—oh, how Nora had admired those matching suits and heels. She yearned to be a teacher and be *somebody*.

But then, in Nora's sixteenth year, her life had fallen apart so swiftly that it still stunned her to remember.

Her brother Herv said he was leaving the Double C. He was moving on to a different ranch in the fall—far away in Oklahoma. And, he said gruffly, he and Marlene wouldn't be taking her.

He and Marlene had taken care of Nora long enough, he said. They had never had a life of their own together, and it was time they did, and that they started raising their own children, not Pa's.

"You got to go back and live with Pa," Herv had said harshly, not looking at her. "He's married now. He's been livin' down 'round El Paso two years now. He's got him a widder woman with a couple girls of her own. Your place is with him. God knows I done my bit."

The shock dazed Nora. Her father was married? And hadn't even told her? No one had told her? He was settled? He hadn't sent for her? That could only mean one thing: he didn't want her. And neither did Herv and Marlene. Nobody wanted her.

She could stay with Herv and Marlene until fall, but that was it, Herv told her. If Pa wouldn't face up to his responsibilities, it was out of Herv's hands. He'd turn the problem over to a social worker.

It was at that dismal point that Gordon Jones entered Nora's life. Home from his second year in college in Texas A&M, he chased her and flattered her and wheedled her, wanting to make love to her. And Nora let him.

She had felt as if she were falling off the edge of the world, and she desperately needed someone to hold her tight, to keep her from disappearing into the black emptiness of space. There was no one except Gordon to hold her.

The result was that she found herself sixteen years old and pregnant.

She married Gordon Jones in a judge's chamber in the Claro County Courthouse. Both Marlene and Herv refused to attend. Only Dottie Jones stood by Nora, and in fact, it was Dottie who'd had to give her away.

If Dottie hadn't been so kind, Nora would have died of shame over what she had done. She bit her lip now, remembering. Even when Gordon failed her, Dottie was always there for her. She helped Nora reach for her dreams.

"You want to finish high school—you finish high school," Dottie had said, even though Gordon had sneered.

"You want to go to college? Do it," Dottie had said. "We'll find some way." Gordon had sulked and gone off to work in the oil fields as a roughneck. He'd done so poorly in college that he'd been glad to marry Nora for one reason: it gave him an excuse to quit.

Now Nora found herself back at the Double C again after all these years. She sat in the shade of the mesquite tree, tracing an aimless design on the limestone with a twig, remembering.

"You still goin' to college?" Ken asked, startling her so much she dropped the twig. It was as if he'd seen into her reveries and followed her train of thought.

She'd been taking all the courses she could in Austin during the school year. Of course she'd also been helping Dottie and taking care of Rory. It would be another year before she finished, but she was determined to do so. She had a straight B average, one of the few things in her life she supposed she could be proud of.

She nodded in reply, feeling shyer than before. She never spoke of her ambitions to anybody but Dottie and Rory.

"Still goin' to teach?" he asked, squinting at the horizon.

"Someday. I hope."

He smiled as if to himself. "I came on you one day, when you first moved here. You were standing alone down on the road where the school bus stops. You were saying sevenses."

She blinked in surprise. "What?"

"Sevenses. You were all alone saying 'em to yourself. 'Seven times five is thirty-five. Seven times six is forty-two. Seven times seven is forty-nine.' Like there wasn't anything in the world except you and numbers."

She laughed, half pleased, half embarrassed. "How could you remember that?"

"You were different. I always figured you'd amount to something."

She shrugged unhappily. "But I didn't. I'm just a waitress."

"Not for always. What'll you teach? English?"

She nodded and hugged her knees, watching Rory recast his line. "English. Like Miss McDuff."

He fell into silence, as if contemplating her words. She took a furtive glance at him. He had an austere face, but she was growing to like it. His cheekbones were high and finely cut, his nose strong, his jaw lean, and his eyes serious. The silver touching his sideburns made him look thoughtful, distinguished.

"Never had a good deal of book learning, myself," he said. "I suppose you read poems. And fancy stuff like that. Hard and fancy."

She picked up the twig and traced a crack in the limestone. "It's not so hard. Once you get used to it."

He nodded, his face serious. He still didn't look at her. "Can you say me something in poetry?"

"A poem?"

"Can you say me one?"

"I—I don't know what kind you'd like."

"Whatever. Just say something in poetry."

She almost smiled at the way he put it. "Something in poetry?"

"I never knew anybody that could do that. Except maybe Beverly Townsend. But she could never say it . . . real, like. She'd put on airs. Like she was in one of her beauty pageants."

Nora did smile. She had never imagined anyone thinking she could do anything as well as Beverly Townsend, who was both bright and beautiful. "All right—I'll try to say you a poem."

She touched a clover blossom growing out of the cracked limestone. She took a deep breath and began. "This is about a flower like this one. It's called 'The Rarest Bloom.'

In a sultan's tended garden—
A thousand flowers grew,
Fragrant, fresh, and fragile,
Bright with every hue.

But I passed by that tended garden—
I rode to rocky land—
No rich earth to feed blossoms,
Only stone and sand.

But one humble flower grew there,
Untended and alone—
And I loved it best, that flower
Its brave root struck through stone.''

He turned his gaze on her and stared thoughtfully at her for a long moment. "You say that nice," he said simply, and kept staring. "Mighty nice."

"Thank you," she said, feeling another frisson of embarrassment. Absently she tried to pick the clover blossom, but the whole small plant came with it, for its roots had made little purchase in the rock.

"Oh," she said in disappointment. It was impossible to cram the delicate roots back into the crevice; now the whole plant would die.

She set it down gently on the limestone. Ken picked it up. It was a small plant, stunted and unprepossessing. He put it into his shirt pocket. She couldn't understand why and so looked away from him again.

"You—you've been nice. Very kind." She gave a helpless shrug. "You didn't have to buy Rory all those fireworks. He loved them, though."

"He can make all the noise he wants out here," he said. "Won't bother anybody."

She smiled ruefully. Her eardrums still tingled from the din of the firecrackers and bottle rockets and cherry bombs. "I like it better quiet, like now. With only the wind and the birds."

"Me, too," he said, then fell silent. The breeze stirred the mesquite branches and the meadowlarks trilled sleepily in the late-afternoon sun.

Rory, tiring of fishing, had taken off his shoes and was stalking frogs at the pond's edge. He liked nothing better than being outdoors, studying nature. He could amuse himself so for hours.

Maybe, Nora thought with a swell of pride, he would grow up to be a scientist, an educated man. Not like her father or Herv. And not like Gordon, who had dropped out of college, and was now driving trucks in some fool scheme in Lubbock with his crazy friend, Charlie. She didn't like Charlie or trust him.

"You know," Ken said, pulling down his hat so it shaded his eyes, "excuse me for saying it, but I know that things—have been—tough for you in the past. I'm glad they're better."

"Things are fine. I've got everything I want. Thanks to Dottie. She's been a pillar of strength for me."

Ken took off his hat and ran his hand through his straight blond hair. He nodded solemnly and stared at the horizon. "You and Dottie are like those two women in the Bible. Ruth and Naomi. The daughter-in-law and mother-in-law. Close."

His words touched her more deeply than she would have thought possible. She remembered the Bible passage in which Ruth vowed to stay by her mother-in-law. It was beautiful:

Intreat me not to leave thee, or to return from
following after thee; for whither thou goest, I will
go; and where thou lodgest, I will lodge, thy
people shall be my people. . . .

"Yes." Nora nodded, feeling an odd knot throbbing in her throat. "We're close. I'd have never sur-
vived without her."

He looked at her again. "And you'd never let anything hurt her?"

"I'd try not to," she said with honesty. Once more
she was disconcerted by his gaze. It was a gaze that all
cattlemen developed eventually—steady, narrowed,
marked by lines at the corners of the eyes. And his eyes
were so blue, as blue as the shimmering July sky behind him.

"Do you ever tell her you're still scared of him?" he
asked. "Of Gordon?"

"Oh," she said, and looked away. She didn't want
to talk about Gordon, or even to think of him.

"I reckon I can guess what he's done in the past,"
Ken said slowly. "It's nothing you should be ashamed
of. He's the one who should be ashamed."

She raised her chin to hide how vulnerable she felt.

"You've never told anybody all of it, have you? Not
even Dottie."

"I don't talk about it."

"Maybe you should," he said quietly. "Talk."

She swallowed hard and remained silent. *I'll pretend I'm not here,* she thought. *I'll pretend this conversation isn't happening. I'll pretend it never happened at all.*

Ken spoke again, almost reluctantly. "I watched your face today," he said. "When his hand reached out, it was like you saw a snake strikin' at you. You shouldn't have to live like that."

Nora hugged her knees because they had started to shake, just a little. Unexpectedly tears stung her eyes. "I said I don't want to talk about it," she said. "Stop."

Ken bent closer. He put his hand under her chin and turned her face to his. "I'll stop. But I still see it in your eyes. I don't want to see it. I want it to go away."

She was surprised at how gently his big hand touched her face. "See what?" she asked, struggling to blink back the hot tears. "Want what to go away?"

"Fear," he said. "He's hurt you before this—and he's hurt you worse than this. Hasn't he?"

"Look," Nora said, trying to escape his touch and turn her face away again. "This isn't your problem. Leave me alone. I can handle it."

"Can you?" he asked, quiet challenge in his voice. "What about the boy? Can he handle it, too?"

She stared at him, more alarmed than before. "What do you mean?"

"Your son—he's scared of Gordon, too. He doesn't want to show it, but he is. He shouldn't have to be."

"Gordon would never hurt Rory," she said in horror. "No—he wouldn't. I'm the only one he's ever—" She couldn't finish the sentence.

A tear spilled onto her cheek. She scrubbed it away furiously, hating that he'd seen it. "With me it was different," she insisted. "I mean, I'm an adult. Rory's only a child. They're flesh and blood. He'd never hurt Rory."

"Why'd he hurt you?" Ken's thumb caressed the spot on her cheek where the tear had been. Then his fingers moved to a strand of her hair that had come loose. She made a gesture to tuck it back, but he blocked the movement and did it for her.

His touch filled her with confusion. Mixed with the confusion was a longing for something she didn't even want to name. *This isn't happening,* she told herself again, with greater desperation, greater vehemence. *None of this is happening.*

"Tell me the truth," he said. "Do you really think the two of you are safe from him?"

Nora's chest constricted, making it difficult to breathe. "I—I'm different," she insisted. "Gordon used to say mean things to me—you know—hurtful things. I got tired of it, so I talked back. He—wasn't used to that. So he started—" Again she couldn't finish. She looked down at her bruised wrist, marked with the deep scratch of Gordon's nail. "I fought back," she almost whispered. "That was why."

"You think that kid won't fight back one of these days?" Ken demanded, leaning closer. "That boy's got the same fight in him you do, the same spirit. You think if Gordon'd hit a woman, he wouldn't hit a child? He's a bully. I knew him when he was a kid, and he was a bully back then. Dottie doesn't think you'll take him back, does she? She's got too much sense for that."

Nora shrugged, wondering why he looked at her the way he did, and why his quiet touch was creating such unquiet within her.

"Of course not. She never—mentions such a thing—she knows—" She let the sentence die away, unable to finish it.

"You never see any other men."

"I don't need any other man," she said with conviction. "I've got Rory, I've got Dottie, I've got a job, I've got school to finish, and someday I'm going to be a teacher."

"I know," he said, stroking her cheek. "I know. You used to say that when you were no bigger than a minute. Once I stopped by to check on your brother, when he had some stove-in ribs. It was summer. All the other kids were outside playin', but you were inside. Readin'. I said, 'How come you're not playin'?' And you said, 'I'm readin' because I'm goin' to be a teacher someday.' Remember?"

"I remember," she said, upset by his strange intensity. "But how do *you* remember? And why?"

"I remember. Because that kid grew up to be you." He paused, staring at her lips. The line of his own mouth had gone rigid with control. "What would Dottie say if I came around to see you?"

"See me? No—I don't think so. Gordon would hear about it. He gets jealous. It's crazy, but he does."

"You're not married to him anymore. And I'm not askin' about him. I'm askin' about Dottie."

"I—don't know how she'd take it."

"What about you? What do you want?" He had both hands cupped around her face now, and she felt dizzied by the steadiness of his gaze. She feared he was going to kiss her. Although the idea gave her an unexpected rush of pleasure, she feared the thought of his lips touching hers.

With dismay she realized that she had never kissed any man except Gordon, and she'd learned to hate his touch with all her being. She was frightened of ever letting any man that close again.

"My God," he said softly. "You're shaking, Nora. Is it that terrible, what I'm thinking of doing? Because to tell the truth, I've been thinking about it for a long time. Even when I shouldn't have."

"Don't," she said tautly. "Rory will see. Please don't. And don't touch me like that. I—don't have feelings that way. I don't want to have them."

"I want to see you again. After today."

"No. I don't want to see—anybody."

"Ever?" His hands fell away from her face, slowly, as if he didn't want to move them.

"Never," she said, the knot in her throat throbbing again. "Never. I mean it. Besides," she added, "I don't want anything to do with cowboys. I've seen too many. Even Gordon tried it." She allowed herself a bitter smile. Gordon had failed as badly at ranch work as at everything else he did. They had spent six miserable months on a ragtag ranch in the Texas panhandle before Gordon got fired. "I've seen all I care to of that life, and I want better—for me *and* Rory."

Almost imperceptibly Ken winced, then his face grew more unreadable than usual. He gave one curt nod, as if what she'd said didn't surprise him.

Nora blinked back the tears, forcing her emotions under control. Her words had been cruel, they hadn't even been completely true, and she regretted them, but she didn't know how else to protect herself from this man.

"It's been—a nice afternoon," she said. "But I think you should take us home now."

A muscle twitched in his cheek. "And not come back?"

She nodded. "Yes. And not come back."

He stood, picking up his hat and slapping it against his thigh. He offered her his hand, but she refused, and scrambled up nervously, watching him as if he might make some sudden, dangerous move toward her.

He put his hat on, pulling it low across his eyes. He wanted to tell her that all men weren't like Gordon Jones or her father or her brother.

He had tried to tell her he worried about her. That he was concerned about all of them—her, Rory, Dottie, too. She hadn't wanted to listen. Ken, at best never a talkative man, was now completely at a loss for words.

If he were like his good friend Cal McKinney, he would know what to say. He would find the right words, clever ones, sweet ones, funny ones to make her smile—Ken would very much have liked to make her smile.

He looked down at her, then looked away. She was so pretty, and her soft mouth looked so defenseless that it made him want to swear and grab her and kiss her anyway.

But that would only frighten her. He permitted himself a small, stiff, self-mocking smile. She was young, educated and ambitious.

In contrast he suddenly felt old and plain. She was twenty-four, and he was almost forty-one. What could he offer her? She was right—he was only a cowboy. A glorified cowboy, maybe, but these days people said that his way of life was dying. Soon nobody would need a man like him anymore. Least of all a beautiful young woman. Was he crazy or what?

Now, as the July breeze stirred and the larks sang, he wanted to reach out to touch her hair once more, but he stopped himself. "I'll take you home," he said.

All the way home he talked to Rory about windmills. The back of the pickup was loaded with windmill parts.

Windmills, he understood.

Women, no.

CHAPTER THREE

NIGHT WAS FALLING, and Ken sat in the swing, his long legs crossed and his booted feet resting on the porch railing. He didn't need to have his hat on, but he always did when he was in a bad mood, and it was pulled down to the angle that said: Don't mess with me.

For years he had lived in the foreman's house on the McKinneys' Double C Ranch. It was a tall, white, Victorian clapboard that long ago had been the original ranch house. It had curli-cues on the porch and the eaves, which Ken thought silly. And it was too big for one person.

In summer the part of the house he liked best was the front porch, which looked over the rolling pasture between his place and the McKinneys'. The porch had a rosebush, almost a hundred years old, that climbed a trellis. Day and night, its red blooms kept the air fragrant.

The porch also had a wooden swing hanging from chains. Evenings he could sit, listening to the whippoorwills and thinking, just thinking. Lately, most of his thoughts had been of Nora. Damn, but he *was* a fool, he told himself.

Beside him on the floor sat a flowerpot he'd gotten from Lettie Mae, the cook at the main house. In the pot, which was far too large for it, drooped one small, withering clover plant, sure to be dead by morning. But he'd planted it, wanting it to live because Nora Jones had picked it and said a poem about it.

I am the worst diddly-damned fool whose miserable ass ever dragged through Texas, he thought, the corners of his mouth grim. *I should be out patching fence or getting drunk. Not potting goddamn plants.*

So deep was he in self-disgust, that he hardly noticed a horseman coming across the pasture, lickety-split.

But then he heard that half-crazy rebel yell that only one person in the world was demented enough to make, and he looked up just in time to see the horse clear the white rails of the fence.

Oh, Lord, he thought, his mood blacker than before, he'd forgotten. Cal McKinney and his fiancée, Serena Davis, were at the ranch home for the long weekend. They'd set up a boot shop over at the Hole in the Wall Dude Ranch, and Cal was also checking as often as possible on J.T., his daddy. J.T. had thrown the fear of God into them all by having had a heart attack.

Although Cal was the only man for whom Ken might admit anything resembling love—he loved him as he might have a rascally younger brother—he didn't want to see him tonight.

Cal was too damned cheerful. Cal took few things seriously, and if he knew about Ken and Nora Jones, he would turn it into an even more rotten joke than it was. Worse, Cal was in love. Being Cal, he was not merely successful in love, he was disgustingly successful. The kid was so happy that Ken wondered why his ass hadn't lit up and turned luminous, like a lightning bug's.

The horse pulled up and reared slightly as Cal slid from its back. He ground-reined it, grabbed a saddle-bag and started up the porch steps, grinning that grin that made even old ladies think young thoughts.

Suddenly, dramatically, Cal stopped and put up his hands as if shielding himself from some malevolent force. He pretended to stagger back down the stairs as if he'd been struck. "Jehoshaphat!" he cried, in mock alarm.

"What's wrong with you?" Ken asked sourly. He was in no mood to amuse or be amused.

"It's the hat." Cal crossed himself as if warding off a vampire. "You got on your *lethal* hat. Spare me. I'm too young and pretty to die."

"That's altogether debatable."

Cal grinned and stood, one hip cocked, with the saddlebag thrown over his shoulder. "I know the slant of that hat brim. Who you gonna kill? And why?"

"You, maybe," Ken said. "And why you runnin' that horse like that in the half-light? He'll step in a gopher hole and break his leg. Who taught you to ride, anyhow?"

"You did. For all intents and purposes. Oh, Daddy and Tyler can sit a horse, but neither is what you'd call your veritable centaur."

"Well, I never taught you that," Ken said with a disapproving nod at the fence Cal had jumped.

"Oh, shut up," Cal said amiably and climbed the stairs. "I brought two six-packs of Lone Star beer and an itch to sit on your porch and look at the stars. When I itch, I scratch. Move and let me sit."

Ken didn't move. "If you brought any beer, you've gone and foamed it up till we can't open it for an hour. It'll foosh all over my porch."

"Then we'll start with yours," Cal said, throwing the saddlebag to the swing. Uninvited, he went inside the house, whistling as he made the door bang.

Ken swore, but moved to make room for the younger man. He called over his shoulder, "Why aren't you with your ladylove? Did she get wise to you?" He put as much sarcasm as possible into the words.

He heard his refrigerator door open, he heard the clink of bottles, he heard Cal say, "Don't you ever clean this thing? I bet there's bacteria in here science ain't even dreamed of yet."

He reappeared, butting the screen door open with his lean hip, and came to the swing. He handed Ken a beer and dropped down beside him. He gazed up at the stars and swore softly in pleased wonder. "No stars prettier anywhere in the world than from this porch. Damn."

Ken didn't bother to look. The stars might as well have been cowpies for all he cared. "I said where's your ladylove? Didn't she come?"

"Course she did." Cal took a drink and sighed with pleasure. "She couldn't be away from me three whole days. She'd wither up like a raisin."

Ken snorted in disdain. "Then where is she? Off witherin'?"

Cal made a grimace. "Ain't you heard? Miss Beverly Townsend is givin' a *weddin' shower*. Ladies only. Tyler'll be along shortly. Ruth's over there, too. We thought we'd come over and bay at the moon with you.''

Inwardly Ken cursed his sorry luck. One McKinney son in love was bad enough. Two would be insufferable.

First, Tyler had found a pretty little California gal to help him in his sacrilegious scheme to turn good Texas pastureland into vineyards. Then Cal, as good a natural cowboy as had ever lived, finally gave up rodeoing—but not to come home and ranch. He'd found a long-legged beauty in Wolverton and was taking up *boot making*. The world was going to hell in a hand basket, sure enough, with neither son eager to take over the ranch when the time came. Ken supposed he would be running this damn ranch alone forever or until Tyler turned it into one giant grape arbor, whichever came first.

Cal took another long swig of beer. ''I'll tell you, man, it's a good life.''

Ken didn't think so. ''How's your daddy tonight? Shouldn't you be at his side?''

''Why, hell,'' Cal said, a wicked glint in his eye, ''you see him more than I do. He's fine. The only thing he's worried about is you. He said today's the first day you took off since he was sick. He's worried that you work too hard. So what'd you do today? See anybody? Where'd you go?''

Ken sidestepped the question. ''Somebody around here's got to work. We can't all be off makin' fancy boots and growin' grapes and pitchin' woo.''

Cal stared up at the stars in satisfaction. He smiled as if at a private joke. His drawl grew slow and taunting. ''Now be careful what you say—I heard you pitched a little woo yourself this afternoon. That true?''

Oh, Christ, no, Ken thought with a sudden wave of bone-weariness. He pulled his hat a notch lower over his eyes and glowered at the gathering dusk.

Cal went unexpectedly quiet. "I'll be damned," he said at last, his voice serious. "It's true. Ain't it?''

Ken drained the last of his beer with one long, ferocious pull. "What the hell are you talkin' about? Crack me one of those Lone Stars. I don't care if it does foosh up like a geyser.''

Cal let another uncomfortable minute of silence spin out. "It's true. You took Nora Jones on a picnic today.''

"I'll get my own damn beer." Ken fumbled in the saddlebag and extracted a cold can.

"Give me one, too," Cal said, still surprisingly serious. He started to set down his empty long-necked bottle in the flowerpot that held the dying clover plant.

"Watch it, dammit!" Ken snapped.

"Watch what?''

"You're settin' your beer bottle smack on my plant, is what. Watch it.''

"What plant? Lettie Mae said you were up at the house askin' for a flowerpot. And—these are her very words—'He was mighty mysterious,' she said. *This* is what you planted? That's nothin' but a dead old clover flower.''

"It's not dead. Keep your hands off it.''

"I'm not hurtin' it. Jesus, what's so special about a dumb old clover? There's a million of 'em out in the pasture.''

"It's special, is all. Leave it alone, that's all." Ken opened his can of beer. It foamed up and spilled onto the floor of the porch. This gave him an excuse to recite all the curses he knew. He did so with dark passion.

Cal sat in the shadows, watching him with the same wonder he'd bestowed earlier on the stars. "I'll be a patch on the devil's long johns. This flower's got something to do with Nora Jones—don't it?"

Ken jerked his hat down until the brim almost touched his nose. "Shut up."

"You took out Nora Jones, you made a shrine to a weed, and your hat just got three degrees more lethal."

"I would not do anything as stupid as plant a flower for some woman. It's—an experiment. In horticulture."

Cal didn't laugh. "No."

"'Tis."

"'Tain't," Cal said with certainty. "I know you."

"So?" Ken demanded.

Cal still didn't laugh. His hazel eyes narrowed, growing almost solemn. "I mean I know you. You don't fool me. How serious is this?"

No answer came. Cal looked worried. "I see. *That* serious. God, Slats, of all the women in town—why Nora Jones?"

Ken threw his hat on the porch floor and stood up. "Get the hell out of here," he ordered. "What do you mean—'Why Nora Jones?' So she got in trouble when she was a kid. So what? Like you were never in trouble? I saved your sorry ass many a time—get outta here before I throw you out."

Cal didn't get up. He folded his arms, settled his feet more comfortably on the rail and looked at Ken, one eyebrow cocked. "Oh, settle down. You're like a bear with a sore head. I didn't mean it like that. I mean, 'Why Nora Jones?' because she isn't exactly out there tryin' to catch a man with a net. She's been hurt. You can see it in her eyes. You don't exactly go for the easy pickin's, do you?"

Ken stared down at the younger man, searching his face for any sign of satire. Then he sighed and leaned against a porch post. He stared out at the night and swore, briefly but eloquently. "I'm sorry."

Cal shrugged and reached down for Ken's hat. He dropped it carelessly on his own head, the brim set back at a cocky angle. "Well, hell," he said with a shrug of admission, "I mean, it took even *me* a little while to get through to Serena. Different problem, but same situation—you know, a man-shy woman. I understand where you're comin' from. That woman was bound to hold out against me."

"Ha," Ken said. "Hold out against you? How long? A half hour?"

Cal's self-mocking smile disappeared, and when Ken glanced at him, he saw pain cross the younger man's face. Cal had never talked to Ken about courting Serena. He'd kept the story to himself, more tight-lipped than Ken had ever known him to be.

Cal shook his head moodily. "I thought she was going to hold out against me a lifetime."

"Ha," Ken gave a laugh of disbelief and stared off into the moonlight again. "I'd like to have seen that."

"No, you wouldn't. I was shameless. I stood on her doorstep and howled like a hound. I got down on my knees and begged like a bum. I stalked her in Wolverton, and she wouldn't have me. I stalked her in Amarillo, and she wouldn't have me still. I pinned my heart to my sleeve with a bowie knife. I was ready to lie down and let her walk on me just to feel her heel prints."

"You're breakin' my heart," Ken said.

"Yeah? Well, she nearly broke mine, which I'm sure you'll find laughable, too."

Ken narrowed his eyes and stared off in the direction of the faraway pond. He remembered the dark blue of Nora's eyes, remembered her soft mouth uttering the words of the poem she'd said for him.

"I don't find it laughable," he said. And he didn't. The idea of Cal desperate for a woman's love was a foreign one to him. Maybe it was a good sign. Or maybe it wasn't. He didn't know. He purely didn't.

"The point is," Cal said, arching a dark brow, "I did not stand around on my porch mopin' and moonin'. Or snap like a dog at my best buddy. I went out and did something about the situation."

"Right," Ken said, folding his arms. "You stood on *her* porch and howled like a hound. You begged like a bum. You stalked her here, and you stalked her there, with your heart on your sleeve. In short, you made a damn fool of yourself."

"So?"

Ken shook his head derisively, but it was himself whom he found bitterly funny. "I already done that. Made a damned fool of myself. She won't have me. She's says she's got no feelin's like that, and that she doesn't want any *cowboy*. She couldn't have made that last point clearer if she poked me in the eye with a

sharp stick. Besides, I'm old enough to be her father—almost.''

"Oh, hell," Cal said with true scorn. "You talk like
you're Grandpa Hank. How much older are you'n
her? Eleven, twelve years?"

"Almost seventeen. And of late, on a winter morning when I get on a horse, I creak more than the saddle. My eyes have got crow's-feet on 'em, and my
hair's going gray."

Ken should have known his luck couldn't last forever. Cal looked at him blankly, then roared with
laughter. He laughed so hard he spilled beer on himself, then laughed even more wildly.

Ken looked away in disgust. "Oh, shut up, you
fool."

"I can't," said Cal, and kept laughing. "Did you
hear what you just said? Your eyes have crow's-
feet—"

"Well, that's what they call them, ain't it?"

"My God, you always said *I* was the vain one. I
never thought you'd be starin' in a mirror worryin'
about crow's feet. I'll phone up Mary Kay Cosmetics
and order you a hundred gallons of wrinkle goo—have
Mary Kay deliver it personal, in her pink Cadillac."

"You ought to go work on a jackass farm—give
brayin' lessons."

"I—can't—help—it," Cal said, holding his side,
"Oh—my broke ribs—ouch—lordamercy. You've
killed me for sure."

Ken, still leaning against the post, swore and turned
away to glower into the night again.

At last Cal's laughter subsided to gasps, and the
gasps, too, dwindled away. He got to his feet and came

to Ken's side. He clapped his hand on the other man's shoulder.

"Sorry," he said, and Ken knew the kid meant it. Cal was irreverent, but he was the most generous man Ken knew, and he didn't have a mean bone in his body.

"Look, hoss," Cal said. "You ain't old, and you ain't so bad lookin'. I heard women say you were right good-looking."

"The hell you say."

"I have. Truth to tell."

"Name one."

Cal thought a moment. "Beverly Townsend. Miss Texas herself."

"*What?*"

Cal nodded. "Swear to it. Beverly Townsend said you were good-lookin'. She said you looked like—like a young Max Von Sydow."

Ken shot Cal a brief, contemptuous glance. "Who in hell is Max Von Sydow?"

"He's a Swedish movie star, is what. Tall fella. Blond. Distinguished lookin'. Nothin' wrong with lookin' like him, that's sure." Cal gave his shoulder an encouraging shake. "Nope. Your problem ain't your looks, and it ain't your age. Your problem is a bad case of the shouldas."

"The whats?"

"The shouldas," Cal repeated confidently. He gave Ken's back a congenial smack and sat down on the swing again, setting his feet on the porch rail. "You're thinkin', 'I shoulda said this. I shoulda said that. I shoulda done this. I shoulda done that.' That's your problem."

Ken said nothing because Cal was too damn right. He should have moved slower with Nora. He should not have touched her. He should have kept things just friendlylike.

Cal took a sip of Lone Star and nodded to himself. "Yep. A terrible case of shouldas. Only one cure for 'em."

"And what's that, Einstein?"

"Simple," Cal said with a guileless smile. "What do you do if a horse throws you?"

"Get back on. Any fool knows that."

"Well," said Cal, "wooin' a woman is like ridin' a horse. If you're dealin' with a creature of mettle and spirit, you're liable to get throwed, especially at first."

"Well, she threw me good today," Ken muttered.

"But—see?—you don't quit. You keep on tryin'."

Ken stared gloomily into the night. "I keep on tryin'."

"Faint heart never won fair lady."

Faint heart never won fair lady. It sounded like more poetry, that was all. But poetry was what she loved.

He didn't know. He'd seen such fear in her eyes that maybe it would be kinder just to let her alone. After all, he was used to being alone. It wasn't so bad. It didn't kill you.

He looked up at the sky, as he'd done often lately, because, despite the earlier spring storms, rain was needed so badly. Not a cloud was in sight. But on the horizon, the lightning flickered and flared, and in the distance the thunder rumbled.

Cal could be crazy as a bedbug, but for some reason the kid's words haunted Ken:

Faint heart never won fair lady.

He stared up at the sliver of the moon and squared his lean jaw.

"Right," he said under his breath to himself and the thin moon. "Right."

"THAT THUNDER," Dottie said in exasperation. "It keeps talkin', but it never delivers. Lawsy, I wish it would rain."

Dottie and Nora sat in the old, mismatched wrought-iron rockers on the back porch, sipping dandelion wine and looking up at the star-spangled sky. It was their favorite way to spend a summer night.

Tonight the song of the crickets was interrupted by the distant rat-a-tat-tat of firecrackers. A skyrocket soared into the darkness, then exploded in a cascade of colored sparks. It was immediately followed by more.

"Oh, look," Dottie said in awe, as a whole barrage of rockets began bursting and lighting up the sky. "Isn't that the prettiest thing? It's too bad Rory fell asleep so early. That boy does dote on his fireworks."

Nora watched the rockets rain down their colored showers: red, green, gold, azure blue. "I wonder if the northern lights are like that," she mused softly.

But she was not really thinking of the northern lights. She kept thinking of Ken Slattery.

She recalled the intensity in his eyes when he looked at her, and the unexpectedness of his touch. The recollection flooded her with strange feelings that were both frightening and pleasant.

Against the dark, a rocket bloomed into showers of fire that looked hot and cold at the same time. *Yes,* she thought, *that's what he made me feel like. Like that.*

She shivered slightly, in spite of the heat. She slapped at a mosquito that wasn't there, just to bring herself down to earth.

No, she told herself, she mustn't think about Slattery, and she wouldn't. Besides, she'd sensed that the outing with Slattery had upset Dottie in some way, and Nora loved Dottie too much to add to her burdens.

Perversely, just as Nora made the resolution not to think of Ken, Dottie brought up his name. "You never said anything about being out with Ken Slattery today," she said slowly and carefully. "Did you enjoy it?"

Nora shrugged noncommittally. "I thought Rory talked enough about everything for the two of us. Yes, he seemed to have a good time."

There was an awkward moment of silence between them.

"I asked if *you* enjoyed it," Dottie said at last.

Nora stared up at the sky, looking for a rocket's colorful blaze to distract her. None came, so she stared at the darkness. "It was all right."

"Do you think you'll—see him again?"

Nora tilted her glass so that the moonlight played on the surface of her wine. "No," she said. "I won't."

"Why not?" Dottie persisted, an odd note in her voice. "I thought he seemed, well, interested in you. He's a nice man, Ken Slattery. A good man, steady. The McKinneys have depended on him for years."

"I don't want a man. I've had one." Nora instantly regretted her words. Dottie had suffered enough over Gordon. Nora didn't need to make her suffer more.

Dottie reached over and took Nora's free hand in hers. She squeezed it. "They're not all like Gordon, honey."

Nora gave Dottie's hand a squeeze in return. "I didn't mean—" she paused, unable to finish, unsure of what she did or didn't mean.

Dottie released her hand and gazed at the treetops. "You never talk about men. You never seem to notice them. If it's because you think *I'd* be hurt or *I* wouldn't like it, well, that's just not so. More than anything, I'd like to see you and Rory settled and happy."

A deep-reaching coldness crept over Nora, as if someone had encased her heart in ice. "Rory and I are fine. We don't need a man."

"Nora—"

"Dottie, I don't want to get married again. Honestly. Being married doesn't automatically make you happy. Look at poor Mary Gibson—sitting home, trying to seem dignified while Bubba runs all over with Billie Jo Dumont."

"Well, yes, but all men aren't—"

"Dottie," Nora interrupted, "tell the truth. Were *you* all that happy married?"

Dottie stiffened slightly. Although she knew most of the town's secrets, few people knew hers. Her husband, Duff, had died the year before Nora and Gordon married. Dottie seldom spoke of him.

"I—" she began, the slightest quaver in her voice. "I was not altogether happy. No. Duff was not a warm person. He was—very stern. I think part of Gordon's problem was that he could never live up to his daddy's expectations. I know I couldn't. Maybe nobody could.''

Nora nodded, almost to herself. She knew Gordon was driven by some inner demon.

"Have *you* ever wanted to remarry?" Nora asked.

Dottie sighed. "No. I'm happy. I suppose in a way I'm married to the coffee shop. God knows it's given me more good company than Duff ever did.''

"That's how it is for me, too. The only marriage I want is to my job.''

"But, honey—''

"No *buts,* Dottie. You and I are the same sort. Neither of us needs a man to feel complete. So don't worry about it. I don't want Ken Slattery. I don't want anybody.''

She repeated the words in her mind, as if they could protect her: *I don't want Ken Slattery. I don't want anybody.*

IN A MOTEL ROOM halfway between Crystal Creek and Lubbock, Gordon Jones sat, slightly drunk and very angry, even though he'd taken a pill to calm himself.

He had a Smith & Wesson Model 10 revolver that he'd been taking apart and putting back together for more than an hour. Gordon always carried a gun, for the world was a hostile place.

Once more he removed the front sideplate screw, setting it in an ashtray to keep it separate from other screws. The blonde he had picked up this morning slept on the other side of the bed, curled into a selfish knot, snoring softly.

She'd demanded safe sex and been so picky and critical of everything, he'd hardly enjoyed himself. He'd also found out she was six years older than he was and that her bra was padded. She was as flat-chested as a boy.

With resentment, he remembered Nora, whose body was young and soft and rounded. But even with Nora, he'd never had as much fun as he should. Nora never responded to him. He should have *made* her like it better.

He should have been tougher. At the time, it had been a relief to let her divorce him. But what was he supposed to do about sex? Now look at him—sleepless in a cheap motel with a skinny old blonde who snored.

He rubbed the cylinder with his T-shirt until the metal gleamed. Sometimes he was convinced that Nora was the cause of all his troubles, all his failures. Other times, like tonight, cause and effect became confused, as tangled as a nest of snakes.

Tonight he resented everyone—especially his mother. Today Dottie had actually rebuked him—her own son. Dottie had time to listen to the troubles of the whole town, but she had no sympathy for him.

What was more, she still wouldn't give him any money. That was why he'd gone to pick up Rory in the first place, to curry his mother's favor. His effort was wasted.

Stubbornly, she'd said he had to grow up, solve his own problems. She was mean, she was cold, she was unnatural, she was selfish.

He couldn't tell her the truth; he was too proud. He was, after all, a man. But he was going to get *hurt* if he didn't get the money. And it was *her* fault. What had turned her against him? Was someone in Crystal Creek working against him lately? Was it Bubba Gibson?

Gordon's jaw tightened. He slid the cylinder back in place and held the gun in a two-handed police grip, aiming it at the door and squinting down the barrel.

He imagined he had Bubba Gibson in his sights. The fat old fool had insulted him, said he wasn't a man.

"Pow," Gordon whispered to his mental image of Bubba, pretending to squeeze the trigger. "Pow." In his mind he blew Bubba away, as if the old man were nothing more than a jackrabbit. The memory of Bubba gnawed at Gordon. He hated the old bastard. He hated him from years ago, when Bubba had wanted to throw Gordon into jail for a harmless, boyish prank.

Gordon and a friend had tried to rustle a couple of calves off Bubba's place to sell. They got caught, and Bubba had called Gordon every dirty name in the book and had wanted to press charges.

Bubba would have saddled him with a criminal record, the vindictive old goat. Bubba's wimpy wife finally talked him out of it, saying, "Think of Dottie."

Grudgingly, Bubba had spared Gordon, but Gordon had hated Bubba ever since, for even thinking of prosecuting him.

Bubba'd better stay away from Nora if the old goat knew what was good for him. Gordon didn't particularly want Nora, but he didn't want anyone else to have her, either. If Bubba crossed Gordon again, he'd be sorry. *Anybody* who betrayed Gordon would be sorry.

The set of his jaw grew grimmer when he thought of Brock Munroe and Ken Slattery—Bubba's companions that afternoon. They'd conspired with Bubba to mortify Gordon, to bully and taunt him in front of his own family. Three against one—that was how cowardly they were.

"Pow," Gordon repeated softly, looking down his gun sight once more at the phantom of Bubba. He pretended to flick the safety off the gun, to squeeze its hair trigger.

"Pow. Pow. *Pow*."

In Gordon's mind, Bubba died again and yet again.

CHAPTER FOUR

NORA WIPED her forearm across her brow. The day wasn't quite as hot as the day before, but she'd been on the run since the coffee shop opened.

Dottie had brought two more fans from home, which kept the room from sweltering, but Nora missed the air-conditioning.

Not a cloud was in the sky today, and no rain was forecast. Would there ever be any relief? she wondered, then told herself sternly to stop feeling sorry for herself. There was work to be done.

Half of Crystal Creek seemed to crowd the coffee shop this morning. Bubba Gibson, looking decidedly hangdog, sat in a booth with his wife, Mary, their daughter and her two children. Mary acted as if nothing in the least was wrong with her life, and if she knew of Bubba's foolishness yesterday, she gave no indication.

"I don't know how she does it," Dottie had whispered in Nora's ear when Mary walked in, arm in arm with Bubba. "If Bubba was my husband, I'd whomp him upside the head with the frying pan. He'd see stars for a week."

Nora had clucked her tongue in sympathy for Mary, but she'd been glad to let Dottie wait on the Gibsons.

The memory of Bubba's would-be amorousness still rankled.

When Dr. Nate Purdy and his wife, Rose, came into the coffee shop, Nora looked around a bit frantically. There was only one more free table.

She set up the table with napkins and silverware, and chatted with the Purdys as she took their order. Then Brock Munroe came in alone, and sat on the last stool at the counter. She took his order, too, turned them over to the cook, then circled the room, making sure all the coffee cups were full, all the ice-tea glasses replenished.

She flinched inwardly when she saw the front door opening again. There was simply no place to seat another customer.

Then her heart gave a painful jerk as she recognized Ken Slattery standing there, looking across the room at her. A strange, tumbling sensation tickled the pit of her stomach.

She didn't remember ever seeing him on a Sunday morning before. He wore a starched, white shirt of Western cut, its sleeves rolled halfway up his forearms. The whiteness set off the bronze of his skin, accented the silvery hair in his sideburns.

His jeans rode low on his lean hips, his boots were polished to a high gloss, and his white Stetson was set at a determined angle.

His blue eyes held hers for a long moment, and Nora wasn't sure if the room went quiet or if she just stopped hearing. He took off his hat, as if in salute to her, and unsmiling, he nodded a greeting. His blond hair gleamed dark gold in the sunlight that poured through the front windows.

Nora's heart flew into her throat and lodged there, fluttering and aching. *What's happening to me?* she thought, slightly panicked. *Why do I feel like this?*

She returned his nod of greeting mechanically. She gave him a small, strained smile. He seemed to study that smile with serious intensity, as if reading what it did say, what it didn't say, what it might say.

She looked for Dottie, who was nowhere to be seen. She had no choice but to approach Ken, who stood by the door, his hat held against his chest, his eyes never leaving her.

Oh, mercy, thought Nora, *oh, mercy, mercy, mercy.* He was so tall that she found his height intimidating. She looked up at him warily, tried to smile again and failed.

"We don't have any room," she said brusquely. "You'll have to wait."

"I didn't come for that," he said, gazing down at her. "I came for something else."

The fluttering feeling in Nora's throat and stomach made her half-dizzy. "What?" she breathed. She was sure people were watching them, certain of it.

You, his eyes seemed to say. *I came for you. I know it. You know it.*

"The air-conditioning," his lips said. "I came to— I came to fix it."

Nora was too startled to speak. She just kept staring up at him, knowing that they weren't really talking about the air-conditioning at all.

"Ken!" Dottie's greeting sounded sincerely happy.

He dragged his eyes from Nora and nodded to the older woman. "I came to look at the air conditioner, Dottie. I figured you wouldn't be able to get anybody to look at it on a Sunday."

Dottie put her hand on his arm and gave him an affectionate squeeze. "Why, Ken—if that isn't the most thoughtful thing. Isn't he thoughtful, Nora?"

Nora gazed self-consciously at the floor. "Yes. He's very—thoughtful."

"You got tools in back, or should I get mine out of the truck?" Ken asked Dottie. His tone was quiet, matter-of-fact, but his voice made the back of Nora's neck prickle.

"There's a big old box of 'em in back," Dottie said. "They were Duff's. Lawsy, I don't know what half of 'em are. I'm not a mechanical person. Why, I can't hardly fasten a safety pin."

"You don't have to be mechanical, ma'am," Ken said gallantly, "when you cook the way you do."

Dottie laughed. "Flattery'll get you everywhere. If you get that air conditioner fixed, your Sunday dinner's on me. Show him where that toolbox is, will you, Nora?"

Nora nodded and kept staring at the floor. She turned and went into the kitchen, all too aware that Ken Slattery was close behind her. She could sense the heat of his long, lean body, and she could smell his after-shave. It was Old Spice.

The kitchen door swung shut behind them. Nora knelt and opened the cabinet under the sink, fumbling to pull out the heavy toolbox.

"Let me." He lowered himself, squatting on his high-heeled boots. His hard shoulder brushed the sleeve of her dress, and his hand accidentally touched hers when he reached for the box.

Nora drew in her breath sharply. They both rose, neither looking at the other. Ken set the old toolbox on the counter and unlocked it. It was rusty, and the tools within were jumbled and dirty.

"I'm sorry," Nora apologized. "Neither of us is very good with tools. I guess we haven't taken care of them the way we should."

"Not your kind of job," he said, reaching for a paper towel to wipe the grease from a wrench.

"Oh, be careful," Nora said. "You'll get your nice shirt dirty."

"Indeed you will," Dottie said breezily, coming through the door with a pile of used plates and silverware. "Don't stand on ceremony with us, Ken. Just slip out of that shirt. You can hang it on the back of that chair there."

"Thanks," he said tonelessly, and began unbuttoning his shirt.

Nora had a glimpse of a hard, tanned chest sprinkled with golden hair. She turned and fled back into the dining room. A few people gave her knowing, conspiratorial smiles, and she was dismayed to find herself blushing.

A few moments later, when she was back in the kitchen, dishing up corn bread and beans, she allowed herself to glance out the back window. Ken Slattery stood, shirtless, bending over the outside air-conditioning unit, a big metal box almost as high as his thigh.

The veins in his biceps stood out as he unscrewed the unit's top, and the ropy muscles in his shoulders bunched. His hair, carefully brushed when he'd entered the coffee shop, fell in a blond hank over his forehead as he examined the exhaust fan.

Nora found she was holding her breath. He worked with total concentration and efficiency. Not one motion seemed wasted; it was as if his body were an instrument perfectly made and perfectly controlled.

Why, he's really a beautiful man, she thought in wonder. *But he's so quiet and self-effacing, nobody ever seems to notice.*

Once more Dottie came bustling through the door, and Nora was embarrassed to find herself blushing again, this time for having been caught staring out the window at Ken Slattery.

Dottie glanced out the window and gave Nora a little smile. "What's the matter? Forgotten what a man looks like without a shirt?"

"I didn't notice," Nora lied, rather desperately. "I just wanted to see how he was doing, that's all."

"Honey," Dottie said, her smile growing smug, "if you don't notice that—" she nodded at Ken's wide-shouldered figure "—you are *not* a well woman."

"Dottie!"

"Well, face it. Do you think he's out there workin' in the hot sun on *my* account? He's taken a shine to you."

"He'll have to shine without me," Nora said stubbornly. "I told you last night, I don't want a man."

Dottie's smile faded and her face became somber. "I've been thinking about it, honey. It wouldn't hurt you to—"

"Please don't think about it," Nora said, cutting her off and turning from the window. "And I wish you hadn't promised him dinner. The less I see of him the better. Besides, if Gordon found out, he'd just make more trouble than usual."

Dottie squared her shoulders. "I've been thinking about that, too. I really have. Nora, you can't spend your life dwelling on what Gordon did in the past and what he might do in the future. Now if any man was to stand up to Gordon, I think that Ken Slattery could be the one to—"

"I don't want to talk about it," Nora said firmly. Expertly she picked up the four full plates, butted the door open with her hip and left the room, Dottie and any further argument.

Dottie looked after her and bit her lip meditatively. She'd meant what she said. None of them, not her or Nora or Rory, should have to live in fear of what Gordon *might* do.

She had seen the look on Ken Slattery's face when he walked in the door today. At that moment, she'd understood that he meant to have Nora, come hell or high water.

More important, she'd also seen the look on Nora's face. That look had gone through Dottie's heart like an arrow. It had told her that in spite of everything, even all the fear, Nora wanted Ken, too. She just didn't know it yet.

NORA LOVED DOTTIE, but she wanted to throttle her. By one o'clock, the air conditioner was humming again, as smoothly as if it had never been interrupted. Ken had cleaned up and put his white shirt back on. Dottie set him down at the most private table, then practically forced Nora to sit with him and take a coffee break.

"Keep him company," Dottie had ordered cheerfully. "It's the least you can do after all he's done for us. The crowd's thinned out. I can handle it. Take a break, sweetie."

It was true. Most people had left, including the Gibsons. Now Nora sat facing Ken, not knowing what to say.

She kept clenching and unclenching her hands in her lap, her coffee growing cold in front of her.

Billie Jo Dumont had come in, obviously in a bad mood because Bubba was with his family instead of her. She looked at Nora and Ken with frank, almost predatory interest.

Why couldn't he be after Billie Jo? Nora wondered in perplexity. *She's beautiful and she wants a man so much she's willing to settle for Bubba. I bet she'd go out with Ken in a minute.*

But Ken didn't seem to notice that Billie Jo was in the room or that she was staring at them.

"What—exactly—was wrong with the air conditioner?" Nora asked at last, desperate for neutral conversation. She kept watching his hands as he ate. He had extremely nice hands for a cowboy. They had the usual scars from barbed wire and hard work, but they were lean and brown with sure, economical movements. She couldn't help thinking of how they had touched her yesterday with such surprising gentleness.

"Just a couple frayed wires. Affectin' the condenser coils."

Nora shrugged and said nothing. She didn't even know what a condenser coil was.

"Are you and Dottie and your boy goin' to the fireworks tonight?" he asked unexpectedly.

Nora looked up at him in surprise, then wished she hadn't. He had long lashes for a man, thick and dark gold, that gave his gaze a counterfeit sleepy look. They almost disguised the true intensity of his blue gaze, an intensity that always shook her.

"The fireworks?" she asked. Each year the Rotary Club and the Fire Department worked together to put on an enormous display on Fourth of July night. The show was at the city park, and people brought blankets and lawn chairs to sit on the hillside and watch the fireworks, which were set off downhill, near the park lagoon.

"Fireworks," he repeated tonelessly.

Nora once again had the disconcerting sensation of feeling hot and cold at the same time, as if tiny rockets were flaring, deep within her.

"Yes," she said, looking away from him again and out the window to where Rory played. "Rory loves fireworks. We always go with the Delaneys. They're our next-door neighbors."

Ken nodded. "I know the Delaneys. He had a stroke. He's in a wheelchair, ain't—isn't he?"

Nora kept staring out the window. The way Ken had corrected himself touched her oddly. She knew it had been for her benefit. He was like many Southwesterners who could speak two distinct varieties of English: the homespun, colorful, casual sort, and the sort that was taught in schools. That he'd bothered to shift his language for her presented yet one more disturbing element of the man.

"I said, isn't he in a wheelchair?" Ken asked.

She nodded, uncertain of what he was getting at.

"I could go with you," he said calmly. "I could help. It's not easy pushing a wheelchair around in a crowd. His wife's not strong enough to do it. Dottie'll be all worn out. That only leaves you. It'd be easier for me."

Nora's spine stiffened. How had she ever thought of this man as shy? Yesterday she'd told him she didn't want to see him anymore, yet today he was back more aggressive than before.

"You don't have to bother," she said crisply. "I'm strong. A job like this keeps a person in shape. I can manage fine, thanks."

"I didn't say you weren't strong. I know you're strong. I said it'd be easier for me."

Rory came bursting in the door, sweaty, with grass stains on his knees, and his hands full of toy cars. "Hey!" he cried, seeing Ken. "I didn't know you were here. I didn't see your truck."

"It was crowded when I came. I had to park around the corner. How you doin', squirt?"

"Fine," Rory said, stepping up to their table. "Did you come to see my mother?"

For the third time that day Nora found herself blushing. "Rory!" she said in a furious whisper.

But Rory was scratching a mosquito bite on the back of his neck and seemed oblivious to her. He was staring up at Ken with frank interest.

"Yeah," Ken said in his slow drawl. "I came to see your mother. And to see if you all'd mind if I went with you to the fireworks tonight. Would you?"

"Come with us? Sure," Rory said, scratching harder. "If you come early, I'll show you my squirrel. He ain't got no tail, but he's tame. He'll sit on your head."

"He hasn't got *any* tail," Nora corrected, grabbing him and wiping the sweat from his face with a napkin. "And you skedaddle into the kitchen so I can clean you up. If you were any dirtier, I could plant seeds on you—and get a good crop. Come on."

Nora rose, upset with Ken for inviting himself, upset with Rory for falling in so guilelessly with the man's plans, upset with herself for not knowing what to do or say.

Ken pushed back his chair from the table and rose. He made his way to the cash register and tried to pay Dottie, who'd been studiously staying out of his and Nora's way.

Dottie waved his money away. "It's no good here," she said with finality. "So put it back in your pocket."

Then she stood looking up at him a moment, mixed emotions in her expression.

"I sort of invited myself to come along with you all tonight," he said. "I don't reckon she appreciates it." He glanced in the direction in which Nora had disappeared.

Dottie looked him up, and she looked him down. She nodded as if giving him some private sort of approval. "Maybe she'll learn to appreciate it," she said.

He stared at Dottie a long moment, then the corner of his upper lip curled up in an almost imperceptible smile. "That might be too much to hope for, Dottie."

"A man can hope for anything he wants."

He allowed his smile to curve a bit more. "You're a good woman. She's lucky to have you."

Dottie shook her head. "No. I'm lucky to have *her*."

"Then you're both lucky. See you, Dottie. Tell Nora good-bye for me. Rory, too."

He turned and left, picking his hat off the rack as he went.

Dottie looked after him a long time. She was alone now in the room now, except for Billie Jo Dumont.

"That Slattery man," Billie Jo said, startling Dottie. "He's after Nora, isn't he? There's something going on between them. You can see it in the way they look at each other. Gordon isn't gonna like *that*."

Dottie steeled her spine and gave Billie Jo a cool look. "Gordon lives in Lubbock these days. We don't see much of him."

"If Nora takes up with somebody, you might start seein' more of him than you think." Billie Jo smirked. "That's one bad boy you raised, Dottie. Sure enough."

Billie Jo drew the fresh daisy from the bud vase on her table and began to pick its petals off.

Dottie narrowed her eyes, struggled to hang on to her temper and said nothing.

"He loves me," Billie Jo said, pulling the last petal from the flower and laying the stem aside. "They say daisies don't lie. Bubba really does love me, you know. He was in here earlier, I know. With that wife of his.

I heard she was just *hanging* on his arm. Did he look like he missed me?''

"You got it part right," Dottie said, ignoring the question. "He was in here—with his *wife*."

Billie Jo sighed lavishly. "I do declare it's just a crime," she said, running her fingers through her long hair, "that love gets so awful complicated. Don't you agree?"

GORDON HAD DITCHED the blonde and was heading home to his apartment in Lubbock. It was a ratty apartment, and Gordon hated it because he deserved better, but he couldn't afford it because of his car payments. Life had never been fair to Gordon. Sometimes it made him want to strike out and hit somebody, anybody.

Gordon's temples throbbed, and he tried to think of Charlie. Charlie had taken Gordon as a partner in Lubbock. He'd let Gordon buy part-interest in a diesel rig. Charlie bought hogs in northern Texas and trucked them down to Mexico. The money was decent, but not enough, and Gordon was sick of the grinding, endless hours on the road, popping uppers to stay awake, and then downers so he could sleep when he finally got to crawl into a bed.

Mostly, he was sick of hauling stinking pigs. He'd grown up in cattle country, and he found it demeaning, being a damned pig jockey. But Charlie was smart and said to be patient. Charlie often spoke mysteriously, saying better days were ahead.

Then, Friday, just before Gordon was going to take off to get Rory, Charlie had finally sprung the news. A couple of trucks going into Mexico, Charlie said, could carry things besides hogs. They could carry, for instance, guns.

There was big money carrying guns, Charlie said. He didn't know what the guns were for or what their final destination was. Guatemala? Nicaragua? It didn't matter.

A man with guts could get rich fast running firearms. And Charlie'd met a man named Eduardo Chessman who'd told him an absolutely foolproof way to smuggle them and who'd pay big money to get them across the border.

Gordon liked to project a macho, fearless aura, but in truth, Charlie's proposition had scared him stiff. Gunrunning was big time, and he was certain the people Charlie was dealing with were capable of violence. Gordon could be violent himself, but he was only an amateur at it. When it came to violence, these people were *professionals*.

Charlie'd slapped him on the shoulder, said he knew Gordon could handle it, to think it over. Give him an answer on Monday, when he got back.

No wonder Gordon had been on edge this weekend. What man wouldn't? If his mother had just handed over the money, he could have told Charlie *no*—he had better prospects. But he didn't. In Crystal Creek everybody had closed in on him, practically suffocating him with their hatefulness.

He thought of yesterday's scene at the Longhorn. He saw *them* all again. Especially Nora and his mother and Bubba. They were the three who'd pissed him off worst.

He cursed Nora; he cursed them all. Well, he thought grimly, he'd show them. He'd take Charlie up on his offer. The next time he went to Crystal Creek, he'd do it in style. They'd all be so jealous they'd turn as green as grass. They'd know they were dealing with *somebody*.

Yeah, he thought, the images still doing their goblin dance through his head, he'd show them, all right. There was nothing to be afraid of.

Gordon knew guns, had always known them. It was a natural pairing, Gordon and guns. He allowed himself a tight smile. It seemed right. It seemed almost— he struggled to find the word—inevitable.

CHAPTER FIVE

RAT-A-TAT-TAT.

Nora flinched. The fireworks display always opened with a deafening barrage of firecrackers that lasted a full five minutes. Then the rockets would begin to soar into the twilight sky, raining down their showers.

She, Ken, Rory, Dottie and the Delaneys had arrived too late to get a close spot. When Emily Delaney had seen Ken, her eyes had lit up as if a guardian angel had appeared. "Why, you're that feller so good at *fixin'* things, aren't you?"

The faucet in Emily's kitchen sink had started to drip Friday night, and by Saturday the drip had turned into an unceasing stream. No plumber could come until Tuesday.

Emily said she was worried sick about all that water going down the drain, with things so dry. Every day radio announcements warned people to conserve water, and the town council had even banned the watering of lawns until the dry spell was over.

Ken had rolled up his sleeves and, using Jack's tools, fixed the leak.

"Such a nice man," Emily had whispered to Nora as Ken reassembled the faucet. And to make sure her point was made, Emily had nudged Nora in the ribs.

Nora, embarrassed, had pressed her lips together and said nothing.

Then it was Ken who'd maneuvered Jack's wheelchair into the Delaneys' van, and after they arrived at the park, it was Ken who'd wheeled the chair up the long hill to the park's highest crest. Jack Delaney was a big man, the chair was not motorized, and the task took considerable strength.

Ken had changed his shirt for a pale blue one embroidered with arrows on the pockets. Nora saw his muscles strain and shift under the thin cloth. It would have taken her and Dottie both to push the chair, she thought, admiring the easy power of his body.

He's making himself necessary, she thought with sudden wariness. *And he's good at it.* When they reached the top of the hill, Dottie had spread out a blanket. Dottie and Emily had settled onto it, but Rory'd said if he sat he couldn't see over the people sitting in front of them.

"No problem," Ken had said, still standing, one lean hip cocked. He'd scooped the boy up and let him sit astraddle his shoulders. Rory had grinned, as if he now possessed the best seat in the house.

Nora stood beside them, watching a series of explosions rain down the sky. "Oooh," the crowd would murmur when a particularly spectacular rocket bloomed. "Ahhh."

As the darkness increased, so did the flamboyance of the display, until almost everyone, even Nora, was oohing and aahing.

Then Nora, her face tipped toward the sky, felt a sudden, pleasantly cool shudder skip over her skin. It was as if elves had tickled her. She glanced at Ken and saw that he wasn't watching the show of flares in the sky; he was watching her.

The changing colors danced over his handsome, serious face, giving it a magical cast. But somehow, no matter what hues lit the sky, his eyes always stayed that same, unwavering blue. She felt her heart wrench more deeply into her chest, and involuntarily she drew in her breath.

She felt a warm, lean hand first brush hers, then fold around it. Wordlessly, but with his usual sureness of movement, Ken had taken her hand in his. Nora's heart jarred even harder, and flutters vibrated deep in her stomach and ran down her thighs.

She should have drawn her hand away, but she did not. She should have taken her eyes from his, but she did not. All the other spectators had their gazes raised skyward, except for Nora and Ken. They saw only each other.

No, Nora thought in rising panic, *I can't do this.* She bit her lip and tried to pull back from his touch.

Something like unhappy understanding crossed his face. He gave her hand a squeeze, as if assuring her that everything was all right, it was fine. Then he let her draw away.

She gazed down at the ground and bit her lip harder. She put her hands behind her back, and squeezed her bruise, where Gordon had hurt her. *Think of that,* she ordered herself fiercely. *Think of that.*

But the intensity of the pain was not enough to distract her. It was as if her other hand, the one Ken had touched, was enchanted, full of strange, dazzling feelings that wouldn't go away, that even pain couldn't wipe out.

No, she thought again. *No.*

And she kept thinking it until the end of the show, when the two big standing displays were lit, one a replica of the flag of the United States, the other the Lone Star flag of Texas. Their colored pinwheels spun and sparkled in fiery red, white and blue.

"There ain't nothin' finer than a good firework show," Jack Delaney said afterward, shaking his head in appreciation. "I could watch it all night."

"Me, too," Dottie said, and Emily and Rory agreed.

"How about you?" Ken asked Nora, his voice low. He'd leaned so close to ask the question that his breath made her ear prickle. She realized, with a start, it was the first time he'd spoken to her since they reached the park.

"No," she said, not looking at him. "I've had enough fireworks for one night. More than enough." Then she began walking faster, so that she would no longer be at his side.

"I'D LIKE to talk to you," Ken said to Nora at the door. He'd gotten Jack and Emily back home and now had walked Nora and Dottie and Rory to their front porch.

"Why don't you come in, Ken?" Dottie invited. "I experimented with a peach and raspberry pie. I'd like a man's opinion."

Rory yawned, but tried to stifle it. "I could show you my video games. Can you play Alien Space Demons?"

Ken shook his head amiably enough in Dottie's direction, but he kept a sidelong glance fixed on Nora.

"Thanks, Dottie. But I need to go. I just want a word with Nora, is all."

Dottie gave both Ken and Nora a short but calculating look. *I see,* her expression seemed to say. The hot night wind stirred the hollyhocks around the porch and from somewhere a hoot owl called.

"But we could play Space Demons," Rory said, looking up at Ken and trying not to yawn again.

"You need to get to bed," Dottie said with sudden firmness. She gripped Rory's shoulder and propelled him through the door. As the screen swung shut behind her, she glanced over her shoulder at Ken and Nora. Her smile was falsely bright. "Take your time," she said. "I'll put this sprout to bed. Then I think it's time for bed myself. But you—you two just take your time."

She closed the oaken front door, leaving them alone. She did not turn on the porch light. Only the moon and stars shed their soft glow. *Oh, Dottie,* Nora thought in despair, *what have you done to me now?*

Among all the shadows and moonshine, only the tall man beside Nora seemed solid and real, uncomfortably real. His height, his nearness, made the elvish tickles once more swarm over her skin.

"I have to go in, too," she said hastily and started toward the door.

But smoothly he stepped in front of her, blocking her way. If another man had made such a move, it might have been rude, yet it did not seem rude from him. Still, his gentle determination frightened her.

"Nora—" he said. He reached out and his fingers closed around her upper arm. His touch flared through her like a wave of electricity.

She stepped backward slightly, but she didn't shake off his hand. It was as if she was caught in some magnetic field that did not allow her to separate from him completely.

"No." She shook her head stubbornly. "I don't intend to get involved with anybody—"

"Things don't always happen the way we intend."

She looked up at his face, but all she could see were shadows and the white of his Stetson, turned a dim silver-blue in the moonlight. She squared her shoulders, still all too conscious of his hand upon her arm.

"I told you—so you might as well quit—" she said, her voice tight.

"And I'm tellin' you—I don't quit easy." He paused. His fingers moved beneath the short sleeve of her blouse, lightly caressing her skin. He paused. "I don't quit easi*ly*," he amended.

Oh, he was doing it again, Nora thought in despair. If he'd brought her roses by the dozens, he couldn't have touched her more deeply. Worse, the feel of his work-hardened hand against the softness of her inner arm confused her even more than his words.

She broke away from his touch and retreated farther from him, sitting on the porch railing. She made a helpless gesture. "What am I going to do with you?" she asked in frustration. "Won't you take no for an answer?"

"I reckon not." He shifted his weight to one booted foot and hooked his thumbs in the back pockets of his jeans.

Nora didn't know whether to laugh or cry at the absurdity of her situation, so she did neither. She tried to think clearly, but it was difficult with the moonlight's inconstant play and the fragrance of garden flowers trying to bewitch her.

Ken, too, was making her head spin, and it frightened her. She'd made herself safe from Gordon, safe from all men. Now Ken was trying to wrest her safety away. She felt desperate. If her cruel words had driven him from her once, perhaps they would do so again.

"I don't understand you," she said, her voice growing bitter. "We don't even know each other. We have nothing in common—nothing."

There, she thought. *That should stop him in his tracks.* The thought gave her both a cynical satisfaction and a sense of emptiness so deep that it hurt.

But he didn't leave. He stood there in the shadows, and she knew, by the prickling of her skin, that he was staring at her again. "If we don't know each other, how can you tell we've got nothin' in common?"

The quiet logic of his statement unsettled her. She shrugged. "I mean, we've been slightly—acquainted—for—what?—twelve years—but—"

"Thirteen. Thirteen years."

Obstinately, Nora tried to persist in her course. She settled her hands into her lap and found that she was clenching her fists. "All right. We've been—acquainted—thirteen years. But we don't *know* each other. And why should we? We're not interested in the same things. Look at us now. We can't even have a decent conversation."

He was silent a moment. His shoulders shifted and squared, and when he spoke, his voice was sardonic. "Well, whose fault is that? Lord knows, I'm tryin'."

"Lord knows you're very trying," Nora said. Impatiently, she ran her hand through her hair. "What could we possibly talk *about?* The last thing I did in school was write a paper about Lord Byron. Do you have anything to say about Lord Byron? I can't imagine that you would."

Now, she thought, crossing her arms. *Now, that should do it. I've been out-and-out mean and snobbish.* The thought filled her with more shame than satisfaction, but she was determined to drive him away.

He seemed just as determined to stay, and his voice stayed calm. "All I know about Lord Byron is they named a cigar after him. That's everything I know about Lord Byron. So why don't you tell me about him? What *should* I know?"

Again his logic disquieted her. Nora folded her arms even more tightly against her chest, as if protecting herself.

"You don't need to know anything about Lord Byron," she said. "You can spend your whole life perfectly well not knowing one thing about him. Not one."

Ken appeared to ponder this. "Well, if he's not important, why are you gonna teach about him? Why you even botherin' to learn about him?"

"Oh!" she said in agitation. "It's not that he's not important. He's not important to *you.*"

"Why not?" Ken persisted. "Maybe I been waitin' my whole life to find out about him. I just didn't know it. How can you tell?"

Nora gave a hopeless shrug and stared up at the bright crescent moon. How could she tell? she wondered. It wasn't as if Ken Slattery was stupid. The longer she talked to him, the more she realized he was an intelligent man, even highly intelligent. He was smart in a different way from her, that was all.

"Look," she said, "I just don't think you'd want to talk about Lord Byron. And I know I don't want to talk about cows. So there's nothing for us to talk about, all right? You should just go home."

To her alarm, he came to the porch railing and settled down beside her. "There's things to talk about," he said. "There's things aplenty."

She gave him a suspicious glance. "What, for instance?"

He stared across the porch. "For a minute up there on that hill, with all the fireworks goin' off, you let me hold your hand. Then you took it away. Why?"

"Why? Because nothing's possible between us, that's why. Haven't I made that clear?"

He shook his head. "I know why you took it away. I want to know why you let me hold it at all, for just that one minute?"

Oh, heavens, Nora thought, looking up at the moon again, he asked her the most impossible questions. He was right. She had stood on that hill, looking into his eyes, and she had let her hand rest in his. It had fit his as easily and naturally as if it had been formed for that very purpose. Why? Why had she let it happen?

She shook her head sadly. "I don't know."

He was silent for the space of two heartbeats. "I see."

"So there's nothing to talk about," she said. "I should go inside, and you should go home—"

"And I said there's a heap of things to talk about," he repeated. "Gordon, for instance."

She looked back at him, surprised and slightly alarmed. "I don't talk about Gordon," she said, her voice tightening.

"Are you afraid of him?"

"I said, I don't talk about him."

"Because you're afraid of him?"

"No." She said it with all the conviction she could. She no longer feared Gordon, she tried to tell herself. She had escaped him. She was free of him at last.

Ken bent nearer. "Is that why you won't have anything to do with me? Because you think he'll hurt you?"

"No." But there was a treacherous quiver in her voice.

"I would never let him do that—hurt you. You know that, don't you?"

Oh, Lord, he's doing it again, Nora thought, closing her eyes and throwing her head back. The intensity in his voice made her fight to keep from trembling. *Why doesn't he just go away? Why can't I send him away?*

Even though her eyes were closed, she sensed he brought his face closer still to hers. She felt the brim of his Stetson brush her bangs. She felt the faint caress of his breath against her lips.

"I mean it." His voice sounded taut with self-control. "I would never let him hurt you."

She could only squeeze her eyes shut more tightly. "I don't want to talk about him."

"We have to. You don't think—you don't worry that he'd hurt *me,* do you? My God, Nora, I can take care of myself. I have since I was fourteen. You're not worried about *me*—are you?"

She let her eyes flutter open and felt tears stinging them. Even in the dim light, she could see the emotions crossing his handsome, serious face.

"Yes," she found herself whispering. "I am. A little afraid of that, I mean. That he'd hurt you. You don't know how he can hurt people."

He brought his hand toward her face, but it hovered there, not quite touching her. His voice was low, strained. "Then those tears in your eyes are for me— a little bit?"

Nora wanted to turn away but couldn't. She felt one tear spill over onto her cheek and make a hot, crooked path down her cheek. "I think they're for us all. Even Gordon. He's a very unhappy person."

"But—?" he said, his hand still poised near her face, his own face lowering itself nearer to hers.

"But—" she managed to say, torn as always by his gentleness, his restraint, "yes, I guess they're for you, too. A little. I didn't want that, either. But—yes. For you, too."

And now he's going to kiss me. And I'll let him. Because I want him to.

She raised her lips to his. His mouth closed over hers with more hunger than she had expected. His hand framed her jaw, guiding her face more intimately against his, so that he could taste her more completely.

His other arm had coiled around her with marvelous strength, drawing her against him. Nora leaned against him, almost dizzied by his touch, wanting to be dizzied even more.

She had the vague impression that his Stetson was gone, that it had been either knocked or somehow thrown into the hollyhocks. His hair felt like silk against her forehead.

He had a wonderful, wonderful mouth for kissing. She never would have guessed, for it was usually set so sternly. But his lips were supple and firm and warm, frankly taking pleasure, frankly bestowing it.

I want you, his silent mouth told her. *This is how much.* Then his lips moved against hers with even greater boldness and yearning, as if to say, *No. No. More even than that. Like this. And this. And this.*

I want you as you've never been wanted in your life.

My body will cherish yours as much as you've ever been cherished in your life.

He kissed away her tears. He kissed her hair, her temples, her eyelids, the soft curve of her jaw, the subtler curves of her throat. Both his arms wrapped her now, pulling her against the hardness of his chest until she was not sure whose heart it was that she felt beating so thunderously, her own or his.

She had her arms around his waist, clinging to him tightly, as if she'd been waiting for him for years, and he'd finally arrived. Her hands moved over his back, loving how his muscles played beneath her fingers, loving the live, solid strength of him.

Abruptly he drew back, looking down at her with concern. The moonlight silvered his hair, his high cheekbones. His brow furrowed. "I've done this ten thousand times in my mind," he said. "Maybe more. Does that scare you?"

She stared up at him, his face at once so familiar and yet so new to her. He reached and smoothed a strand of hair from her cheek, tucking it behind her ear. Her heart knocked crazily in her breast. She was happy, but frightened, too.

"Yes," she said, trying to keep the tremor out of her voice. "It scares me."

Then she thought of Gordon and the happiness in her fell away, dying into fear.

Ken must have seen the change in her face. His frown deepened. "What's the matter?"

She shook her head and tried to pull away. He held her fast. She looked away, out at the moon-silvered lawn, and wondered if she really wanted him to let her go.

"I didn't mean for this to happen," she said, still not meeting his gaze. "I didn't want for this to happen."

"I know."

"You should let go of me now."

"I know," he said, but still he held her tight against his chest. He stroked her cheek lightly, again and again, as if amazed by the feel of it.

"You should go home."

"I know that, too. Better than you, maybe."

"We shouldn't have done this, and you should go home and forget about it."

"My God, Nora. How could I forget?" Slowly, caressingly, he continued to stroke her cheek.

"Oh," Nora said miserably. She felt overwhelmed, buffeted by too many emotions at once. She had fought Gordon for years, never giving up once she started. But she was exhausted from fighting this man for a mere few days. Defeated, she laid her face against his shoulder. She would not forget what had happened tonight, either. How could she? But even as she rested in his arms, she was frightened of him and angry at herself.

"You made this happen too fast," she said against his shoulder. Through his shirt, his chest was hard and warm against her cheek. "I need time."

He ran his hand over her hair, smoothing the tumbled waves. He kept doing it, a hypnotic motion. "I figured you would."

"And I mean it," she said, hating the tears that began to sting her eyes again. "We don't really know each other. So this is crazy. This doesn't fit my plans. This can't fit into my life."

"Shh," he said, sensing her agitation. "It's all right. There's a lot to talk about, is all. Startin' with Gordon."

She shook her head and shuddered. "I can't talk about him."

He soothed her again, still stroking her hair. "Then start with Lord Byron, sugar. I reckon we gotta start somewhere."

As distraught as she was, she gave a weary laugh. "You're crazy."

"Be that as it may. Come on, sugar. Here. Just lie back and let me hold you. Look up at the moon and talk to me."

He made her turn around so that she could lean back against his chest and look up at the sky. He held her, his jaw resting against her hair. "Now," he said, kissing her ear. "Tell me about Lord Byron. What was he—besides a cigar?"

"You really are crazy," Nora said, almost smiling, "and your hat's in the hollyhocks."

But she stayed, nestled against his chest, safe in his arms, gazing up at the stars, and they talked and talked that way, until nearly morning.

CHAPTER SIX

GORDON HAD AWAKENED so early that when he'd looked out his window, the sky was still black. Nightmares had hounded his sleep, tormenting him. His heart beat so fast that it scared him.

Gordon had dreamed that Brock Munroe and Ken Slattery held him, arms pinned back, while fat Bubba Gibson hit him in the face again and again.

The worst part was that all the time Gordon was being beaten, Nora, his mother, and Rory looked on, almost impassively. But then Nora broke into tears; she threw her arms around Bubba and begged him to stop. Bubba turned from Gordon and kissed Nora possessively. He began to undo the buttons of her uniform, and Nora, whimpering, let him.

"No," Gordon had screamed in his dream, "he's a dirty old man—no!" He'd begun to fight with the sweaty sheets.

Then with the illogical shift that dreams take, Gordon was driving his livestock truck toward the border. The truck was full of guns, but every time it bounced or jounced, the guns would be jolted from their hiding places.

The barrels poked out, bristling from every niche until the truck looked like some monstrous, mechanical porcupine. No highway exit offered refuge, and

Gordon was trapped, hurtling down the road with the guns plainly visible.

Then the guns began falling off the truck, leaving a trail of weaponry, and Gordon went cold with terror, knowing he would be caught at any moment. He heard sirens. They came from both directions, and overhead a police helicopter appeared, deafening him with its hellish chop-chopping sound.

As if by magic, a police barrier loomed before him, and desperately he tried to run it. Bullets shattered his windshield, cracking it with spiderweb shapes. Blood was in his eyes and—

Then suddenly Gordon was back in Crystal Creek, in bed, sore and weeping, but safe in Nora's arms. As long as Nora held him, he would be protected. He would not have to prove anything to anyone.

He tried to hold Nora down and take her, roughly and quickly. But he couldn't. She vanished as if she were no more substantial than a will-o'-the-wisp.

Gordon could stand this whirligig of torture and humiliation no more, and he'd awakened.

He sat up in the shadowy room. He leaned his elbows on his knees and held his face in his hands.

He was edgy, that was all, because he was going to tell Charlie, yes, he'd run those guns across the border. He was nervous because he'd never done anything of this magnitude before.

His stomach twisted and kept twisting. *Damn,* he thought in anger, if only he didn't have to prove anything. If only he didn't have to pay off those bitching gambling debts. If only, if only.

He was still so sleepy that the distinction between dream and reality blurred. In his dreams, Nora had been the only one to help him.

The Nora of his dream had been more desirable than any of the women he'd had since they'd parted. He wouldn't have taken up with the skinny blonde if it hadn't been for Nora. He'd wanted to make her jealous, he realized that now. He'd done it all for Nora.

It was Bubba Gibson's fault, too. Bubba was a letch, and everybody in town knew it. The old holier-than-thou bastard had a gleam in his eye for Nora—he always had. And he'd been trying to order her around as if he owned her. No wonder Gordon had lost his temper. How could he help it?

He swore softly and stared into the darkness. In the ever-shifting cavalcade of Gordon's desires, he suddenly realized what he really needed. He needed to get Nora back.

She needed him, too; she just didn't know it. If he had her back, the breach with his family would be healed, and Dottie could loan him the money to pay off Steponovich, and his life would be sane and sensible and safe.

Then bastards like Bubba Gibson and his friends could go to hell. And Gordon could go home again. Home.

If Nora would just say, "Come home," he could forget about Charlie and the gunrunning. Dottie could help Gordon get on his feet. Wasn't that what mothers were for?

Gordon had half a bottle of rum, and a half-filled glass of the liquor sat on his night table. He'd needed the rum to get to sleep. Now, again needing fortification, he drained the glass.

He switched on the bedside light and took up the phone. His fingers shook as he dialed Dottie's number, and he lit a cigarette to steady his nerves. He prayed Nora would answer, not Dottie. He didn't want to explain himself to *two* women. After all, he was a man. He had pride.

Nora, I think it's time I came home again, is what he'd say. *You're still mine. Mine. You don't belong to nobody else. Never.*

MAYBE, MAYBE, MAYBE, sang an early meadowlark. It seemed to Ken like a song about Nora. Maybe she would be his. Maybe.

The first gold streaks of dawn were paling the eastern sky when he pulled up beside his house.

He whistled softly to himself as he got out of the truck, and he had a hollyhock flower thrust through his buttonhole. Nora had put it there. His step was light, and a slight, private smile touched his lips.

He stopped dead when he saw Cal McKinney on his porch swing, one booted leg cocked up on its seat, rocking lazily. Cal grinned like a Cheshire cat, and Ken's smile died. He'd wanted to slip back to the ranch unnoticed. It was nobody's damn business how long he'd been with Nora, and he didn't want the lateness of the hour reflecting poorly on her.

"What are *you* doin' here?" he demanded.

Cal held a mug of coffee. He hadn't shaved, which made his dimples more shadowy when he grinned. "Couldn't sleep. My back's actin' up. I got up and made some coffee. Looked out the kitchen window and saw you wasn't home. Decided to come wait. Have a good time?" He injected a maximum of amiable lechery into the question.

"Till now it was fine," Ken said grumpily. He climbed the stairs and looked down at his friend.

Cal eyed him up and down with satiric interest, his gaze settling on the blossom stuck so jauntily in Ken's buttonhole. "Hollyhocks? First clover flowers, now hollyhocks—what next? Daffodils growin' outta your ears?"

Ken was not amused. "I'll tell you where to grow daffodils."

Cal laughed. "Sit. Have some coffee. I brought a thermos jug."

"Your 'coffee'? You could float horseshoes in that gunk. I need sleep, not company."

"Why sleep?" Cal asked smugly. "You only got to get up in an hour or so. Daddy said you was riding fence this morning." He shifted to make room for Ken, and as he did so, his smile turned into a grimace of pain. "Damn!" he said with passion. Gingerly he touched his back.

Ken paused a moment, staring down at the kid with both disgust and concern. He sat, pulling his hat down a notch lower. "You're lucky Serena pulled you outta that rodeo before some horse tromped out the few brains you got."

"Oof," Cal said, settling back again. "I got brains to spare. It's vertebrae I'm runnin' out of."

"You ain't got much of either."

Cal ignored the gibe. Instead he narrowed his eyes at Ken's shirt, then reached over and tweaked his collar. "Is that *lipstick?* Bless my soul. And yesterday you was ready to give up wooin' altogether."

Ken shoved the hand away. "Oh, give me a cup of that tar and stop starin'. It's none of your affair."

Cal passed him the thermos. "Oh, I've seen lipstick before."

"I don't doubt *that*."

"We saw you at the fireworks. Only you was too intent on your own private fireworks to notice. That's the lipstick of the lovely Miz Nora, I take it?"

Ken gave him an impatient glance. "It's not lipstick. It's—hollyhock juice, is all."

"Hmm." Cal smirked and settled more comfortably against the swing.

Ken frowned and pulled his hat brim lower. "Just keep your mouth shut, hear? Don't get any ideas. All we did was talk, dammit." To prove what he said, he added, "We talked—about Lord Byron."

Cal started to laugh.

Ken turned to him, scowling harder. "Oh, shut up, you ignoramus. You probably think Lord Byron's nothin' but a cigar."

"Well, ain't he? A cigar, I mean?" Cal began to laugh harder.

"Yes, he is," Ken snapped. "But he was also a poet. A rebellious sorta fella. Not that you'd ever appreciate anything high class."

"I appreciate poetry. I can *recite* poetry. Listen— 'There was an old man from Nantucket—'"

Ken's strained patience broke. "*Stop* that, you baboon."

Painfully Cal hoisted himself into a straighter position. He clapped a hand on Ken's shoulder. "Aw, hell, Slats, I'm funnin'. I don't mind poems. Mama was ever partial to poetry, you know.''

Ken said nothing, thinking back to Cal's mother, Miss Pauline. She'd been a real lady—the first Ken had ever known. She'd been a kind of ideal to Ken. An ideal that no younger woman had ever matched—except Nora.

Cal, seeming to understand, sobered. He leaned against the back of the swing again. ''That's okay, Slats. If you don't want to talk about her. I just want things to go right for you. That's all.''

Ken nodded pensively. He took off his hat and leaned his elbows on his knees, staring out at the sunrise again.

He and Nora had talked all night long, and she had fit into his arms just right, the way he'd always figured she would. She'd fit so perfectly that the memory of it hurt his heart and tightened his groin.

Could he make her love him? He didn't know. He wanted her hard enough to pray for it, and he hadn't prayed for anything since he was a kid.

The uncertainty gave him a sick feeling in his stomach. Oh, she'd agreed to see him again, but he'd seen the worry appear in her eyes again as soon as she said she would.

''I didn't come over here just to give you a bad time,'' Cal said.

Ken, pensive, kept staring at the dawn's changing colors. ''That's a switch. What did you come to give me?''

''This. Here. Take it.'' Ken glanced over his shoulder at the younger man. Cal offered him a silver-colored key. Ken raised a quizzical eyebrow.

"It's the key to the lake house. On Lake Travis," Cal said. "Serena and I were going to use it next weekend. Only we got to work at the boot shop. You take it."

Ken frowned. "Your family's lake house?"

Cal nodded, holding up the key so that it glittered softly in the morning light. "Take 'em all there—Nora and Rory and Dottie. Spend the whole weekend. Why let it stand empty? Use the boat, swim, fish—hell, do anything at all."

Ken stared first at the key, then Cal. "I can't do that—" Ken struggled for words. "—let Tyler—let Lynn—"

"Tyler and Ruth and Lynn and Sam are all goin' to Arkansas. Visit a winery and look at some horses in Hot Springs. Daddy and Cynthia got plans of their own. Here. Take it. Keep it in the family, so to speak."

Neither of them spoke for a moment. They gave each other the steady, dispassionate look of men who like and respect each other but would never tell each other in words.

At last Cal shrugged. "Take it," he repeated, his tone careless.

Ken took the key and slipped it into his shirt pocket without looking at it. J.T.'s lake house was a beauty, and Nora and Dottie and Rory had probably never stayed at such a place in their lives. Nora would feel like a princess there, which was how she always ought to feel. Would she agree? It'd all be right and proper with Dottie there.

Out in the pasture, the lark broke into song again: *Maybe, maybe, maybe.*

"Thanks," Ken said gruffly and started to turn to stare at the dawn-stained sky again, but Cal's voice halted him.

"I brought you more besides." Ken glanced at the kid again. Cal picked up a book from beside him on the swing. He offered it to Ken. The book was old, thick, and its pages edged in gold. The green leather cover was well-worn.

Ken took it and looked at it, one eyebrow going up, the other down. "What's this? I can't take this—it's Miss Pauline's book, your mother's book. What are you givin' me this for? Here. Take it back."

He tried to give back the book, but this time it was Cal who stared at the horizon, and stony-faced, he waved away the attempt. "It was one of the poetry books Mama liked best. Give it to Nora. She likes the same things Mama did. It's fittin'."

Ken frowned and kept holding the book toward the younger man. "I can't take it. I remember this book— it was always by her chair in the study. You should keep it."

Cal shook his head stubbornly. "No. There's lots of books. But I know that's one Nora'd like, 'cause Mama did. It's fittin'. Mama always liked you. She'd want this. I know."

He said 'I know' with such conviction that Ken clamped his lips together tightly and studied the book's cover with its gold lettering: *Great Poems of the English Language*. Nora would love it. He knew that.

He could say nothing. As a kid and a rodeo tough, Cal had once been irresponsible as hell, yet always generous to a fault. Now he was a man about to marry, irresponsible no more, but generous still. He was as good a friend as a man could ask for.

Ken heaved a harsh sigh and fingered the book's cover.

"Besides," Cal said, "maybe that'll make up for some bad news. There's somethin' you should know."

Ken stared at Cal. "Bad news?"

Cal gave him a sidelong glance. "Serena and I went dancin' last night at Zack's. We ran into Wayne."

"Wayne Jackson? The sheriff?"

Cal nodded and scratched his unshaved cheek. "Yeah. He took me aside. He asked about Gordon."

Small bolts of wariness shot through his nervous system. "Gordon Jones?"

Cal's eyes met his. "Yeah. Gordon's workin' with some guy in Lubbock named Charlie. Charlie Foss. Charlie Foss has some rough friends. Suspicious friends. And Gordon's been makin' a lot of runs to Mexico lately. Some good old government boys came round here last week, makin' *discreet* inquiries about Gordon. If you get my drift."

Ken's muscles tensed. "What kinda government men? What kinda inquiries?" A litany of sinister initials ran through his head. FBI, DEA, ATF.

Cal shook his head. "Wayne wouldn't say. But he looked serious, worried. He knows you're my friend. He saw you with Nora tonight, same as everybody else did. I think he wanted me to get word to you, warn you. Whether for your sake or Nora's, I don't know. Be careful, is what I'm tryin' to say. I don't want you to worry, but I thought you should know."

"Jesus," Ken said softly. He shook his head. Hadn't Gordon given Nora enough trouble? What sort of hellfire was he stirring up now?

"Maybe it's nothin'," Cal said, but he didn't sound convinced. "I hope it's nothin'. Are you gonna tell Nora?"

Ken's mouth took on a grim slant. "I don't know."

"Grandpa Hank's been havin' some of his funny dreams lately," Cal said, watching Ken from the corner of his eye. "This time they're about you. Did you know?"

Ken lifted one shoulder skeptically. Some said that Cal's great-grandfather, Hank, had psychic powers. He didn't want to hear about the old man's dreams. They were often too spooky. Ken felt an unfamiliar emotion rising in him. It was so unfamiliar that it took him a moment to identify it: fear.

Not for himself, but for Nora. Cal's words kept echoing in his mind. And so did her name. *Nora*.

Nothing was going to hurt her again, he told himself. He wouldn't allow it. Nobody would hurt her again. Ever. He'd die himself first.

Maybe, sang the lark. *Maybe.*

DOTTIE HEARD the phone ring, glanced at the bedside clock and swore softly. She rose, not bothering with slippers and robe. She didn't want the phone to wake Rory—or Nora.

Tired as Dottie was, she remembered how long Nora had sat on the porch with Ken Slattery, and she smiled to herself. Dottie had awakened when she heard Ken's pickup pull away. She'd glanced at the clock then, too.

God be praised, Dottie had thought, marveling at how long Ken and Nora had talked, *maybe my sweet girl's come round at last. I'd like her to be happy.*

But the phone kept ringing, and her smile died. She padded swiftly down the hall and into the living room. She snatched up the receiver, irritated. At this time of night, the caller could only have dialed a wrong number.

"Yes?" There was a long moment of silence.

Then she was stunned to hear Gordon's voice. It had an insistent, angry whine. "Ma? Get Nora. I gotta talk to her."

Shock rippled up Dottie's backbone. She glanced at her watch to be sure of the time: it was just past five o'clock. What did Gordon want? Was he calling because he was drunk? He sounded a little drunk.

"Gordon," she whispered furiously, "do you know what time it is?"

"I gotta talk to Nora." His tone was self-righteously petulant.

"She's asleep. I won't wake her up. Not at this hour."

"Ma—I need to talk to her. It's important. Look, I've been thinkin'—"

"No. You haven't been thinking at all. Or you wouldn't call up at this god-awful—"

"I want Nora. I *want* her."

Dottie spoke softly so as not to wake Rory or Nora, but despair shook her voice. "What do you want her for? If you want to apologize—"

"Ma!" Gordon's voice was suddenly so anguished that it sent a chill creeping over Dottie's flesh. "I want

her *back,* Ma. I want to come home again. Don't
stand in my way. Help me. Please."

Oh, Lord, Dottie thought, closing her eyes and
putting her hand to her throat.

Her skull ached and she leaned her forehead against
the wall. This was the sort of call that Dottie dreaded
most. *I want to come back, Ma. I want to start over.
I've changed. Let bygones be bygones. You're my
mother. Help me. Take me in. Help me, I'm your son.*

"Gordon, I've heard this so often before. So has
Nora. Don't put me through it again. Please."

"Mom—" his voice broke slightly "—I need for
you to understand me. Nobody ever understands me.
It isn't fair."

Dottie felt shaky, but she kept her voice steady and
cold. "What is it, Gordon? Are you in trouble? That's
what usually brings on these fits of homesickness. Do
you realize you do this almost every three months? As
regular as clockwork? What is it this time? The gambling again?"

Her pulses hammered so forcefully she wondered if
they would rupture. Her breastbone hurt, and she
found it hard to draw her breath.

She was saying terrible things to her own son,
heartless things. Her words pained her almost beyond bearing, yet what else could she do, could she
say?

For years Gordon had played his irrational game.
First he inflicted hurt, then he pleaded for forgiveness
and promised to change. But change never came, and
Dottie's forgiveness had worn out years ago, and so
had Nora's.

Besides, Dottie knew, to her sorrow, that Gordon didn't mean what he said.

Yesterday he had spoken as if Nora and Dottie conspired against him, plotting his downfall. Today he spoke as if they alone could be his saviors.

Often he blamed them for all his failures. Sometimes, paradoxically, he claimed they were his only hope. Neither version was true, but Gordon could never realize it.

"What is it now, Gordon?" Dottie said from between her teeth. "You want money from me, no matter how you get it. Is that it?"

"No." He sounded insulted, but then his tone changed, became more beguiling, more sly. "Well—I could use some. Just a loan. I slipped. I wasn't going to bet anymore, but I slipped a little. 'Cause I thought so much about you and Nora."

Dottie's tone went frigid. "I've paid enough of your debts, Gordon. More than enough. And Nora doesn't want you back. You hurt her too often and too much. You lost her, and it's nobody's fault but your own."

"I just want to *talk* to her."

"Gordon," Dottie said fiercely, "leave her *alone*. She's got a right to her own life. She's making a future for herself—a good one. She's—"

"She's my wife—dammit. She's the mother of my son—"

"She's *not* your wife. Not—"

"The hell she's not—and why are you comin' between us? What kind of mother are you? What's the matter? Has she found somebody else? You hate me so much you'd rather she had anybody else than me?"

Dottie's distress was so intense that it had set off her ulcer. She felt as if someone was poking and twisting a sharp stick through her stomach. She was unable to speak. Tears burned her eyes.

He took her silence for consent. "She's found somebody else—hasn't she? I saw Bubba give her the eye. I heard how he talked about her. He wanted to fight me over her. My God, Ma. First he practically ruins my life because I made one little mistake. Now he wants my wife, too? I'll kill him first."

"Gordon, don't talk like that," Dottie ordered. "Bubba flirted with her a little, that's all. There's no call to talk of killing—"

"Why not?" Gordon asked bitterly. "You're all trying to kill me."

"We're not—"

"Well, I can take care of myself," Gordon sneered. "I can take care of myself fine. I got opportunities. They're dangerous, but I ain't no coward. And if I want Nora back, I'll come take her. You can't stop me. And if Bubba Gibson gets in my way, I'll knock his—"

"Gordon, don't—"

But Gordon didn't let her finish the sentence. He swore and hung up, banging the receiver so hard that Dottie flinched.

Oh, Lord, she thought. She hung up the receiver then ran both hands through her hair. What had she done to deserve Gordon? What had any of them done?

And what did he mean, that he had opportunities, but they were dangerous? Why was he suddenly obsessed with Bubba Gibson?

She bit her lip. What if Gordon found out about Ken Slattery? What then? Would he be jealous, resentful? Would he be vengeful?

And what would Nora do if she found out about this insane phone call? Would it frighten her as much as it did Dottie?

Maybe this is a fluke. Maybe it'll burn itself out, Dottie thought, praying it was true. *Maybe this call will get things out of his system. Such things have happened before. Maybe Gordon really is drunk, so drunk he won't even remember this.*

She shook her head and went into the kitchen to make herself a cup of coffee. She wouldn't sleep again, she knew that. Gordon had seen to that.

She felt ill with apprehension. She would not tell Nora of Gordon's call. Not just yet. There was no need to worry her about something that might amount to nothing.

Besides, who knew how it might affect Nora's attitude toward Ken? Why should Gordon's pleas and threats come between Nora and Ken when they were just starting to discover each other?

Dottie sat down at the counter, willing her heartbeat to slow. It did not. She felt so unwell, it frightened her.

She was alarmed to realize that she had never made any provisions for Nora and Rory should anything happen to her. She put her elbows on the counter and buried her face in her hands.

She had never made a will. She'd been superstitious about it. But if anything happened to her, she would leave behind money and property. Gordon would be back for sure, making Nora's life a living hell. *That mustn't happen,* Dottie thought, her heart drumming harder.

She would see Martin Avery, the lawyer, as soon as possible. She would put things in writing and sign them, even though she would feel she were signing in heart's blood. Gordon had left her no choice.

Rory and Nora were the ones she must protect. The bitter irony was that she had to protect them from her own flesh and blood, her own son.

Her confused, tormented and possibly dangerous son.

CHAPTER SEVEN

NORA AWOKE to sunshine pouring into the room. She stretched in the brightness and warmth.

She felt a strange mixture of content and excitement. Why? Luxuriously, she stretched again.

Then she remembered Ken, and her sense of well-being fled. Her body tensed.

She'd spent almost the whole night in Ken Slattery's arms. She'd lain against the hardness of his chest, her head resting against his shoulder. From time to time, he'd kissed her ear, her hair, her cheek. And she'd closed her eyes and let him. She—Nora Jones, who'd sworn never to let a man near her again.

No, she thought, *I didn't do that. I couldn't have.* But she had, and a shiver ran over her.

What had they talked about, all night long? Nothing and everything. They had even laughed, softly as befitted the softness of the night. Because he had always looked so serious, she'd been surprised by his humor, which was quick, sharp and ironic.

When, at last, she'd told him that he must leave, they'd stood on the porch, embracing, each reluctant to let the other go. He had kissed her so fiercely and sweetly that she hadn't wanted him to leave.

And when he'd fetched his hat out of the hollyhocks, she'd found herself fastening a flower in his buttonhole, then smiling up at him, waiting, happily, for him to kiss her again.

She closed her eyes and relived the moment of that kiss. It made her body seem as if it were full of hummingbirds, wild and tumbling and drunk on nectar.

She snuggled more deeply into the sheets, wondering if this was how other women felt when they were in love.

Love? Nora's eyes flew open. She couldn't be in love with Ken Slattery. Her heart was barred and locked against it. Her plans did not allow it.

And yet . . . she'd agreed to see him again—tonight, in fact. She mustn't do it. She'd vowed never to become involved with a man.

No, she thought in confusion. *I do want to see him again. He made me feel things I've never felt before.*

She snatched the pillow and buried her face in its depths. What sort of intoxication was settling over her? She had a child to raise, school to finish, a job that took all her energy—

Her job! Nora sat bolt upright. Anxiously, she glanced at the clock. Ten forty-five.

Oh, heavens, she thought in guilty panic, she'd slept until nearly noon—what was wrong with her? What would Dottie think? She scrambled out of bed.

But then she noticed a note propped against the clock radio. It was scribbled in Dottie's nervous, slightly quavery handwriting:

Sweetie—
I thought you deserved to sleep late for once in

your life. Take your time. I've got Rory. I hope
you had a good time last night.

Love, D.

Nora's guilt swelled. She reread Dottie's note with
perplexity. Dottie sounded *happy* that Nora had dal-
lied away the night.

Oh, Lord, thought Nora, her pulse pounding. Was
Dottie trying to play matchmaker? Dottie of all people should know that Nora was burned out on marriage.

She snatched up her clothes, fled from the bedroom to the bathroom and scurried to ready herself for
work. She was so shamefully late that she didn't take
time to eat.

She paused only long enough to try to phone Dottie to say that she was on her way. Poor Dottie—she
must have handled all the business with no help other
than Tillie, the cook. How could Nora ever apologize?

But when she lifted the receiver, the phone was
dead. No dial tone hummed in her ear; there was only
silence.

How odd, she thought. Had there been a storm
while she slept? Had lightning knocked out telephone
service?

A glance out the window showed her it was foolish
to think of storms. The sky was as hot and monoto-
nously cloudless as it had been for days.

Nora pressed the phone's plunger button several
times, trying to coax the line to life, but it stayed silent. What could be wrong? The bill was paid. Nora
knew because she herself had mailed the check.

At last she shrugged philosophically; the phone company was so computerized nowadays, who knew what gremlin might have slipped into the system, ready for mischief?

She snatched up her purse and swung open the front door, but paused when she saw the front porch. Memories of last night surged through her again, tickling and taunting her.

She looked at the wide railing. She and Ken had sat precisely *there*, next to the clematis trellis. That was the spot where they had kissed for the first time.

The memory gave her the sensation of pinwheels spinning dizzily in her midsection. For a split second, she was giddy.

Stop it, she commanded herself, her cheeks burning.

Then she was further dismayed to see that Dottie had left the car for her. Fresh guilt assailed Nora. Walking the six blocks to the coffee shop wouldn't hurt Rory, of course. Rory had energy to burn.

But Dottie had seemed so tired of late. She shouldn't have walked, especially in this heat. Nora bit her lower lip hard, to punish herself. She'd get to work as fast as she could, then send Dottie home to rest.

As she unlocked the car and got in, Emily Delaney appeared on the porch next door, carrying a throw rug to shake clean. She gave Nora a smug, conspiratorial smile.

"Well, Nora, did you have a good time last night? That man of yours surely did stay late—I heard his truck when he finally left. And a fine fella he is, too. That's one you should *grab*. Get your hooks into him, girl."

Grab? Get her hooks into him? The thought repelled Nora. "Can't talk, Emily. I'm late."

Nora started the car and backed it out of the drive, anxious to escape.

During the short drive to the coffee shop, she scolded herself. She wouldn't get involved. She hardened her heart against memories of Ken. In determination, she squared her jaw. She would, she vowed, stay safely numbed to feeling. She didn't ever want to *need* any man.

Nora's resolve lasted until she parked in front of the coffee shop and got out of the car. At that moment, Ken walked out of the coffee shop, and his eyes met hers.

Momentarily paralyzed, Nora stood as motionless as a statue. It was as if his sudden appearance had bewitched her, taken her prisoner.

Oh, but he was handsome, she thought helplessly. His white Stetson hid his hair except for the silver of his sideburns. The brim cast a shadow over his face, making the bronze of his brows and lashes seem darker still.

The moment he saw her, the lines bracketing his mouth had tightened. But they relaxed as he stared unwaveringly into her eyes. At last he smiled, almost imperceptibly, and something within Nora melted. She smiled back.

He walked toward her, and she sucked in her breath. His body seemed all height and leanness and wide shoulders. He swept off his hat, and the noon sun glanced off the gold of his hair. When he reached her side, he stood, looking down at her, his hat held over his heart.

Neither of them spoke. Neither of them had to.

INSIDE THE COFFEE SHOP, Dottie paused by the front window, a pitcher of ice tea in her hand. She watched as Ken reached out his free hand and tentatively took Nora's, lacing his fingers through hers.

At his touch, Nora looked both terrified and radiant. The complexity of emotions that played across her face made Dottie's heart ache. *Oh, Nora,* she wanted to say, *let it happen. Just let it happen, honey.*

He said something to her, and Nora's shy smile grew stronger. Then she whispered something in return, and Ken nodded, smiling back. The two of them stood, hands linked, staring into each other's eyes, apparently unaware that the rest of Crystal Creek existed.

"I'll be swoggled," said Shirley Jean Ditmars, who worked in the business office of the telephone company. She was a short, plump, inquisitive woman. "Ken Slattery—and Nora?"

Shirley had a round face with bright black eyes, and when she cocked her head, she reminded Dottie of a bold, curious little bird. She looked up at Dottie and cocked her head now. Dottie had the irrational desire to feed her a handful of seeds.

"Do you approve, Dottie?" Shirley asked. "I mean she was married to *your* son. Does it bother you, her findin' someone else?"

Dottie refilled Shirley's glass with tea. "It's not for me to approve or disapprove. It's not our business. It's theirs, and theirs alone."

Shirley, never one to take a hint, cocked her head on the other side. A slyness crept into her expression. "Dottie, is this why you had your phone turned off at the house today? Does it have something to do with Nora? Did anybody tell you how much it'd cost to turn back on? Plus, it's going to be *very* inconvenient.''

"Inconvenient doesn't bother me," Dottie said shortly. "I chose to turn it off. And don't mention it to Nora. You hear me, Shirley Jean?''

Shirley blinked her button-bright eyes. "It's Gordon, isn't it? Gordon's calling again—isn't he? Is it because he knows—" she nodded significantly toward Ken and Nora "—about *this?*''

Dottie set the pitcher down on the table with a thump. "No," she said, putting her hand on her hip. "He doesn't know. And he won't—unless some bigmouth tells him.''

Shirley was not fazed. "He's calling again? But Nora doesn't know? My goodness, what's he saying? Why don't you report him to your service representative? Why inconvenience yourself by cutting off your phone? I always say, the phone is the lifeline of modern—''

"I know what you always say," Dottie snapped. "And no, Nora doesn't know he's calling, and she doesn't know I shut the phone off. She won't know either thing—I repeat—unless some bigmouth tells her.''

Shirley, as usual, was blissfully impervious to personal insult. "Well, how on earth will you explain it? Won't Nora suspect something?''

Dottie narrowed her eyes. "I'll say that the phone company's screwed it up. It won't be the first time it's happened.''

At last, Dottie's remarks seemed to ruffle Shirley. "Well, I don't think *that's* nice. But if you're going to tell a fib, you might as well tell a big one. What about here, though? Gordon can call you here. How do you intend to handle that?''

"I just make sure that I answer the phone first," Dottie said, with both hands now on her hips. "And if he keeps at it, I pull the plug. *That's* how I'll handle it."

"Hmmph." Shirley shrugged rather grandly and looked out the window again. Nora and Ken still stood, their heads close together, her hand in his.

"Ken Slattery—holding hands in public," Shirley said, shaking her head. "Him, of all people. I never thought I'd see the day."

"Leave them be," Dottie said curtly and picked up the pitcher. "Let them discover each other in peace. Nora deserves a little happiness, God knows. Let her enjoy it."

The phone behind the counter rang, and Dottie stiffened as tensely as if she'd heard a shot. She hurried to answer. Shirley watched her with frank curiousity.

"Longhorn Coffee Shop," Dottie said and braced herself, hoping the answering voice wouldn't be Gordon's.

But it was Gordon, and he sounded both irritable and resentful. "I tried calling Nora. Now the phone company says the phone's disconnected. What is this, Ma? What are you tryin' to do to me?"

"I'm having the number changed," Dottie said.

It was not a total lie. She did intend to change to an unlisted number when the phone was turned back on. Perhaps if she could have thought more clearly, that was what she would have done in the first place.

But Gordon had rattled her too badly to think straight. Ever since his call, her temples had throbbed. An out-of-order phone would sound less alarming to Nora than a sudden change to a private number. She didn't want Gordon harassing Nora, and she didn't want Nora worrying about him.

Gordon stayed silent for a long, ominous moment. When he spoke again, his voice shook with accusation. "You shut the phone off? You hate me that much? What kind of woman are you?"

Dottie took a deep breath and tried to sound calm. "I'm a *tired* woman, Gordon. And I don't hate you. It'd be easier if I did. I just don't want you bothering Nora. You don't love her. You never did. Stop trying to fool yourself—and us, too."

"You stay out of it," Gordon said savagely. "Is she there? She's there, ain't she? Let me talk to her."

"No."

"Ma, you're coverin' up something. It's Bubba, isn't it? He's dumped that Dumont woman and took up with Nora. And you're gonna let it happen. Why? Because he's got that big ranch? What's he gonna do—divorce his wife and move you all out to his *ranch?* I'm not good enough? I'm your own son, but I'm not good enough?"

Dottie closed her eyes; her head was aching harder than before.

"Stop calling, Gordon. Stop—or I'll have this phone turned off, too. I'm sick of this."

"It's true, isn't it?" Gordon persisted. "She's mixed up with Bubba Gibson, and you got dollar signs in your eyes. Bubba—after what he tried to do to me! Deny it—go on—*try* and deny it."

Dottie put her hand to her forehead. "What good would it do, Gordon? You always believe exactly what you choose."

"You'd rather have her mess with Bubba than come back and be my wife again. You would, wouldn't you? You know what you are? You're unnatural."

Dottie's patience was stretched too far. "Yes," she snapped, "I *would* rather see her with Bubba than you. I'd rather see her with anybody—"

She heard the sound of Gordon's receiver crashing down. *Oh, Lord,* thought Dottie wearily, her eyes still closed. *Why did I say that? What a stupid thing to say. Now he'll think Nora's interested in Bubba. Lord, forgive me; I can't think straight.*

She stood, her eyes squeezed shut, the receiver held to her breast. A small, cold, logical corner of her mind told her that what she had said didn't matter.

Today he might hate Bubba. Tomorrow he would hate someone else—whoever was the first to raise his ire. Tomorrow he might even forget about Nora completely—who knew what direction his thoughts might take?

In the meantime, it was better that he fume over imagined slights by Bubba than know the truth about Ken. Who knew how crazy a real rival might make him?

She had meant what she told Shirley about Ken and Nora: *Leave them be. Let them discover each other in peace. Nora deserves a little happiness, God knows. Let her enjoy it.*

"Dottie?" Shirley's voice pierced her consciousness. "Are you all right, honey? You don't look well."

Dottie forced her eyes open. The room seemed a bit blurry, a bit unsteady. She hung up the phone, then firmly pulled its plug from the jack. *There,* she thought. *Gordon can't reach us now.*

"I'm fine," she said. "Just fine." But she knew she wasn't.

"Was it Gordon?" Shirley pried. "What did he say? What does he want? What does he—"

"Hush!" Dottie commanded, cutting her off. "I told you—don't say a word about this. Here comes Nora."

Nora came in the door, smiling, but with a slight furrow in her brow. The conflict in her expression rent Dottie's heart. *It's so hard for her, learning to care again,* Dottie thought. *I won't let Gordon spoil it for her. I won't.*

IN LUBBOCK, Gordon was so angry his hands shook as he redialed the coffee shop. He got a busy signal.

He smashed the receiver down, then picked it up, dialing the number for the third time. Another busy signal—she'd really done it, he thought in fury. She'd unplugged the phone on him. His own mother.

And she'd flaunted Bubba in his face—fat, old, foolish Bubba. What could Nora see in such a man? How could Dottie tolerate it? Money could be the only answer.

Gordon took another tranquilizer and washed it down with a swallow of warm beer. Was money the tune that made those women sing? Well, soon he'd have plenty of money. Charlie'd told him how much it was worth, running guns over the border. A fortune.

Tomorrow he would start. And when he got back, his pockets jammed with money, he'd confront Nora. He'd punish her, of course. But he'd take her back. As for Bubba, he'd beat the old man senseless if he got the chance.

He drained his beer and felt so nervous that he popped open another one. He had all day Monday to himself because of the long Fourth of July weekend, and he was frustrated and sick with a sense of betrayal.

How could Nora even *think* of Bubba Gibson? It made Gordon's flesh creep. She just had to be leading him on, that was it. Leading him on to make Gordon jealous. That was it—she *wanted* him jealous.

Gordon took a long drink of beer and thought of all the things he'd like to do to Bubba Gibson. Starting now—starting right now. He would make the old man live in terror of him. He'd show Bubba. He'd show them all.

He dialed information. His hands still shook, but not as badly. He asked for the number of the Gibson ranch and wrote it down on the cover of a matchbook. Then he finished his beer, opened another and dialed Bubba's number.

The phone rang three times, then, as if three were a magic number, Bubba answered. "Hello?" he said.

"Stay away from my wife," Gordon said in his most menacing tone.

"Say what?" Bubba sounded truly perplexed.

"Stay away from my wife, you bloated old toad. She ain't no Billie Jo Dumont. You mess with my woman, and I'll string your innards from Austin to

Lubbock and back. I'll dance in your blood, old man."

"Who the hell—?"

"I mean it. I'm gonna find you alone. You don't know who you're dealin' with, mister. I'm a dangerous man."

"Gordon? Is that you, you damn fool? What in hell you talkin' about, boy?"

"I'm talkin' about *vengeance,*" Gordon said, sick with hate. "I'm talkin' about *honor.* I'm talkin' about what's *mine.*"

"You're crazy. I shoulda throwed you in jail years ago, when I had the chance."

"You listen to me, you old—"

Bubba swore and crashed down the receiver so hard that it hurt Gordon's eardrum. Gordon swore, too, and hurled the phone across the room and against the wall. He kicked the leg of the table. He was so angry that he shook.

You can't get away from me, he said to himself. *You can't. I'll win, goddammit.*

He picked up the phone from the floor and listened at the earpiece. The dial tone still hummed. "I'll make your life hell," he promised Bubba as he dialed again. "Living hell."

ON THE GIBSON RANCH, Bubba stood in the living room, glaring at the phone. Gordon had called so many times, Bubba'd unplugged it. He was pale and breathing hard.

"What*ever's* going on?" asked his wife, Mary. She'd come creeping into the room as silently as a mouse. Their tall daughter, Sara, was right behind her.

"Who's been calling? Why did you unplug—" Mary asked timorously.

"Some nut. Leave it unplugged," Bubba replied harshly, then turned away. He couldn't stand the worry in her eyes. The whole long weekend Mary had been looking at him with martyrdom written all over her face, driving him crazy. His daughter, too. Both women looked at him sadly, as if his infidelity had turned him into some kind of monster.

Mary usually kept her chin up and her feelings hidden, but now that she had her daughter home and on her side, she was making him as nervous and guilty as hell. Good Lord, couldn't she understand? He wasn't going to leave her or anything. Billie Jo Dumont was just something he had to work out of his system.

"Have you gone and got yourself in some kind of trouble, Daddy?" Sara demanded. All weekend she had taken that tone with him, self-righteous and holier-than-thou. "What have you gone and done *now?*"

Bubba sighed heavily. "I ain't done nothin'. It's crank calls, is all it is."

Sara gave him a cold look. She took her mother's hand. "Come on, Mama," she said. "Or your brownies will burn."

Mary nodded sadly, and Sara kept staring accusingly at Bubba.

Bubba's head hurt. He watched stonily as Sara and Mary left the room. Damn, but it was awkward, and he was having a *terrible* time with Sara and the kids home, and the irony was that Billie Jo was mad as hell at him for spending the entire holiday with his family. His family—in its overly polite and ladylike and long-suffering way—was making his life sheer, hellacious misery.

Bubba glanced at the phone as if it were an instrument of torture. Why, in the name of all that was holy, was Gordon Jones calling *him?* That boy was crazy. Always had been.

NORA WAS WORRIED. Dottie was acting funny, not at all her usual self, and for some reason she kept the phone unplugged. She'd made a hurried excuse that some children kept calling up as a prank, and she'd finally lost patience. Nora didn't believe her.

She took Dottie aside after the noon rush was over. "Dottie, what's wrong? Has Gordon been calling? If he is, you should tell me."

Dottie shook her head. She reached up and smoothed a stray curl of Nora's back into place. "Don't worry," was all she said. Then she got a distracted look in her eyes. "Oh, heavens—I forgot to defrost the cherries for the cherry pie." She hurried into the kitchen.

Nora looked after her, her face shadowed by trouble. Since she'd awakened, her emotions had gone up and down and back and forth and around and around.

She'd vowed not to go out with Ken again, but her resolve had melted at her first sight of him. She'd promised herself to break their date, but she was still going to see him again—tonight, after Rory was in bed.

She'd stood, like a love-struck teenager, holding his hand and staring up into his eyes—in public!—for all the world to see. It was insane. It was wonderful. It was insane.

Since she'd seen him this morning, strange, irrational waves of happiness had been sweeping over her, making the day shimmer with brightness. Then the happiness would vanish, chased by a cold and shadowy foreboding. Something was wrong, something was badly wrong. She could see it in Dottie's strained face.

Only Gordon could upset Dottie like that. The thought frightened Nora. Was Dottie worried about what Gordon might do if he found out about Ken? Nora, herself, did not know how Gordon would react. If she gave him grounds for jealousy, who knew what terrible and punishing force she might set into motion? She did not dare do such a thing; she *must* not.

She shook her head sadly. Rory came bursting in the door, excited and calling for a jar because he had caught a little gray lizard. She welcomed the distraction. She gave him an old gallon jar that had once held pickles.

Rory put the lizard into the jar and regarded it with satisfaction. "I'm gonna make a terray—terray—terrarium," he said. "And I'm gonna name this lizard Pickle."

"Pickle it is," said Nora.

He looked up at her, his face suddenly going sober.

"Are we gonna go to the ranch again? Back at that pond? I could get some mossy rocks. It had good mossy rocks."

Her smile died. "I don't think so. Don't count on it."

"Why not?"

Nora swallowed hard. "Well, Mr. Slattery took us there. And maybe he won't ask again. I—just don't think so."

Rory chewed his lower lip thoughtfully. "If you marry him, would we all live at the ranch? Grandma, too? Could you stop working here?"

Nora stiffened in shock. How, in so short a time, had Rory come to think of marriage? Had someone been talking nonsense to him? She could think of nothing to say. She stared at him, her mouth slightly open.

He set his jar on the table and put his hands into the back pockets of his denim shorts. "Well?" he said, studying her face, his expression solemn.

"Well—you surprised me. Those aren't questions I've ever thought of. No. Nobody's getting—married."

Rory cocked his head and chewed on his lip again. He traced an aimless design on the floor with the toe of his sneaker. "Well—*if* you got married, would he be my father, then? Instead of the one I got?"

Nora shook her head helplessly. "Rory, why are you asking these things?"

He looked away and shrugged. He kept tracing his toe across the floor, back and forth, back and forth. "Because," he said and shrugged again, "I wouldn't mind it if you got me a different father. I—don't much like the one I got."

He paused and looked up at her with eyes that seemed too old and too worried for a child. He shrugged for the third time. "He's scary," he said quietly, then looked away.

"Oh, Rory," Nora said, kneeling and pulling him into her arms. She hugged him fiercely, almost convulsively, and tears burned her eyes. "Oh, Rory," she said, and buried her face against his warm, sweaty little shoulder. "Don't be scared. Please don't be scared, sweetheart. Please, sugar. Don't. Please."

But deep in her heart she wondered how she could comfort the boy, when she herself was so unsure and so frightened.

CHAPTER EIGHT

KEN TALKED a reluctant Nora into returning to the pond where he had taken Rory fishing. Once there, he feared it was a mistake.

Last night she'd seemed happy to be with him. Tonight she was abstracted and uneasy. She told him that she didn't want to see him again.

The words struck him like nails hammered into his heart, but she looked so unhappy when she said them that he found himself reaching to her, wanting to comfort her. Then somehow, she ended up in his arms. She felt right there, and he wondered if it felt as right to her.

There was lightning in the distant sky, but it was only heat lightning, and no true hint of rain stirred the sluggish summer night.

A thousand reflected stars danced on the pond's surface as they stood beside it. Ken held Nora, who was crying against his chest. Her body shook with each sob, and every time it shook, his heart contracted so painfully he had to fight against wincing.

He held her more tightly. "Nora," he said against her hair, "you are the most up-and-down woman I ever saw."

Nora cried harder, so he gathered her still more closely to him. "Oh, Lord," he said with a helpless sigh. "Hush, darlin'. Hush, sugar. Hush, love."

His words seemed only to upset her more. She pushed away from him and stuggled, briefly, to extricate herself from his embrace. "I'm not your darling. I'm not your sugar. I'm not your love. Oh! Why can't I tell you goodbye for once and for all?"

"Because you ain't hardly said hello. I mean, you haven't hardly said hello. Why do you want things to be over before they're started?"

"Nothing's started," she protested, "nothing can be started." But she was lying, and they both knew it. She collapsed against his chest again.

"Oh, Nora," he said, folding her into his arms again. "Nora."

Although she'd said she didn't want to see him again, paradoxically her arms were now around his waist, and she held him almost as tightly as he held her.

"Come on," he said, his lips against her ear. "Sit down. Talk to me."

He led her to the limestone slab where they had sat the first time he'd been with her. It was blue-white in the starlight. Behind them, from the pond, the frogs sang, the crickets whirred.

He lowered her to the stone, then settled beside her, taking her in his arms again. "Shhh," he said, and smoothed her tumbled hair. His shirtfront was damp with her tears, and when he saw the streaks on her face glinting in the starlight, he felt a terrible wrenching within him, as if his ribs were being broken from the inside.

She shook her head. "I don't *want* to want you," she said, her voice ragged. "I only came with you to tell you—no. That it's impossible. I don't want to want you."

He kissed her behind the ear. She shivered, and the shiver ran through him, too. "But you do," he said. "You do."

"It's impossible."

"It's not. Look me in the eyes and tell me that. It's not."

She drew back and stared up at him, her lips trembling. They were such soft, beautiful, vulnerable lips he wanted to kiss them until he died of making love to her, but he held himself back. He only allowed his hand to move to her face, his thumb to stroke away a tear that shimmered in the starlight.

"We can't—" she said. "We don't—we're not—"

"We can. We do. We are."

He couldn't help it. He lowered his mouth to hers and kissed her until she kissed him back, her lips answering his: *yes, yes, oh, yes.*

He lay back against the stone, drawing her with him. She gasped against his mouth, and once again his heart lurched hard enough to crack his ribs. He felt her shudder again, and this time he knew the shudder was fear, not desire. He forced himself to slow.

"I'm sorry," he said brokenly, drawing back. "It's just—I love you."

"No." Her voice was as strained as his. She put her finger against his lips and held it there. "Don't say that."

"I love you."

"No." She shook her head.

"Yes."

"You can't."

"I do. You know I do." He took her hand in his and kissed the palm. He kissed it long and lingeringly, the way he wished he could kiss every part of her.

"No," she breathed, pulling away and sitting up. "No!"

He raised himself and took her hand again, pressed another kiss against her palm. "I'm not sure this is something you have a choice about," he said, looking into her eyes again. "It happens or it doesn't. It's happening."

She drew back from him. She put her arms around her legs and hid her eyes against her knees. "I only came here to tell you goodbye," she said miserably. "That's all. And to get some—some mossy rocks. For Rory."

"I'll get him all the mossy rocks in the world. All the tadpoles and toad-frogs. Whatever he needs—I'll see he has it."

"Oh," she said, hugging her knees tighter. "Why are you so good to me? Why do you do it?"

His chest tightened, and he fought the urge to take her in his arms again. "I told you. I love you."

She refused to look at him. She kept her face hidden. "No."

He said the only thing he could think of. "I love you."

"Don't *say* that." Tears quavered in her voice. "I can't get involved with anybody. There's—there's Gordon. He's already driving Dottie crazy. She won't admit it, but he is. I know."

Gordon, he thought blackly. *Is she still afraid of Gordon? Jesus, how long does Gordon have to shadow her life?* He wouldn't tell her what Cal had said about authorities asking about Gordon. He couldn't stand for her to worry any more than she already was.

"Look," he said, his voice suddenly harsh, "he's hurt you enough. He's taken up enough of your life. Don't let him take any more."

She turned to him, her chin lifted. "That's easy for you to say. I don't know what he'd do—if he found out about—this."

"What *this?* You keep tellin' me there's no *this.*"

Nora shrugged in frustration. She pressed her lips more tightly together.

"Gordon's your past," he said. "He's not your present. Or future. You shouldn't have to be afraid of him. Neither should Dottie." He paused for emphasis. "Neither should Rory."

Her shoulders stiffened, and she looked away from him, out at the stars reflecting and shifting on the pond. He knew he'd scored a point by bringing up Rory, and he pressed on relentlessly.

"Are you all goin' to spend the rest of your lives worryin' about what Gordon might do? Maybe he's too much of a coward to do anything—if there's a man to stand up for you. Did you ever think of that?"

She raised her chin higher. "Gordon's—unpredictable."

"Do you think—for a minute—I'd let anybody hurt you? Or yours? Do you?"

She turned again and looked at him for a long moment. Tears rose again, glittering in her eyes. "No," she said at last. "I don't suppose you would, would you?"

"No," he said simply, holding her gaze. "I'd die first."

She looked away. "Don't say that," she said, furiously scrubbing her tears away. "Don't talk about dying. It makes me feel like a goose walked over my grave."

"I mean it. I wouldn't let him come near you. I wouldn't let him come near Rory. I don't understand why you do. Is it because you're scared?"

Nora pushed her bangs back from her eyes. She stared pensively out at the night. "I—I—he wanted to fight over custody. He was just making trouble. I talked to Martin Avery, to the lawyer. He said, let Gordon have custody every other weekend. He said Gordon would hardly ever use it—he was right."

She took a deep breath, hoping to steady her voice. "This weekend was a fluke. He said he wanted to take Rory fishing. We found out he just wanted to butter Dottie up. For money. But I'd *wanted* to believe that Gordon could act like a father for once in his life. For Rory's sake. And Dottie's. The way Gordon is—it's hard on Dottie. Gordon's been—strange lately."

She paused. "I worry about Dottie. She's been through so much. I know that Gordon's got her all nervous and upset. And it's on *my* account."

He took her chin gently in his hand and made her face him again. "Do you think she wants you to spend your whole life scared of what he'll do? Do you?"

She shook her head. "No."

He bent nearer to her. "Nora, could you love me back? A little? Even a little'd be enough."

"Oh, stop," she said, "you'll make me cry again. I already feel like a—a sponge."

"I wouldn't mind you bein' a sponge—if you'd be my sponge."

He put his arm around her. With a sigh she sank back against his chest, her cheek pressed against his heart. "What am I going to do with you?"

"Whatever you want, I reckon. Except lose me. I ain't—I'm not allowin' that."

She shook her head. She lifted one hand and shyly toyed with his shirt button. The gesture, so simple, so small, made his heart turn over and sent fire coursing through his blood. He wondered if she could hear how hard his heart thudded. He did not trust himself to speak.

She continued to play with the button, her touch so light it made him catch his breath. "Ken?"

He nodded.

"I told you I didn't want a cowboy. That I wanted better for Rory and me. Didn't that bother you?"

He laid his cheek against her hair. "Yeah," he said, staring at the starlight on the pond's surface. "It bothered me."

"I didn't mean it. Not really. It was just something I said to make you go away."

"It didn't work."

"No. It didn't."

He allowed himself a tight, wry smile. He owed Cal for that, for telling him not to quit, come hell or high water.

He drew back slightly and tilted up her chin so that he could look into her eyes. "I've got some things to tell you," he said solemnly. "I know I don't have much education. I know I'm only a cowboy. But I'm no drifter. I'm a steady man. I've been with the

McKinneys fifteen years, I've been foreman for thirteen, and I've saved my money. I saved a good deal of it.''

Nora squirmed a bit, as if his words made her uncomfortable. "You don't have to tell me—"

"Shh," he said softly, touching her lower lip with his forefinger. "These are things you should know. I got no particular bad habits, though I take a drink now and then, and I like a game of cards. Well, all right, I cuss from time to time. I got a house that's way too big for me, and I—I—" He stopped, searching for words. "What I'm tryin' to say is—what I'm tryin' to ask—"

She imitated his action and put her finger on his lips. "No," she cautioned him, her tone full of intensity. "No. Don't say any more. Please."

"Nora, honey, it's gonna get said, sooner or later. It might as well get said now."

She shook her head. "No. Not now."

He let out a jagged breath. He let his hands frame her face, lace themselves through her silken hair. "Because it's too soon? It's not too soon for me—I know. But if you don't—"

"I don't know what I know," she said, tracing the line of his upper lip. "I don't understand what you make me feel. I don't know so many things. I don't even know your full name, do you know that? If it's Kenneth or Kennard or what."

"Kendell. Kendell John. Ask me whatever you want, Nora. I'll answer anything. Though God knows, I'd rather kiss you. I want to kiss you so much it hurts."

She shook her head and pressed her finger more firmly against his lips. "Don't say that, either. It scares me."

He bent and kissed her anyway, a long kiss, but a gentle one. He forced himself to be gentle, not hungry. He tried to tell her by his touch that he would never want to frighten her, would never want to hurt her. When he finally broke the kiss, he gathered her into his arms. Once again she laid her cheek against his heart. He stroked her hair. "Listen," he said. "We'll take as long as you want. And I got something to ask. Cal gave me the key to the McKinneys' lake house for next weekend. I'd like you all to come—Rory and Dottie, too. I'm not proposin' nothin'—anything improper. I'd just like us to be all together. Would you?"

She went very still in his embrace. He wondered if once more he'd been overbold, pushing her too quickly.

"Nora?"

She was silent for a moment. "Rory won't be here," she said at last. "He's going camping with his Cub Scout troop. Dottie'll be gone, too. She's shutting down the coffee shop and going to visit her sister in Dallas. She always does in July."

Suddenly the thought of having her to himself all weekend swept through him like a flash fire.

"Oh," he said, and kept stroking the silk of her hair.

He imagined having her alone with him in the lake house, imagined her lying in his arms. He thought of the big bed in the master bedroom. He remembered that bed well. It was an antique brass one that Miss Pauline had had shipped up, unassembled, from an antique shop in San Antonio, and Ken had been the only one who could figure out how to put the thing together.

He imagined Nora lying in that beautiful bed—her naked body next to his—but he clenched his teeth and said nothing. He could not ask her to go there with him alone.

It was as if she sensed the direction his desire was carrying him and how hard it was for him to keep control of it. "I should get back home," she said against his chest. "Neither of us got much sleep last night."

"I guess we didn't. You still got your purse full of mossy rocks for Rory?"

She gave a little laugh and looked up at him mischievously. "I think I dropped it over there. When I started being a sponge. And where's your hat? Have you lost it again?"

"I don't know. Maybe a toad-frog hopped off with it. Help me look."

He rose, and helped her to her feet. "Oh," she breathed, "look at the lightning on the horizon. But it's still just heat lightning. Won't it ever rain again? Won't things ever be fresh and clean and green and growing again?"

"Yes." He smiled his solemn smile down at her. "It'll rain. And things will be fresh and clean and green and growin' again. I promise you."

"You can't promise a thing like that."

"I do."

Then, to seal the declaration, he kissed her again. But the false lightning flickered and played on the horizon, as if mocking him, mocking them both.

CHARLIE FOSS, Gordon's partner, was a large man who, like Gordon, lifted weights. His body bulged with muscle and his neck was as thick as a bull's. He wore his hair cut so short his head looked nearly shaved, but he had a sweeping dark walrus mustache. He kept its ends waxed to sharp points.

The two men sat in the kitchen of Charlie's apartment. The kitchen, like the rest of the apartment, had a Spartan neatness that was marred only by a large motorcycle leaning against the wall. Charlie had once been in a motorcycle gang, a fact that impressed Gordon.

It was morning, but Charlie was drinking beer and so was Gordon, even though he had taken two tranquilizers before coming over. The longer he thought about the Mexican run, the more nervous it made him.

When Charlie went to the bathroom, Gordon dug into his pocket and popped another tranquilizer, washing it down with beer. His hands were starting to shake, and a strange buzz echoed in his head.

Charlie came out of the bathroom, fastening a gold ring in his right ear. He said the earring was his lucky piece, and he always wore it when he undertook a hazardous enterprise.

Charlie sat down again across from Gordon. "Now," he said, eyeing Gordon, "you got it straight? You make your first run tomorrow. Today it's business as usual. And when the time comes, you actually don't *know* what's on that truck, understand? You get out and say, 'Load her up, boys.' Then you leave while they do it. Understand? Them's Chessman's orders."

Gordon nodded, his mouth dry.

"You go through the border at a little town just west of Langtry in Val Verde," Charlie said. The morning light twinkled on his earring, transfixing Gordon. He felt giddy, almost hypnotized.

"You cross the border as close after midnight as possible," Charlie said. "Time it right. Chessman owns the guards on that shift. Also, ain't nobody gonna go pokin' around them hogs too much, anyhow." He laughed.

Gordon managed a weak smile. He wished Charlie would offer him another beer.

"Same thing once you cross the border," Charlie said. "You go to the drop point in Monterrey. You ask for Luis. You do the same thing you did stateside. You say, 'Unload her, boys. Take off whatever you want.' Then you split, man. Till they're done. You don't see nothin', you don't know nothin'. Got it?"

"I got it." Gordon looked away from Charlie's earring because it made his head buzz more loudly.

Charlie raised one heavy eyebrow. "You look kinda green around the gills, boy. You sure you're okay?"

"Hell, yes," Gordon said with false heartiness. "It's just I got a bellyache. I ate a bad burrito last night." He paused, wondering how to make his story more plausible. "Besides," he said, "I had woman trouble over the weekend. Some jerk tryin' to put the move on my ex-wife."

Charlie raised his other eyebrow. "You go round and round about that woman. You like her, you hate her. Don't you know your own mind?"

Gordon felt wounded, defensive. "I just don't like the idea of nobody puttin' the move on her, is all. This ol' boy, he's rich, but he's no good. He made me damn mad.''

Charlie shrugged, then rose from the table. He got another beer from the refrigerator, but didn't offer one to Gordon. He sat down again. He cracked his knuckles.

''An old boy took it into his head to flirt with Irma once,'' Charlie said. ''I put him in the hospital. I put more than one man in. You ever shoot anybody?''

''Hell, yes,'' Gordon lied. The thought of shooting someone made him sweatier, but it gave him a strange sense of comfort, too.

''I shot a man in Baton Rouge,'' Charlie said thoughtfully. ''He'd done got on my nerves. I waited across from the bar till it closed. Then he come out, and I leveled a shotgun at him—blam—and then just drove on.''

''You kill him?'' Gordon asked, impressed.

''I don't rightly know. I just kept on drivin'.''

Gordon rubbed his forehead. ''I don't think this old guy's worth shootin'. It ain't like my woman cares for him or nothin'. That'd be different. I'd shoot him in a minute then.''

Charlie laughed, a short, sarcastic bark. ''Hell, Gordo—you want that woman *back?* You told me she was intolerable uppity.''

''Well, I'll just take the uppityness out of her. I can do that, too.''

Charlie's smile seemed sarcastic.

Damn! thought Gordon. *Doesn't he think I'm man enough?* Gordon wondered, with a sudden chill, if Charlie sensed his fear and indecision and was inwardly laughing at him.

"Gordon," Charlie said, "you do love to talk big. Ain't you got work to do? You're supposed to drive a load of yams to Odessa."

"Yeah," Gordon challenged. "And what do you do today?"

"I gotta talk to Chessman some more. And I make my run this afternoon. Blaze a trail for you. Are you sure you're up to this? You look jumpy as a cat."

Gordon stood. He knew he couldn't stay in the apartment any longer. He needed to get out and have a couple more beers to calm himself.

"I'm up to it as much as you are," he said to Charlie and forced himself to glower as menacingly as he could. "Make sure *you* don't screw up."

Charlie only grinned. He raised his beer can in a mock toast to Gordon, then drained it.

Gordon turned and walked away. When he went down the stairs of Charlie's apartment, his legs felt like rubber. His eyelid started to twitch, and it wouldn't stop; it was out of control.

He drove his car to the nearest 7-Eleven and bought himself a six-pack of beer. When he paid for it, his hands were shaking again.

If he drank any more beer, he'd have to pop uppers to drive clear to Odessa and back, but it seemed a small price to pay. His own adrenaline was trying to kill him.

He drove to a deserted spot beside the river and parked. He stared out at the low water of the river, drinking beer and trying to sort his thoughts.

Damn! he thought. He didn't want to drive any damn guns into Mexico. But at this point, with Steponovich on his tail, he had no choice.

Well, he'd get the money, pay off Steponovich, and then he'd by God get *out*. He'd go back to Crystal Creek. First, he just had to get the guns to Monterrey, then pick up a load of goats in Val Verde and haul the goats to Fort Worth.

That, he figured, would get him back to Lubbock by Friday. He'd pay off Steponovich, rest for a day, and Sunday he'd go to Crystal Creek, safe and free. In the meantime, he'd scare old Bubba Gibson half to death.

If the old man really were a threat, Gordon realized he would have no compunction about killing him. But he couldn't imagine Nora, who was so particular, really messing around with Bubba. If Gordon ever found she was fooling around with somebody in earnest—why, he would shoot the bastard—like *that*.

He did want Nora back, he'd decided. And if he wanted her back, he'd take her. How had he gotten her the first time? He'd made her pregnant. It was that easy. He'd do it again.

Maybe she'd protest, at first, but what the hell. Women secretly liked the masterly type; Nora was just too snobby to admit it. Besides, she *owed* him; she'd put him through a lot of hell. She had it coming.

BUBBA HAD PLUGGED the phones back in that morning, trying not to think of Gordon. He wasn't about to live in terror of a fool. Besides, the kid was so unpredictable, he'd probably moved on to some newer grievance, real or imagined.

Bubba felt cheerier today, because last night he'd been with his sweet young thing, Billie Jo Dumont, and she'd forgiven him. She couldn't help it. He'd given her a gold and garnet bracelet he'd bought at a discount store in Dallas for just such an emergency. Soon she was purring like a kitten. He, wearied by his terrible weekend, had been too tired to purr.

When the phone rang for the first time, Bubba jumped. He was in his office, wrestling with his money problems. He told himself the caller wouldn't be Gordon and stayed bent over his tangled accounts, letting Mary answer the ringing.

He was unpleasantly surprised when a few moments later she pushed open the door of his study. She never came into the study uninvited. It was one of Bubba's rules.

At first, he wondered if she was sick; her face was pale and her eyes seemed enormous and full of pain. She looked at him for a long moment. And somehow, he *knew*.

"Bubba," Mary said in a small voice, "what have you done now? That was Gordon Jones on the phone. He said—he said that you and Nora—is it Nora now? I can't believe that, Bubba. She wouldn't—she's not—"

Bubba swore. Then he blustered. "Mary, if brains were money, that boy wouldn't have a red cent. I never touched Nora Jones. I never looked at Nora Jones. I was over at the Longhorn, and he mistook something I said—"

"Was that the day Brock Munroe brought you home?" Mary asked with a sarcasm that startled him. "Oh, Bubba, why don't you just take a hammer and break my heart? Why do it the long, slow way?"

"Mary!" he said, truly shocked. Mary was usually careful to hide any hurt from him; it was one of the things that made her a good wife. "Honey—I'd never hurt you. This is an *accident*—I'm *innocent*. Look, honey, if he keeps callin', I'll tell the phone company. They'll—''

"No," Mary said sharply. "I won't air our dirty laundry in public. Don't you dare tell anyone that this is happening, Bubba. Don't you dare. I am *ashamed*."

The phone on Bubba's desk rang again. Both he and Mary looked at it as if it were a snake, coiled and ready to strike.

After a moment, Bubba snatched up the receiver angrily. "Stop terrorizin' my wife and stop lyin' to her," Bubba shouted, "or I'll mash you like a turnip at Thanksgiving."

"You keep your dirty thoughts off my wife," Gordon retorted. "I'll kill the man that comes between me and her. You understand?"

"Understand *this*, you pinhead," Bubba snarled, and crashed the receiver down so hard that the desk shook.

He looked at Mary, his face suffused with rage and humiliation. "That punk is talkin' about killin' people. I'm gonna report him. I'm gonna call the sheriff. I'm gonna tell Dottie—"

"Leave Dottie out of this," Mary returned, tears flashing in her eyes. "That poor woman has had enough problems. So you just be quiet and take your medicine like a man, Bubba Gibson. You brought it on yourself."

She turned her back on him and closed the door between them. Bubba stared at it, feeling guilty and helpless.

The phone began to ring again, impossibly shrill. It rang and rang. He sank back into his desk chair and put his head between his hands.

"ALL RIGHT," Dottie told Nora, nodding at the coffee shop's phone. "I unplugged it because Gordon *was* calling. And that's why I had the phone turned off at the house. But it has nothing to do with you. Absolutely nothing."

Nora glanced at the phone warily, then back at Dottie.

Dottie shrugged and tried to keep a poker face. She hated lying but felt she had no choice. "All he wants is money—I told him we'd reached a dead end on *that* subject, and he knew it. We went through *that* fight last year."

Nora nodded and began to look less suspicious. She knew about Gordon's borrowing. Since the divorce, Dottie had loaned him hundreds of dollars, actually thousands—he'd never repaid so much as a cent.

Gordon would be fine for a while, then he'd go off on a spree and be back, begging for money. Dottie had kept paying because she didn't want him to get in trouble.

But at last Dottie, driven to distraction and an ulcer, had talked to her doctor, Nate Purdy. She'd also talked to her minister, Howard Blake, and her lawyer, Martin Avery, whom she trusted implicitly.

They'd all told her the same thing. Gordon didn't need money. He needed what Howard Blake called "tough love." If he was ever to grow up, he must control his own behavior, learn to solve his own problems, clean up his own messes. Dottie shouldn't yield another inch to him.

"Well," Dottie went on with her story, "this time he wanted *five hundred* dollars more than he'd asked for before. *Imagine*—after the way he'd been acting! Believe me, I told him what was what."

Nora shook her head in disapproval. "Is it gambling again? Did he say it was gambling?"

"Yes," Dottie answered, glad that at least that much of what she said was true. "He said he'd 'slipped' again."

"Why can't he learn his lesson?" Nora asked with a sigh. "Did he take it well?"

"Take it well?" Dottie said, her eyes widening. "When did he ever take an argument well? And it was an argument—a red-hot one. I was still mad over how he'd acted the other day. I suppose I said more than I should. Well, for once in my life I let it out."

"You should," Nora said loyally. She moved to the counter where Dottie stood and patted the older woman's freckled hand. "You keep too much bottled up inside. It's not good for you."

Dottie gave another shrug. "Still, all I did was set him off on *me*. He said he'd keep calling until I gave in. Well, I'm not putting up with *that*. I'm keeping that phone unplugged all week. I'll show him."

"Good for you," said Nora and gave her hand another pat. "But why didn't you just tell me?"

Dottie waved away the question as if it were a buzzing insect. "Oh, fiddle, he had me upset. I didn't want you—or Rory—concerned on my account. I've calmed down now. But I thought I should explain. I'm the one he's mad at. He never even mentioned you."

Nora seemed to relax. Dottie squared her shoulders and went on. "It's nothing. I'm just showing him I won't be manipulated. I'll keep the phones off for a week. By that time he'll probably have forgotten all about it. You know Gordon."

Nora gave her a rueful smile that said, yes, she knew Gordon all too well. But, Dottie noticed, after she'd confessed to Nora, the girl seemed to go about her work with a lighter step and the worry that had haunted her eyes for the past few days faded.

Dottie watched with relief. She'd lied to Nora, but only because she wanted Nora happy. And she also wanted her to give Ken Slattery a chance.

Last night, when Nora had gone out with Ken, Dottie had been scared sick that the girl was determined to break off with him.

Dottie had feared that Nora would be back in half an hour, saying she'd told Ken goodbye for good. But Nora'd returned late, quite late. And this morning, at breakfast, her face had had a radiant, almost dreamy quality.

Dottie had known then that if she wanted that look to stay on Nora's face, Nora had to be shielded from any fear of Gordon. And so, she'd hatched her lie.

Now, in the coffee shop, Nora sang to herself as she crossed the room. She adjusted the blinds against the strong morning sunshine.

Dottie watched her out of the corner of her eye. *She's falling in love,* she thought with satisfaction. It was, Dottie thought, a wonderful thing to see, and it gladdened her heart.

Gordon would eventually find out, of course. *But not yet. Definitely not yet,* Dottie thought as she smiled at the dreamy look on Nora's face.

CHAPTER NINE

OUTSIDE NORA'S WINDOW, the sparrows chirped a desultory song in the afternoon heat, and no breeze stirred.

"Wear your new blouse," Dottie said, fussing, "the pink one. You always look good in pink."

"But we're just going to the ranch," Nora protested. "He'll think I'm putting on airs."

"It's a very simple blouse. You wear that and your good jeans. Now here—let me put your hair up in a French braid, like I saw Beverly Townsend wear hers the other day. I think I can do it. I used to be good with hairdos."

Nora sat at her dressing table, capping her lipstick. She felt giddy and didn't know why she'd agreed to let Dottie do her hair. *Look at us,* thought Nora. *Two grown women and we're as nervous and giggly and keyed up as teenagers.*

"I don't want a French braid," Nora said nervously. "I'll look silly. Beverly's a beauty queen. I'm not."

"You're every bit as pretty as she is," Dottie said, starting to plait her hair. "Or would be if you'd work at it as hard as she does. You never take the time to do girl things. Hold still. You're as squiggly as Rory."

"Ouch," Nora said, "you're pulling." But she held still, studying herself in the mirror. With lip gloss, powder, blusher and mascara, she looked younger and rosier and brighter-eyed than usual. Maybe she looked too young, she thought, and it would make Ken reconsider the difference in their ages. He would think she was only a child and that he'd made a mistake. And who knew? she thought in frustration, maybe he had, and maybe so had she.

"I can't go out with my face painted up like this," she said, fretting as she reached for a tissue.

"Your face is *not* painted up," Dottie contradicted, holding her in place. "You've only got on a dab. In fact you could stand some more eye makeup. How about eye shadow? I used to have some, someplace."

"No!" Nora almost yipped at the thought. "Oh, Dottie, what are you doing to me? He'll think I'm out to trap him, all got up like some *femme fatale*. I can't do this."

Dottie had pulled back Nora's hair and was still working on the intricacies of the braid. She had fluffed Nora's bangs, and let little wisps and tendrils curl around her temples, ears and the nape of her neck.

"Hush," Dottie commanded, "I think I'm getting my touch back. Oh, I used to enjoy this. All through high school, this is what Vera Wagonner and I did. This is what most girls did. We'd giggle and pretty up and fix each other's hair and play records and practice dancing."

Nora found herself staring at her image again. Who was the girl emerging in the mirror? Nora both knew her and didn't. Dottie's words affected her strangely. *All through high school. This is what most girls did.*

Halfway through high school Nora had been married and a mother. She'd never been to a pajama party or a prom. She'd never belonged to a set of friends; she'd felt too shy and shabby. Other girls walked the high school halls in pairs and groups, giggling and whispering confidences. Nora had walked alone, her head down, her books clutched protectively to her chest.

She hadn't gone to football or basketball games; she'd never been asked to a dance; she'd never actually been on a real date. Gordon had never taken her to so much as a movie. He'd put all his money into maintaining his car, and when he'd taken her out, they drove around, then parked, that was all.

Nora blushed and tried to look away from the girl in the mirror, but she couldn't. It was as if she'd hypnotized herself. She looked into her reflected eyes, trying to see the girl-child she had once been, but she could find no trace. Gordon had destroyed that childhood, that girlhood.

Why, in a way, she thought in wonder, *this is my first real date. A man has actually asked me to supper, and he's coming to pick me up and take me out. It's like being sixteen again. It's like having another chance.*

"Now when he brings you home," Dottie said, making minute adjustments to the braid, "ask him in. There'll be chocolate cake. As I recall, Ken's partial to chocolate cake. I'll have coffee on the stove, ready to perk. If he'd rather have sherry, there's some in the pantry."

Dottie inspected her handiwork, uncoiled one more tendril of hair at Nora's temple, then nodded her approval. "There," she said with satisfaction. "You plumb look like a princess. All you need are some fancier earrings." She drew a pair from her apron pocket. "Here. Let's put these on you."

"Dottie! No—those are your genuine gold earrings from Neiman-Marcus. I can't wear them," Nora protested. "Those are your special-occasion earrings."

"This is a special occasion," Dottie said firmly, fastening the thick gold hoop into place.

She thinks I'm in love with him, and he's in love with me, Nora thought in rising panic. *Everybody thinks that, but it's too soon.*

The air seemed to thicken in her lungs, choking her. "No, you're making too much of this."

Dottie attached the second earring to the lobe of Nora's ear. "Honey, I'm enjoying this. I like seeing you happy."

Nora's throat grew tighter, her chest more leaden. A stricken look crossed her face. "I—I'm happy enough by myself," she said to Dottie. "As long as you and Rory are here—"

Dottie put a freckled hand on Nora's shoulder and squeezed. Her eyes met Nora's in the mirror. "No, honey. You've been *content* with Rory and me. Today you've been *happy.* There's a difference."

"Happy," Nora mused, the beat of her heart playing painful games. She put her hand on Dottie's and clasped it. "Happy. Is that what I've been?"

Dottie nodded, her expression loving, yet tinged with sadness. "Yes, honey. That's what you've been. Don't you even recognize it?"

"I don't think I'm used to it," she said, shaking her head with uncertainty. "It scares me."

Dottie swallowed and licked her lips. She knelt beside the chair and took Nora's face between her hands. "Sweetie," she said, her voice trembling, "I know. But don't be afraid. Don't be afraid of *him*. He's not like Gordon, honey. Not at all. He's a good man—a real one."

But Nora's eyes kept their troubled look. She knew what frightened her so deeply about happiness.

It tasted so sweet, so intoxicating, so rare, that she knew if she drank deeply of it, then lost it, it would be like dying. Yet how could she *not* lose it?

Ken Slattery was a real man. But she was not sure she was what some people would consider a real woman. Gordon had killed her sexual feelings. She'd even been grateful for that little piece of murder. It had seemed a mercy.

To be kissed by Ken was one thing, sweet and warming and addictive. That she liked it surprised no one more than herself. But to let him make love to her was something else. The prospect terrified her. She didn't know if she could allow herself to do it.

She would have to face the question soon—not tonight, thank God—for she and Ken wouldn't truly be alone tonight. But soon she would have to confront the reality of sex. She didn't want to. It held too many bad memories.

All she knew about sex was that it was connected to pain. It could imprison a person like a trap; she knew, for it had imprisoned her, and she was lucky to have escaped, scarred as she was.

Ken Slattery wanted a complete woman. She was not sure she dared even to *try* to be one. She was not sure at all.

AT FIVE O'CLOCK that afternoon, Ken stood shirtless before the bathroom mirror, shaving for the second time that day. He was to pick up Nora and Rory in town at five forty-five.

A sudden hammering at the front door startled him into knicking his chin. He swore under his breath. The knock sounded again, louder than before.

"What?" Ken yelled, grimacing as he stabbed at his cut with a styptic pencil. "I'm busy."

"So am I," came Cal's voice. "But it don't make me antisocial."

Ken sighed. He'd heard that Cal and Serena were coming to the Double C for another few days. With their second boot shop open at the Hole in the Wall, the two of them were hopping around like fleas these days. This was how the kid settled down?

"Come in," Ken said with resignation. "Unless you've got your ladylove with you. I ain't fit to receive ladies." He glanced down at his jeans. They were zipped, but at the top, the copper button was still undone. Hurriedly he fastened it, managing to get shaving cream on his flat stomach. He wiped it off and tried to concentrate on his face again.

He heard Cal's boot heels striking the hall's bare floor; then in the mirror he saw Cal's reflection appear behind his own. Cal wore jeans, a brown shirt, a tan Stetson and a sardonic smile.

He leaned against the doorframe, folding his arms. "Behold." He smirked, nodding toward Ken's reflection. "He beautifies himself. Gentlemen who do twilight shavin' have twilight nuzzlin' on their minds."

Ken shot him a brief glance, then concentrated on his own jawline. "You haven't thought about anything except twilight nuzzlin' since you were nine years old. Also mornin' and noon nuzzlin'. Where's Serena? Or did you nuzzle her insensible?"

Cal shrugged amiably. "I have, on occasion. But not today. She's in the kitchen, helpin' Lettie May. She is, in fact, helpin' Lettie May make a pizza for *you* tonight. Serena just happens to be the best little pizza maker in Central Texas."

"Just so it ain't in the shape of a boot," Ken said. "Or taste like one." He finished the left side of his jaw and started on the right.

"You must be bringin' both Nora and Rory out here. That's how I've got it figured."

Ken gave him a sharp glance, then nodded. "Yeah. But I didn't tell anybody. Just *how* did you figure it?"

Cal edged into the bathroom and sat on the edge of the old claw-footed bathtub. He crossed his legs and pushed back his hat to a cocky angle.

"Easy," he said with obvious self-satisfaction. "First you asked Lettie May for pizza. That means there's a kid involved. You're a true waddy. If it ain't steak, you don't stick a fork in it."

Ken only grunted in reply.

"Second," Cal said, jerking a thumb toward the living room, "you rented a VCR from the Armadillo Video Store. I saw the sticker on it. Third, you also got a passel of rented video games on your couch, including Alien Space Demons from the Planet Droog. I don't think you and Nora are gonna play it."

"Humph," said Ken, and wiped the last of the lather from his face. "You're a goddamn Sherlock Holmes, ain't you? Are you a-sittin' on the edge of my shirt? I was usin' that tub for a shirt hanger."

Cal looked down and edged away from the white shirt draped over the bathtub's edge. Then he squinted up at Ken, his handsome face half serious, half taunting. "On top of that, I heard that you asked Daddy if you could borrow old Sparkplug for the evening and saddle him up. *I* learned to ride on him. So did Lynn. So did half the ranch hands' kids. He's the official teach-kids-to-ride pony. You gonna teach Rory?"

"He wants to learn," Ken said. He reached for his shirt and shrugged into it. He rolled the sleeves halfway up his forearms, then began to button the front.

Cal let out a soft whistle. "You're gettin' domestic, Slats. Pizza and ponies and video games. Never thought I'd see the day."

"You're seein' it," Ken said laconically. He tucked in his shirt. He reached for his belt, which hung over the doorknob. He began lacing it through his belt loops. It was a hand-tooled Mexican belt with a large, elaborate silver buckle studded with turquoise.

"Jeez-louise," breathed Cal, watching Ken fasten the belt. "It's the Gawd-a-mighty belt buckle. I thought that was reserved for sacred occasions."

"It is." Ken stepped into the bedroom, paused before the bureau and combed his hair. He examined himself critically in the mirror.

The belt buckle was the only truly rich piece of finery he'd ever owned. Years ago he'd gone with Cal to Nuevo Laredo, where, for one of the few times in his life, Ken had gotten pie-eyed drunk. He'd somehow ended up with his wallet two hundred dollars lighter and the belt, buckle and all, slung over his shoulder like an ammunition belt. He'd remembered none of the particulars.

"Why in hell'd you buy *that?*" Cal had asked. "It's big as Las Vegas. It's *shinier* than Las Vegas. When'll you ever wear it?

"Someday," Ken had vowed, swaying slightly, "a day will come important enough—to wear—this here—buckle."

"When?" Cal had demanded, still astounded.

"I don't know it—now," Ken had said solemnly. "But I'll by God know it when it comes." Then, just as solemnly, he'd hiccuped, which had pitched Cal into a snickering fit.

Over the years, to bait Ken, Cal had repeated the conversation dozens of times, complete with the hiccup.

Now Cal had risen and was leaning his elbow against the frame of the bathroom door. He looked at the fancy silver buckle and shook his head. His smile was no longer sardonic. "You reckon this is a sacred occasion?"

"Close enough," Ken said. He reached to the dresser top, took up his white straw Stetson and put it on. "I've gotta go. I promised to pick them up."

"Yeah," said Cal. "I understand. Hey, Slats?"

"What?"

"You'll need my help. Feel free to ask."

Ken's eyes narrowed. "Your help?"

"Yeah," Cal said with a smug smile. "I bet you ain't worth a cow pie playing Alien Space Demons. That little kid is gonna eat your lunch. You'll need coachin'. That means me." Cal stabbed his thumb against his chest.

Ken shot him a wry look. "*You* can play Alien Space Demons? Since when?"

"Since I've been minglin' with Serena's nieces," Cal answered. "Don't laugh. I've won the rank of Supreme High Universal Commander of All Galactic Forces. You'll be lucky to make Space Cadet. A geranium pot from Jupiter will fall on your head and kill you, sure enough."

Ken shook his head and started toward the door, concealing a smile. "You've done mastered more ways to waste time than I ever thought of."

"You're jealous, is all." Cal ambled carelessly behind him and followed him outside to the pickup truck. He had one of his favorite horses, Grumpy, tied to the porch rail. He unknotted the reins. "Did you give Nora the poetry book yet?"

Ken slammed the truck door and shook his head. "I'm savin' it. For Saturday."

On Saturday he would have been seeing Nora for a full week. That was an anniversary of sorts. He didn't suppose the fact would mean much to her. Someday it might. Maybe.

He met Cal's eyes. "I'll tell her where it came from. That'll make it special to her. She liked your mama."

"What about the lake house?" Cal asked. "You gonna use it?"

The question was a fair one, but Ken didn't want to consider it. He looked away, off toward the horizon, his expression moody. He shook his head. "I don't know yet."

He wanted Nora to go with him to the lake house. But asking her to go there with him alone would sound like a sexual invitation, and he didn't want to hurry her in that department. He could tell that Gordon had left her with only bad memories about sex. In his arms she could seem intoxicatingly warm and eager. But always, just beneath the warmth of her response, he could sense her fear as well.

That conflict in her tore at him. Would she always fear him more than she wanted him? He didn't know if he could coax her and gentle her past her fear. Maybe it couldn't be done. But he aimed to try. God in heaven, he aimed to try.

That was why he had asked her to bring Rory with her tonight. So she'd feel safe. Besides that, he knew that to win Nora, he'd have to win Rory over, as well. There was an old saying he remembered: To take the mother by the heart, take the child by the hand. What's more, he genuinely liked Rory. The boy had so much of Nora in him.

"I see," Cal said.

Ken nodded noncommittally. He put two fingers to his hat as a signal of goodbye, started the truck and pulled away. Cal gave one of his wild whoops, making Ken glance back over his shoulder.

"Remember," Cal said with a laugh, "you'll beg me to teach you that damn game—you'll see. That kid'll whip your ass."

Ken allowed himself a small smile and turned his attention back to the road.

Cal gave another yell of pure high spirits, then leaped on Grumpy, and raced Ken down the lane to the highway. When they reached the road, he reined in the horse, waved his hat and laughed again. "Watch out, world. Slats is courtin', and he means bidness!"

Ken glanced at him in the rearview mirror and allowed himself another slight smile. He was indeed going courting, and he did indeed mean business. The sacred belt buckle proved that, he supposed.

He also supposed that somehow, clear back in Nuevo Laredo, even in his cups, he had known that one day he was destined to go after Nora Jones, to make her his own. Or to die trying.

CHAPTER TEN

"THANK YOU," Dottie said to Martin Avery. She sat down stiffly in one of the leather-upholstered chairs in Martin's law office.

The smile pasted on her face felt artificial, but she tried to keep it in place. "I appreciate your staying after hours for me," she said. "I didn't want Nora to know I was coming. I want to keep this—confidential."

Martin nodded. He was a trim man of average height, handsome in a sharp-featured way, with a full head of graying hair. He was fifty-five, three years older than Dottie, but looked younger. Life had been quieter for him and kinder to him.

Dottie cocked her head toward the office door, which was slightly open. As hard as she tried to force her smile, it faded.

Billie Jo Dumont sat at the reception desk in the outer office. She had on earphones and was transcribing from a portable tape recorder, her fingers dancing over the keys of her word processor.

"I didn't expect *her* to be here," Dottie said pointedly. "Like I said, I want this confidential. Can I close that door?"

Martin smiled. "The air-conditioning isn't working in my office—just in there. This dadblamed heat has burned out half the units in town. I'm a coolant vampire, sucking Billie Jo's cold air into my room. Relax, Dottie. She's working overtime transcribing. Besides, she's the soul of discretion.''

Some soul of discretion, Dottie thought darkly, *gallivanting all over town with somebody else's husband.* Martin was bright enough as a lawyer, but Dottie sometimes thought he was naive about women.

When Billie Jo had taken the job as Martin's secretary, it had been clear to everyone except Martin that she had set her cap for him. But Martin seemed a confirmed bachelor, and Billie Jo's wiles had gotten her nowhere. On the rebound, she'd taken up with Bubba, who was not so impervious to her charms.

"Believe me," Martin said. "Billie Jo knows more than she ever tells. It goes with the job. She minds her manners.''

Dottie, dubious, said nothing. She couldn't help it; the open door and Billie Jo's nearness made her nervous. But what Martin said was at least partially true. The air in the room was close, the only relief the slight flow of cool seeping in from the outer office.

Martin took off his glasses and loosened his tie. "So what is it, Dottie? What can I do for you? What don't you want Nora to know about?''

Dottie gripped the leather arms of the chair. "A will," she said, trying to keep her voice calm. "I want to make a will.''

"A good idea," Martin said smoothly. "In fact, you should have years ago. Everybody should have one.''

"I want to leave everything to Nora and Rory," Dottie said, forging ahead while her resolve was still firm. "Everything—except some money in savings. I want to give Gordon two thousand dollars. That's all. I want you to make it so he doesn't get any more—and that he *can't*. He'd take it and gamble it all away. Make me a will he can't break, Martin. One so iron-clad he won't even try."

Martin's expression grew more serious. He put his glasses back on. A frown line appeared between his brows. "You've thought this out? You're sure?"

"Positive. And I want Nora to be executor of Rory's share. If she wants to sell the Longhorn, she can. The house, the business, everything—it's theirs."

Martin studied her for a long, uncomfortable minute. He picked up a pencil and tapped it on his desk blotter. "I see," he said.

Dottie wiped her palms nervously on the skirt of her flowered dress. "Martin, Gordon's getting *worse*. It's like he's possessed. I want to rest knowing he can't get his hands on what should go to Nora and Rory. If he does—I'll come back from the grave and haunt you, I swear I will."

Martin shook his head and laid down the pencil. He folded his hands before him. "Let's not talk about graves yet, Dottie. I think I can do what you want."

Dottie opened her big white straw purse and drew out a sealed envelope, addressed to Gordon. "Here," she said, "I want to leave this in your hands, too. It's to be given to Gordon if I—die. It tells him in no uncertain terms why I'm doing this. And that I want him to leave Nora and Rory *alone*. I love him, but I can't let him make everyone's life miserable."

Martin took the envelope and set it on his desk beside a file folder. "I'll do what you want, of course.

But you should know, Dottie, that no letter can guarantee that Gordon stays away, especially from Rory. I mean, he does have visitation rights—''

"That's another thing I want to talk about," Dottie said, gripping the chair arms again. She squared her jaw and tried to keep her face controlled, emotionless. "What'll it take to end his visitation rights? And what would it take for somebody else to—to adopt the boy?"

Martin's chiseled mouth curved downward, and his frown line deepened. He seemed to be choosing his words carefully. "Dottie, you can't do anything about visitation rights. That's between Nora and Gordon. Nora would have to have grounds—''

"I'm aware of that," Dottie said impatiently. "There *are* grounds. Gordon hasn't paid a cent of child support—ever. He's only asked to take Rory once in the past four months. He also blessed out Nora in front of the boy and a lot of other people—*and* grabbed her. He left a bruise. He's in debt. He gambles. He—talks wild, he talks crazy—he's not himself, Martin."

Martin avoided her eyes and scribbled something on a yellow legal pad. "I'm sorry to say he sounds exactly like himself, Dottie. Only more so. Has he made any specific threats? Especially against Nora or Rory?"

Dottie's brow furrowed. Her head was starting to hurt again. "Specific threats? He said something about—about *taking* Nora back. I can't remember how he put it. And he talked about having 'dangerous business' or something like that. He actually talked about killing—well, killing somebody. I know he didn't mean it, but I'm worried, Martin. He sounded so out of control I had the phone at the house turned off. I stopped answering it at the coffee shop.''

Martin looked up and met her gaze. He put one hand to his glasses, a studious pose. "Dottie, this *is* Gordon we're dealing with. He might have forgotten everything he's said to you by now. He could be off on a completely different tangent. This may just be another one of his—episodes.''

Dottie shook her head. A vein leaped in her temple. "The episodes happen more often, Martin. They're getting worse. I'm his mother, and *I can tell*. They scare me. If Nora took him to court, how much would it cost? So that he couldn't see Rory?''

Martin shrugged. "I can't say. It depends on if he tries to fight it.''

"And a protective order,'' Dottie said, putting her hand to her forehead. "That's what you call it, isn't it? Couldn't we get a protective order to keep Gordon away?''

"An order's serious business,'' Martin said, looking grimmer than before. "Is he actually threatening or attempting to commit some specific wrong involving Nora or Rory?''

Dottie let her hand drop into her lap and curl into a fist. "I want to stop him before he does.''

Martin shook his head in sympathy, but his expression didn't change. "That's not how the law works, Dottie.''

She clenched her fist tighter. "It's how it *should* work.'' What did the courts want? she wondered in despair. Couldn't they stop harm before it was done?

Martin's eyebrow raised ruefully. "The law is not a perfect instrument. I'll be the first to admit it."

Dottie's mouth twisted. She realized she probably sounded nervous and irrational to Martin. Why did Martin insist on making things difficult? All she wanted to do was protect Nora and Rory—and make sure Nora got her chance at happiness.

"All right," she said. "Just try to figure out how much money it would take to revoke Gordon's visitation rights."

"I told you," Martin said with quiet patience, "it depends. Are you sure that Nora's going to want—"

"Yes," Dottie practically snapped. "I'm sure Nora's going to want to. Listen to me, Martin. You probably think I'm a hysterical woman, who's got a bunch of funny notions, all of a sudden. You're thinking, 'Oh, she's worked too hard,' or 'Oh, the heat's got her,' or 'Oh, she's at that age.' Well, I'm not hysterical. I *sense* Gordon's going to make trouble, I feel it, and I'm trying to stop it before it starts. Nora never wanted Gordon to have any visitation rights—you're the one who said, 'Don't worry. Don't fight him. It won't be any problem.' Well, you were *wrong*. It is a problem. Or it's about to be."

Martin sighed and leaned back in his chair. He began to toy with the pencil again. "Touché," he said unhappily. "You're right—I was wrong. And I don't think you're hysterical. If the whole county was as sane as you are, I'd be out of business and so would the sheriff. So would the social workers."

Dottie sank back against her seat. "I'm sorry, Martin. I didn't mean to carry on. But he worries me. He's sometimes—very jealous about Nora. Before, there was never any reason to be, I suppose. But now—''

Her sentence died, unfinished. Martin completed it for her. "But now Ken Slattery's in the picture. Don't look so surprised, Dottie. Everybody knows it. This is a small town. But you talked about adoption. Surely this thing between Nora and Ken hasn't gone that far, that fast?''

Dottie's face went hot with embarrassment and she looked away from Martin, staring at the pattern in his Oriental rug instead. "No—of course not. I was just wondering. Rory needs a real father. Ken's been watching Nora for months—for months I've guessed how he's felt. He's good to her. He's good to Rory. I hope— He seems— Nora acts— He—''

Once again words failed her.

Martin set down his pencil and rose from his chair. "Let's take one thing at a time, Dottie," he said, smiling kindly. "Let me make out the will. Then Nora needs to come to me about the visitation business.''

"But I'm the one paying your bill," Dottie objected. "Every extra dime Nora's got has gone into schooling. She's trying to build a future for her and Rory.''

Martin shook his head. "She has to be the one anyway, Dottie, no matter who pays. I know you. If you could, you'd fight all the battles for the people you love. But Nora has to be the one to go to court. And if she and Ken decide to marry, then they need to come to me about Ken adopting Rory.''

Dottie colored more deeply, feeling like a foolish, meddling woman. "I just wanted to know the facts,'' she murmured. "I just wanted to know the legalities ... what's involved ... the costs ..."

"I'll try to give you a general idea," Martin said. "But not here. Not now."

He offered his hand to her. She looked at it and took it.

"I know," she said. "You're telling me to leave. I've bothered you enough, asking questions about things that are none of my business."

He helped her to her feet, but kept hold of her hand, placing his free one over hers in a clasp of friendship. "No. That's not what I'm telling you. I'm telling you let's talk about this as friends, not as attorney and client. I'll take you to Zack's, buy you a drink. I could use a tall cool one. I know that Rory's your business. Nora, too. They're your business because you love them."

Dottie looked up at him in surprise and gratitude. "Why, Martin. How kind you are. Why do I always forget how kind you are?"

He laughed and released her hand. "Because I'm a lawyer. The reputation always smirches me. You know the joke—how do you scare off killer sharks? Throw a lawyer in the water. Come on. Let's get that drink. Visions of gin and tonic dance in my head."

"I'll buy," Dottie said, touched by his concern and his courtliness.

"I'll buy," Martin said firmly. "For old times' sake. And we've been through some times, haven't we, Dottie? Remember that tornado on Halloween, back when we were in high school ... ? I was a senior, you were a freshman ...."

BILLIE JO DUMONT watched them leave. She took off her earphones, and one of her lovely auburn brows bent itself into a frown.

Martin Avery was taking Dottie Jones for a drink? Why, Dottie was as old as *he* was. Why didn't Martin ever take out someone young and attractive and sexy? Someone, such as, say, herself?

She'd worked in this office for two whole years. In that time, Martin had never volunteered to take her as far as the coffee shop or to buy her as much as a one-scoop root beer float. Sometimes Billie Jo wondered darkly if Martin wasn't secretly a sissy boy.

She narrowed her eyes. And that old cat, Dottie, hadn't trusted Billie Jo to hear her *private* conversation with Martin. The nerve!

As if Billie Jo didn't eventually find out everything that happened in the office anyway. She had clearly heard Dottie ask about closing the door. Billie Jo's tape had ended, so she just pretended to be busy. And, for spite, she'd made sure she heard every word.

So Dottie didn't trust her? Who did Dottie think typed up those wills? Who did Martin's paperwork for every single thing he did—including protective orders and adoptions?

Still, Billie Jo thought, it was interesting, the way even Gordon Jones's own mama had turned against him. And now it sounded as if Gordon was making threats against Ken Slattery over Nora. She wouldn't want to be in Ken Slattery's boots. No, indeedy.

Billie Jo gave a dainty shudder. Gordon Jones had always given her the horripilations. Why sometimes, when a person looked into his eyes, it was as if nobody was at home in there.

She'd heard how Gordon had almost pounded on Bubba last Saturday. Well, she thought, clearing her desk, *that* had been a tiny little incident, and it had almost served Bubba right, he'd been so hateful to Billie Jo and so neglectful of her that whole long weekend.

She might even break her professional ethics and tell Bubba about Gordon's own mother turning against him. Bubba always rejoiced over the misadventures of his enemies. On the other hand, maybe she wouldn't say a word.

After all, Martin had defended her ethics, and well he should. Billie Jo might have her flaws, but she seldom told tales out of school. No, she decided, she wouldn't say a word to Bubba. She liked having earned Martin's compliment the way she had.

But if she *wanted* to say something—oh, yes, she thought with satisfaction—if she wanted to, she could let a cat or two out of the bag.

THE AFTERNOON SUN was low and hot on the horizon and shining directly into Gordon's eyes as he drove west toward Mexico.

He'd pulled the shade flap down, but it didn't help. Dozens of little phantom suns seemed to have burned themselves into his eyeballs. They danced and spun, ghostlike, over everything he saw.

He had the air-conditioning on in the cab, but he couldn't stop sweating. He couldn't quite believe he was doing what he was doing, and he half wondered if he was dreaming.

Even when the truck's wheels hit a pothole, he felt as if the truck wasn't quite substantial, and the jolt from the pothole wasn't actually... actual. All physical sensations seemed filtered through a veil of buzzing haze.

He had left the truck alone while the men—two Anglos, one Hispanic—had loaded it. Now it was full of hogs, but hidden under the truck bed were rifles, hundreds of them, Charlie had said. Gordon didn't even know what kind.

Gordon didn't want to think about the rifles. They seemed as strange and dreamlike as the little suns dancing dizzingly across his vision. When it periodically hit him that everything about this trip *was* real— the guns especially—such a wave of nausea swept over him that he truly thought he might die of it.

God, but he wished he'd stop sweating. He supposed it was the uppers, the amphetamines in his system—that made him sweat. He wanted to take another downer, to counteract the effect, but if he got drowsy and ran the truck off the road—oh, Lord, what then? What *then?*

At that thought, another flood of sickness swept over him, so intense that it brought tears to his eyes.

He pulled out a bandanna handkerchief and wiped his eyes, but they still stung. Keeping the steering wheel steady with the pressure of his thigh, he fumbled to tie the bandanna, piratelike, around his forehead to keep more sweat from dripping into his eyes.

Then, just as he'd fastened it, his leg gave an involuntary jerk, and the truck went swerving half out of its lane and directly toward a church bus trundling down the road.

Gordon seized the wheel with both hands, his heart turning cold and leaping up to choke him. The church bus blared its horn, and the noise made him feel as if someone had stuck thousands of ice-cold needles into every square inch of his flesh.

Shaking, he managed to keep the truck's path steady. He swore inwardly—a church bus? What if he hit a *church bus,* and the cops found all those rifles? Good God, they'd lock him up and throw away the key and he was still a young man, and everybody knew what happened to good-looking young men like him, in jail—no, no, no no no no no no.

He reached into the glove compartment, opened his bottle of tranquilizers and popped one, swallowing it without water. It almost gagged him and left a bitter taste on his tongue.

A beer would have been better, he thought helplessly, a beer he could have controlled the effect better, but he had to do something, now, fast; he couldn't go on killing himself with worry the way he was doing.

Oh, to be done with this nightmare, he thought, scrubbing the sweat from his lip with the back of his hand. Oh, to have it over, over, over.

He wanted to go home to safety and sanity again, to a place where people had to love and respect and obey him.

Nobody would hurt him there. He was forcing his enemies into submission there, he was whipping them into submission, starting with old Bubba. Every time he stopped the truck for gas or for anything, he made sure he phoned Bubba. The phone rang, somebody would pick it up, swear and bang it down again. Old Bubba. Scared even to *talk* back.

Bubba had better stay scared and stay away; Gordon was coming home.

His heart beat madly, his head buzzed more thickly than before. The phantom suns danced and winked in his vision.

He was going home. Home. Home.

Where he would take his young wife to bed all the time, whenever he wanted, whether she liked it or not. He'd show her, for once and for all, who was running this show.

And where his mama would again love him unconditionally and forever. And she would forgive him for everything and keep him out of money trouble.

That was his dream. God help the man who tried to come between that dream and him. That man was dead.

CHAPTER ELEVEN

CAL HAD BEEN RIGHT, dammit. Rory hadn't merely beaten Ken at Alien Space Demons, he had annihilated him.

Ken pulled Nora closer, kissed the edge of her ear and smiled at the memory. She stirred drowsily, snuggling more deeply into the crook of his arm.

Now Rory lay soundly sleeping down the hall, sprawling across Ken's bed, where Ken had carried him and Nora had drawn down the quilt so that the boy's head could rest on the pillow.

"We should go now," Nora murmured against Ken's chest, but she made no move to draw away from him.

He tightened his embrace and nuzzled her ear more languorously. His breath softly stirred her hair. It was warm and it tickled her.

He laughed, low in his throat.

"What's funny?" she asked, pushing him away slightly so that she could look up into his eyes. They seemed deceptively lazy, and his one-sided smile was partly rueful, partly shy.

"I got killed nineteen times tonight," he drawled, shaking his head. "I never even made space cadet. Those dadblasted geranium pots from Jupiter kept fallin' on my head."

"They're terrible," Nora agreed, but she really wasn't thinking much about geraniums from Jupiter. She was admiring the way the light gilded the strong planes of his face. "They've killed me dozens of times. I don't know how kids do it. What's Rory? Major General of the Solar System?"

"Solar system, my foot," he said, tracing the line of her cheek with his forefinger. "He's Warlord of the Galaxy."

She smiled. "You were a good sport."

He let his finger rest in the soft cleft in her chin. "What choice did I have?"

"He had a wonderful time. He loved the pony. He's always wanted to know how to ride."

"I'll teach him." He turned his hand so that the backs of his fingers trailed across her cheek.

"I remember that pony. I always wanted to ride him. My brother said I was too old."

He frowned slightly, but kept stroking her cheek. "You never learned to ride?"

She smiled. "Just barely."

"I'll teach you, too."

"Do you think you could?"

"I could try." He touched his thumb and forefinger to the edges of her lips. "My God," he breathed, his eyes holding hers, "you're so soft."

His smile faded, his lips parted, and he bent to take hers. Something leapt sweetly in Nora, making her giddy and eager for his touch. His warm mouth conveyed so many contradictory things: strength, yet sensitivity; hunger, yet restraint; tenderness, yet increasing mastery.

She found her lips opening to allow him greater intimacy. His tongue tasted hers, toyed with it, dared her to explore him as he was exploring her.

Shyly, the tip of her tongue entered his mouth, lightly tracing its most private contours. At the same moment, she raised her hand to play with the button at the throat of his shirt. He inhaled so sharply that she gasped and sank into his embrace, letting desire enclose her like a cloud of darkness and stars.

Somehow, the button she had twisted so artlessly came undone, and she felt the bare warmth of his chest against the backs of her fingers. The crisp hair and the hardness of his muscle grazed her knuckles.

Startled, she began to draw her hand reluctantly away, but his hand closed over hers, guiding it back to rest against his chest once more. The beat of his heart thudded beneath her fingertips, as if saying, Touch. Touch. Touch.

Slowly she let her fingers glide over the sculpted planes of his chest. He gasped harshly, then deepened his kiss.

His hand fell from hers to clasp her waist and draw her nearer. Then it rose, sliding up her rib cage until it framed her breast, but did not quite touch it.

Her body tensed, yet throbbed with such desire that she could not bring herself to move away. She stopped stroking his chest. He stayed motionless for the length of two heartbeats, then three, then four.

Nora's taut muscles could not resist him. With a sigh, she relaxed against him, letting the roundness of her breast brush his tensed hand.

Slowly, gently, his fingers moved to cup her, hold her. His other hand moved up underneath the back of her blouse. His fingers were roughened, but they were deft and sure upon the fastening of her bra. It tightened slightly as he undid it, then seemed to sigh free of her flesh.

She realized that there was nothing now but a loosened wisp of lace between her bare breasts and his hand. Shakily, she held her breath, waiting for his touch. Her pulses beat so quickly that she could feel them tingling in her fingertips.

His mouth drew away from hers, just barely. When he spoke, his breath felt first warm, then cool against her moist lips. "Nora? Do you want me to touch you? If you don't—"

She could not answer *yes* or *no*. Once more she tensed, almost to the point of shuddering. She kept her eyes tightly closed. *This should seem so wrong,* she thought in confusion. *This should seem so ugly and shameful. But it doesn't. Not with him.*

He bent his head to kiss her between her breasts, his mouth hot against the thin silk of her blouse. He kissed that deep valley until it tingled, then moved to caress the curves and aching tips of her breasts.

"Oh," she whispered. She knew she should pull away but did not. "Oh."

His fingers were undoing her buttons, one by one, so swiftly and gently she'd hardly realized it.

"Oh," she repeated helplessly.

"I know," he said harshly. "This isn't the time. This isn't the place."

"Rory..."

"I know. I know."

"Please," she said, anxiety closing over her, its chill driving away the warm urgency of wanting him. No man except Gordon had ever touched her breasts. The memory of his roughness came surging back, chilling her. "I—I—"

"Wait," he murmured, drawing back from her, his breath ragged. "Wait. Just let me see you. That's all."

Suddenly panicking, she thought she heard Rory stirring in the bedroom. The coldness clamped her more tightly. She winced, pulling away from Ken and clutching the edges of her shirt together.

Rory, she thought, certain again that she heard him. *He mustn't find us, he mustn't see this, I mustn't do this—*

She bit her lip hard and kept her eyes squeezed shut. She fumbled to refasten her bra. As she did, her shirt fell open, and Ken leaned and began to kiss her breasts again, his hands taut on either side of her bare waist.

"Oh, please," she begged, still struggling to fasten her bra. "I don't know how to do this. I'm hopeless."

His mouth moved down her torso, to the smoothness of her stomach. He kissed her long and lingeringly, just above the navel. Nora felt almost faint, fear and desire mingling with nearly equal strength.

But once again she heard a noise, and it galvanized her into escaping Ken's touch. *I don't want this, I don't want this.* The words ran through her mind, an echo of the fearful old times with Gordon. Yes, that was precisely what she'd always thought in Gordon's rough embrace: *I don't want this.*

She jerked away from him and began to button her blouse. She hurried to tuck it in and to smooth her hair. She refused to meet his eyes. She could hear his breathing. Like hers, it was shallow and rapid.

"Nora, I'm sorry," he said, his voice gruff. "I promised I wouldn't—"

"Mom?" A sleepy voice called her from the bedroom. "Mom? I had a dream."

She sprang to her feet. Ken rose at the same moment, buttoning his half-opened shirt. He reached for her hand. "Nora—"

She eluded him and sped toward the bedroom, her face burning. Her lips still stung from his kisses; her whole body tingled. But she struggled to put on a natural face for Rory, to act as if all was normal.

"Hi, sweetie," she said briskly as she came into the room. She didn't turn on the lamp. Enough light from the hall fell into the room for her to make her way to him.

"You fell asleep," she said in a chirpy voice she immediately hated herself for using. "It's time we went home. Get up."

She felt Ken's tall figure looming behind her. His shadow joined hers on the wall.

"I'm tired, and I had a bad dream," Rory said, cranky. He rubbed his eyes and squinted unhappily at the hall light. "Carry me."

He was too big to be carried, but Nora felt too guilty to argue. She sighed and bent to lift him.

"He's heavy," Ken murmured. "Let me." He scooped Rory up and held him, the boy's head resting sleepily on his shoulder.

Nora looked at the two of them in the shadows, the tall, rangy blond man, the dark-haired little boy. An odd wrenching feeling tore at her within for reasons she didn't understand.

"You shouldn't," she said to Ken." You'll spoil him—"

Then she clamped her mouth shut, because she was being illogical. She had been about to carry Rory herself. She bent and picked up his shoes. Then once more she found herself staring at the man and the child. Rory's head lolled against Ken's shoulder, his eyes already fluttering closed again.

"It's all right," Ken said. "Everything's different. That's all." He reached and took her by her free hand, lacing his fingers through hers.

They stepped into the hall. He looked down at her. "It's all right," he repeated.

He seemed waiting for some kind of signal, some kind of sign from her. She looked away, unwilling to meet his eyes.

She resisted the desire to squeeze his hand, even shyly, just once. She was afraid of failing him, of failing herself. She needed time, she told herself. But what if even time wasn't enough? What then? Ken wanted a warm and loving woman, not a frigid one. Oh, she didn't know what to think. She didn't want him to know how confused she felt.

"We'd better go," she said, her voice clipped and cool. "It's after midnight."

IT WAS JUST after midnight. Billie Jo Dumont thrashed about in her bed, pounded her pillow into a more submissive shape, settled against it and tried once more to relax.

She could not. She sighed in frustration.

Bubba was supposed to spend as many evenings with her as possible. Ordinarily at this time, she would be playing elaborate kissy-face games with Bubba, telling him goodbye the way he liked. Tonight, she hadn't even been able to tell him hello.

When she got home, she'd found a message from him on her telephone answering machine. "Sweet thing," he'd said, "you're gonna have to do without me tonight. I'm not feelin' so good. I got the heartburn something terrible. I'll call you tomorrow, cupcake. Love-'ems, wuv-'ems, li'l woozle."

Billie Jo had replayed the message six times. She most definitely perceived something *weird* in Bubba's tone. He didn't sound at all like his usual bluff and hearty self.

Maybe he was telling the truth, that he did have heartburn. He was prone to it, and that wife of his fed him way too much. Billie Jo kept her medicine cabinet full of bicarbonate of soda and Alka-Seltzer on his behalf.

He did say he'd call her. And he did say "wuv-'ems" and did call her "woozle," which was his most extraspecial pet name for her.

But out of the past five nights, he had been with her precisely *once*. And Billie Jo couldn't help but notice on that last night he'd been closemouthed about his long weekend. Everybody in town knew he'd made some sort of pass at Nora Jones, then had a scene with Gordon, but Bubba refused even to speak of it. He was upset with his wife and daughter, but he wouldn't talk about that, either.

Billie Jo rolled over, hugged her pillow and rested her chin on it. She stared into the darkness, her nerves alternately running hot and cold.

The fear that kept coursing through her the strongest was always the same. What if Bubba was trying to get rid of her? What if he was dumping her? Was that why he'd been paying attention to Nora?

Billie Jo had always been sweet as pie to Bubba, far sweeter than he deserved. She'd also let him be flagrantly open about their affair, because it seemed to give him pleasure. Why, she had let her reputation get absolutely *tarnished* on his account.

What had happened? Had his wife and daughter double-teamed him and worked him over so badly that he wanted to give her up? After she'd practically stood on her head to please him?

The thought both chilled and angered her. Billie Jo felt incomplete without a man; she needed someone to take care of her.

Bubba had seemed such a good candidate. He obviously no longer desired his wife. He delighted in having someone young and warm and willing to make whoopee. Billie Jo put up with his multitude of flaws in the hopes that someday he would be honest, leave his wife and marry *her* instead.

She'd never told Bubba of these hopes. She didn't want to scare him off. She made as few demands on him as possible. This past weekend had been an exception. Couldn't he have gotten away from his wife and daughter for just a few hours? Was it so much to ask? Billie Jo was so sick of being forgiving, she could explode.

Oh, she thought, rocking her head back and forth on the pillow, something was wrong, wrong, wrong; she knew it.

Bubba's voice on the answering machine had sounded strained and weary. If she didn't know better, she would have said he sounded frightened. Was he nervous because he was fixing to tell her goodbye?

She'd hate him. She'd want to scratch his eyes out.

Then her emotions, like a pendumlum, swung in the opposite direction. What if something was *wrong* with Bubba—what if he was seriously sick and didn't want to tell her? He really hadn't been himself last night. He'd been jolly on the surface, but underneath, something had seemed to gnaw at him. What? Was he ill? Was he in trouble of some kind?

If it was anything she could fight, she would fight it with all her jealous heart. She considered Bubba to be *her* Bubba, and any enemy of his that she could smite, she would. She would crush that enemy without mercy—and without a second thought. She was a desperate woman. And her patience had been worn dangerously thin.

IT WAS slightly after midnight. Gordon was across the Mexican border. During the border check, his flesh had crawled the whole time, as if it wanted to detach itself from his body and creep wetly off into the night.

He'd gotten the sweats again, and his muscles kept contracting so jerkily that he could hardly hand over his papers. The guards had looked at him and then exchanged loaded glances with each other.

One of them had told Gordon to get out and stand free of the truck. Gordon still wasn't sure how he had managed to do so without being sick. Then the guard had walked around him, slowly, looking him up and down with suspicious eyes.

Gordon had taken a deep breath. He could feel the acid stripping the lining off his stomach walls. He hadn't known what to do, so he'd silently prayed. The only prayer he'd been able to think of was this:

Mathew, Mark, Luke and John,
Bless the bed that I lie on.

He'd known there was more to the prayer than that, but had been too nervous to remember, so he just kept repeating the same two lines.

The guards had muttered to each other in Spanish so rapidly that Gordon's head felt as if it were full of chattering squirrels. He had no idea what they were saying.

Finally, after it seemed that he'd twisted in hell for an eternity, the guards gave him a last suspicious look and waved him through.

He'd driven just out of sight of the checkpoint, then stopped the truck. He'd staggered from the cab. His legs barely carried him to the highway's edge before they collapsed beneath him. He fell down in a sitting position and threw up.

Finally the retching ceased. He buried his face in his shaking hands and wept. He wept because he'd been so frightened. He wept because he was still frightened. He wept because he'd made it across the border. He wept because he still had to make it to Monterrey. He wept because he was exhausted. He wept because he had no beer.

He cried, great, dry, choking sobs, until he could cry no more. Then he sat, spent, staring up at the starless Mexican sky.

He had to move on. He reached into his shirt pocket, uncapped his pills and took two more uppers to give him strength to get to Monterrey, and half a downer to keep him from flying out of his own skin.

Then he forced himself to get to his feet. He moved around the truck, his gait lurching slightly, and got in. He was so weary that he bowed his head against the wheel and prayed again:

Matthew, Mark, Luke and John,
Bless the bed that I lie on.

He felt he was going to cry again, but he steeled himself against it. He was, after all, a man. He straightened, rubbed his aching eyes, blew his nose.

God, he thought, staring out at the strip of Mexican highway leading to Monterrey, was this what it was like to be in a war?

Was he a veteran now that he had crossed that border bearing his dangerous cargo? He had succeeded, though, he told himself. He'd done it. What did they call it? Was he *blooded* now?

Yeah, he thought, he was blooded. He'd been tried by fire. And he was almost to Monterrey. He was almost free of the stinking guns. He was almost safe.

Then he would go home. Where his mother waited for him. Where she'd been waiting all this time for him to come home. She'd always known he would someday, and she was right. That was what a mother was for, to know such things.

And his wife. His pretty little wife that he had saved from that lecherous old hog, Bubba Gibson. Nora was back home, probably asleep by now. Asleep and alone. But she wouldn't be sleeping alone for long. Oh, no.

Gordon was almost ready to start back to her. His loyal mother. His little Nora. His. His.

NORA PUT Rory to bed. Ken waited downstairs for her. She dawdled with the boy, half-afraid to face the man again.

"I *can't* sleep," Rory insisted, fighting a yawn. "I'm afraid I'll have another nightmare. I want to stay downstairs and have cake, too."

She knelt by his bed to refasten his pajama top, which he'd buttoned crookedly. He'd fallen fast asleep in the truck on the way home, but didn't remember.

"You won't have another nightmare," she told him. "And you can have cake tomorrow. You ate enough pizza for an army tonight. You'd get a stomachache. Lie down."

"It was the best pizza I ever ate," Rory said, sinking back into his pillow. "Maybe I ate so much I got the nightmare. Could that be?" This time the yawn overpowered him. His mouth stretched open in a small, dark O, but he remembered to cover it.

Nora drew the sheet up to his shoulders and gazed at him fondly. "Just what was this terrible nightmare? Bears? Monsters?"

He finished his yawn and blinked sleepily. "Dad," he said and rubbed his eyes.

Nora's heart went cold. Her hand tightened on the sheet. "You—had a nightmare about your father?"

He nodded and yawned again.

Her heartbeat took a hobbling, painful pace. "What was it? Your dream?"

He shook his head, his eyelids lowering. His lashes were dark against his cheek. "Don't remember," he muttered. "He was coming after us. Or something."

"Well, he's not," Nora said, although the thought shook her so much she felt half-sick. "So don't worry. Sleep and dream something nice instead."

"Pony," he said softly. "Pony."

"Yes," she whispered, bending over him. "Dream of the pony."

She kissed his cheek. His lashes gave another sleepy flutter, then went still. His breathing grew slower and deeper.

"Oh, Rory," she breathed, "don't have bad dreams. Please don't, honey. I'll take care of you."

She rose, her emotions tangled in all the old knots. *Gordon,* she thought helplessly, *will you haunt us all forever?*

Slowly she descended the stairs. When she entered the kitchen, Ken stood next to the stove, holding a mug of coffee. She looked away. She knew what questions lay in his eyes. They were both the most primitive and most intimate questions a man could ask a woman.

"Want a cup of coffee?" he asked, although she knew coffee wasn't what was on his mind.

"No." She shook her head and moved to the sink. She braced her hands on the counter and stared out the window into the darkness of the backyard. "Dottie made a cake. Can I cut you a piece?"

She said it in a tone that she hoped told him that she wanted him to go home. Tonight he had taken her to extremes of feeling that she knew were but a first frontier. Not only had he frightened her, she had frightened herself.

"Thanks. I'm not hungry—for cake."

She stiffened slightly and kept staring out the window. She thought again of Rory's nightmare.

What would Gordon do if she fell in love with someone else? Would he hurt Ken? Her? Rory? All of them? How could she think of that—along with everything else?

"Nora?" His voice was quiet, as always.

"I'm sorry," she said, taking a deep breath and bowing her head slightly. "I guess I'm tired, that's all."

She felt him move behind her. The tingling that prickled along her spine warned her of his nearness.

He said nothing for a long time. Then he put his hand on her upper arm. His touch sent an almost painful physical awareness of him jolting through her system, like a shock of electricity.

She tried to move away from his touch, but she could not. She could only stand, confused and torn, as motionless as an animal paralyzed by fright.

He turned her around to face him. She did not protest, but she refused to look at him. She stared stubbornly, unseeingly, at the white expanse of his shirtfront.

He put his hands on her shoulders. "What I feel for you," he said slowly, "and what—you seemed—to feel for me, it ain't—it isn't wrong."

She could not help herself. She sank against his chest and rubbed her forehead against the crisp whiteness of his shirt. The warmth of his hard flesh radiated through the cloth and seemed to soothe her.

He held her. And she held him, her arms tentative and cautious around his waist.

"I—I was never—with any man except Gordon." She paused, for it was difficult to go on. "It wasn't good. I got so that I hated him to touch me. I've never thought—never believed—I could ever feel what it is I'm supposed to feel for a man."

She felt his arms tense around her, almost imperceptibly. But they tensed. She wanted to press nearer to him, but felt it wasn't right. "And maybe I can't. Maybe at the last moment, I'll always pull away, always hate it. I don't know. I can't know. I—I'm afraid to find out."

His hand moved up her back. He pressed her nearer to him. Without volition, her arms tightened around his waist.

He said nothing. He asked her nothing. He merely held her. One hand moved up to cradle her head more firmly against his chest. Once more she felt the dependable beat of his heart against her cheek.

She realized he could have done a hundred things. He could have made a hundred sorts of promises, plain and fancy. He could have vowed a hundred sorts of vows, all high-sounding. He could have tried to kiss her into excitement or caress her into submission, but he did none of them.

He simply held her, tight and protected, in his arms.

Oh, she thought, *as terrifying as it is, I have to take the chance. How can I not, when he makes me feel the way he does?*

"I scare you," he finally said against her hair. He gave a broken sigh and pulled her even more securely into his embrace.

For a moment she leaned against him, holding him almost as tightly as he held her. But then she drew back. Now she wanted to look him in the eye. His face was serious and troubled, but strong. She thought it might be the most beautiful male face she'd ever seen, because it was his.

"Yes," she said with total honesty. "You scare me. But I scare me worse. Because—I think I want you. Oh—I'm *afraid* I want you. And—I don't understand these things."

They looked into each other's eyes and, without saying anything, they both understood.

Yes, she thought, *I do want you. I really do. It's like something was broken in me, but the longer I'm with you, the more it heals. Be gentle. Be slow. Be patient. Help me. Show me. Yes.*

She would go with him to the lake house this weekend. He wanted to make love to her, and she wanted it, too. At least, she hoped she did, because she cared so much for him.

He was not a foolish man. He wasted no time on words.

He bent and kissed her. He kissed her the way a woman was meant to be kissed.

CHAPTER TWELVE

WEDNESDAY DAWNED hot and cloudless. Just outside the Longhorn's door was a thermometer. By mid-morning its mercury had climbed until it was a solid red stripe, filling the tube from top to bottom, as the temperature sweltered at well over a hundred.

"It's too hot to live," Shirley Jean Ditmars said.

She was on break from the telephone company, and her round face was flushed with heat from her walk to the coffee shop. "It is simply," she said, "too hot to live."

Dottie smiled wanly. Everyone in the coffee shop looked slightly crushed by the heat and humidity outside. Everyone, that is, except Nora. She moved briskly and cheerfully, as if she were sheltered in a private bubble of coolness.

Shirley eyed her suspiciously. "Why's Nora so perky?" she asked. "I feel like a limp tea bag. Is it true she was out with Ken Slattery again last night? They're becoming quite the item. I don't know that I approve of things happening that fast. There *is* a child involved."

"I don't think it's up to anybody to approve or disapprove," Dottie said dryly. "And Ken's quite good with the boy."

Shirley cocked her head. "You honestly wouldn't mind Rory having another father? Instead of Gordon? Honestly?"

Dottie's lips thinned. Sometimes she had the very real urge to brain Shirley with a coffeepot. She tried to keep her tone even. "Honestly. Nothing would make me happier than for Rory to have a real father. Nothing. I'd be a completely happy woman if I knew he had that."

"You're very hard on your own boy," Shirley said, lifting her nose. "*Very* hard."

A sudden wave of weariness swept over Dottie. "I'm not a hard woman," she said. "I just face facts."

She turned away. She didn't want to talk to Shirley any longer.

"Speaking of facts," Shirley called after her, "is something wrong with Bubba Gibson? Hardly anybody's seen him lately. Do you suppose he's called it off with Billie Jo? Or maybe he's sick?"

Dottie shrugged and kept walking. She had no interest in Bubba Gibson. None whatsoever. He had nothing at all to do with their lives.

BUBBA WAS indeed sick. He had heartburn so intense he felt as if his chest was full of hot rocks. He kept unplugging all the phones. Mary kept plugging them back in.

Just as soon as he thought maybe the torture had stopped, Gordon would call again. He was starting to sound as crazy as a slaughterhouse rat.

Bubba wished he could escape into Billie Jo's sweet arms so he could forget his multitude of problems.

But his stomach hurt too much, and quite frankly he felt *unmanned* by all this loco business. He had a deep-down secret fear that his ill health and his tension might make him unable to, well, *perform*.

The thought of failing Billie Jo in that department terrified him so much that he was putting off seeing her. He didn't even have the nerve to talk to her in person. He just left excuses on her answering machine.

He shook his head in sorrow. He'd always thought of himself as a stallion of a man. That he should sink to this—it was *tragic*, sure enough.

And it wasn't even fair. He wasn't even interested in Nora Jones. But now he had a jealous ex-husband on his hands, and woman trouble besides. Billie Jo would be losing patience with him soon—he knew it.

What he needed to do was to talk to someone, someone sensible, understanding, tolerant. But who? Most of his friends had been cool to him since he'd taken up with Billie Jo. He figured that deep in their hearts they were jealous of him, even though they'd never admit it.

But surely, somewhere, there was one friend old enough and good enough to turn to. Bubba hated suffering alone and in silence. He was the sort who needed sympathy in large amounts, and these days he wasn't getting it anywhere, from anyone.

NORA TOOK her lunch break at one o'clock, and she and Rory went to the park to meet Ken. She and Ken could each spare only an hour during their workday today, but they wanted to spend it together.

Rory was too young and energetic to be slowed by the heat. And Nora was so full of soaring emotions, she didn't notice it at all.

The pavement was hot, but her feet hardly touched it. She hurried toward the park as effortlessly as if carried on a lovely, cool cloud.

When she saw Ken, tall and lean, standing in the shade of the elms by the picnic table, her heart made a crazy, happy bound so strong it hurt.

He wore his usual low-slung jeans and again had on his belt with the ornate buckle. His immaculate white shirt had the sleeves rolled halfway up his forearms. His straw Stetson threw his face into shadow, but she could see his shy smile and found herself smiling back with all her heart.

What if I can really love him? she thought with a sense of dazzled wonder. *What if I can love him in all the ways a woman can love a man? In mind and soul— and body, too? What if I can?*

Ken gave her a chaste, short kiss on the mouth— Rory was, after all, watching and not missing a thing. Then Ken picked the boy up and whirled him around once, making Rory squawk with delight, and set him on the picnic bench.

Ken had brought them ice cream sundaes from the Dairy Bell Ice Cream Stand, Rory's favorite. Rory wolfed his down, then went to play on the swings.

Ken and Nora kept forgetting to eat. They talked of seemingly inconsequential things, but every word seemed freighted with such sweetness and excitement that Nora felt intoxicated.

Then they noticed their ice cream had melted and laughed sheepishly. Nora accidentally got hers all over the fingers of her right hand. Ken smiled, picked up her hand and started to lick the vanilla from her fingers. His tongue flicked over her flesh, lazy and teasing and savoring.

Nora was astonished at the surge of sensual pleasure that swept through her. It seemed to flood every part of her body, shaking her. *Oh, my,* she thought, as he nibbled at her knuckle. *Oh, my.*

Then he took a paper napkin, scrubbed the last of the stickiness from her hand, raised it to his mouth again and kissed her on the inner tip of each finger and her thumb.

At last, he simply locked his fingers through hers, and with their elbows resting on the table, he and she sat that way, wordless, staring into each other's eyes.

He gave her his slight, quiet smile. "I love you."

Nora's lips parted. "I—" she said, then paused. She took a deep breath. "I love you, too," she said, amazed at her own words. She had never before uttered that simple sentence to a man. She had wanted to be able to say it to Gordon, once, years ago. But he hadn't wanted to hear it. He said only sissies talked about love. What he wanted from her was sex. But this was different. So different.

She smiled at Ken and wondered why she felt like crying.

"It's okay," he said, squeezing her hand and nodding. "Everything's going to be okay, Nora. I promise."

She bit her lip and nodded, too.

He leaned over and gave her another short, simple kiss on the mouth. But despite its brevity it somehow gave Nora a heart quake that shook her with delight.

"I do," she said. "I love you." She blinked back tears. He smiled and squeezed her hand again.

"Hey!" Rory yelled from the swings. "Will you guys stop smooching—and will somebody give me a *push?*"

"Duty calls," Ken said, but when he rose, he kept her hand in his.

She smiled when he made her sit down on a swing, too, and he took turns pushing both her and Rory. Nora held on to the swing's chains and leaned back, looking up into the flawless blue sky. She felt liberated and lucky and giggly and girlish.

Girlish, she thought. Yes, it was as if Ken were somehow giving back her lost girlhood. She laughed, Rory laughed, and Ken teased them both.

Then it was all over, too soon. Ken had to be back at the ranch. Nora and Rory walked him to his truck. He held them each by the hand. When he said goodbye, he looked down solemnly at Rory.

"Mind if I steal just one more? She's so sweet, your mama."

Rory shrugged and gave him a knowing look. "Help yourself," he said, sounding surprisingly sophisticated.

Ken bent and gave her a last kiss. It was as short and plain as the others, but it gave Nora another happy heart quake.

"I'll see you tonight," he told them. He had promised to take them into Austin to the movies. He'd told Nora they should include Rory in their plans because the boy would be gone for the weekend. She was touched by his consideration.

And she and Ken knew that on Friday she and Ken would truly be alone together. They smiled goodbye, knowing that they would be at the lake all weekend if they wanted. The thought made Nora excited and frightened and guilty and shivery by turns.

When Ken drove off, she and Rory waved goodbye, then started back to the Longhorn. She was surprised Rory let her keep holding his hand. Maybe he wasn't as secure about things as he seemed.

"Does it bother you?" she asked carefully. "That he—well—kisses me?"

Rory gave another of his philosophical shrugs. "No. It's nice. I never saw a guy kiss you before."

She gave his hand a squeeze. He frowned and looked thoughtful. "I never saw Dad kiss you," he said. "I can't remember anything like that at all."

She nodded sadly and said nothing, thinking the conversation was over.

But then he went on, and his words chilled her. "All I remember," he said, bitterness in his voice, "is how he hit you. He threatened to hit me the other day. And he said he'd beat on me if I ever told. But I don't care. Someday I'll be big, and he can't."

Oh, Rory, Nora thought in dismay, *I've got to protect you from this. I've got to.*

Something was going to have to be done. If Gordon was actually threatening Rory with his violence, she had to act. She would see Martin Avery. She would do whatever she had to. Her face, which had been smiling so shortly before, grew troubled.

"I don't think Ken would ever let Dad hurt us," Rory said, shaking his head somberly. "Do you?"

Nora wanted to stop and hug him, but she knew it would only embarrass him. So she ruffled his hair as lovingly as she could. "No," she told him with conviction. "I don't think he'd ever let anything hurt us. He's such a good man, Rory. The best man I've ever known."

Rory was silent a moment. He swallowed. "But, Mom? One thing bothers me."

"What, sweetie?"

"Ken doesn't have a gun. Dad does. He's got a *lot* of them."

In spite of the heat, the marrow of Nora's bones went icy. She shook her head. "Rory," she said, "let's not even think such things, okay? Let's just not think about something like that."

Rory nodded, but he looked more worried than before. "Mom?" he said again, his voice a bit shaky.

"Yes?" She held his hand more tightly and patted it.

"There's something else I didn't tell you or Grandma."

Nora felt the cold within her grow icier. "Yes?"

"Dad's taking pills. A lot of different pills. I—saw him."

Pills, Nora thought in panic. A lot of different pills. Of course. That would explain everything. Why Gordon's behavior had become so much more erratic, so much more unpredictable lately—

Oh, no, no, no, she thought. *I* have *to do something—right now, right away, as soon as possible.*

Back at the coffee shop, she gave Rory a handful of quarters so he could distract himself with the jukebox. Then she drew Dottie into the kitchen.

When she told Dottie what Rory had said about the hitting and the pills, Dottie's face went gray. She clutched Nora's arm spasmodically.

"Dottie," Nora said, "I have to do something. I'll have to ask a lawyer what can be done. I'll have to see Martin Avery—"

Dottie squared her shoulders and took Nora by the upper arms. "I've already talked to him, sugar. I've been worried about something like this. Make an appointment. I'll pay for it. I've got money put away for an emergency, and this is an emergency. I felt we might have to do something like this."

"Dottie—you've already been to see him?"

"Honey," Dottie said, taking Nora into her arms and hugging her tightly, "I want you and Rory to be happy. Gordon's hurt everyone enough. I won't let him hurt you anymore. *I won't.* I'd rather die first."

"Oh, Dottie," Nora said, laying her cheek on the other woman's shoulder. "I love you so much. I really do."

She took great comfort from Dottie's closeness. But she wished Dottie hadn't spoken of dying. It scared her. Too many people were talking about dying lately.

Too many things scared her these days.

It frightened her.

"So she's goin'," Cal said. He sat on Ken's old couch, his hat cocked low over his eyes, his booted feet crossed. One hand toyed with a strap of the saddlebag he'd brought with him. "To the lake house, I mean."

Cal's pose was deceptively lazy. Ken sensed tension in the younger man, in spite of Cal's one-cornered smile.

Ken sat shirtless in a chair across from him, polishing his boots. He was about to set out to pick up Nora and Rory. He tossed his friend an impatient glance. Things had reached such a point with Nora he didn't feel right talking about them. "I don't believe it's gentlemanly to discuss her."

Cal picked up a long-necked bottle of beer and sipped at it lackadaisically. "Gentlemanly," he repeated.

"I know it's a foreign concept to you," Ken said. It wasn't a fair shot, because Cal had changed his ways since Serena. But the closer the weekend drew, the more apprehensive Ken became. He wanted everything perfect for Nora.

Cal slapped his flat stomach and pulled his hat brim farther down over his eyes. "I just wanted to have a little heart-to-heart with you, Slats."

Ken set down one boot and took up the other. "Save it for Serena."

"This is man-to-man talk," Cal said, setting his jaw. "You and Nora are gettin' so closelike, I thought I oughta talk to you about protection."

Slowly Ken lowered the boot. His face darkened, and he lifted one brow in displeasure. "Are you *crazy?*" he demanded. "*I'm* the one that made you put those packets in your billfold when your mama thought you wasn't carryin' nothin' but your library card. If it wasn't for me, you'd have probably screwed yourself to death by now."

Cal pushed back his hat and cast Ken an indolent hazel glance. He sipped the last of his beer. "True." He set down his bottle and patted the saddlebag. "But—"

Ken threw the polishing rag at him in disgust. Cal ducked, but he didn't laugh. He barely smiled.

"Butt out," Ken ordered. "I don't need advice from *you*. I'm a grown man. I'm a responsible individual. I can take care of myself—and my woman."

Cal's forehead creased and his brows lowered. "I'm sincerely tryin' to give you a tip, old stag."

Ken yanked on first one boot, then the other. He took a blue shirt that hung from a doorknob and thrust his arms into the sleeves. "Why don't you give me some goddamn privacy instead? Or you want to come to the lake house *with* us? *Coach* me, maybe?"

Cal's face grew grimmer. "We got plans, thanks."

Ken relaxed slightly and began buttoning his shirt. "Thank God for small blessings."

Cal's face grew more sober. "Don't thank anybody until you've heard what I've got to say."

Slowly Ken raised his eyes to meet those of the other man. He finished buttoning his shirt and rolled up the sleeves. He didn't like the troubled look in Cal's normally laughing eyes. "What *are* you tryin' to say?"

Cal lifted one shoulder, but the gesture wasn't nonchalant. "I'm tryin' to talk to you about a—different kind of safety."

Ken made an expression of disgust. "Will you get off that, dammit? It's *personal*. And I'm able to take care—"

Cal reached into the saddlebag and drew out a holster and gun, a Smith & Wesson .38. "I'm talkin' a little more basic type of protection."

Ken's eyebrow rose. He recognized the gun. It was Tyler's. He stared at Cal, his expression wary. "What the hell . . . ?"

"Gordon Jones is what the hell," Cal said without a flicker of emotion. "I think he's comin' back. I think he's comin' for Nora. And I think he's in a real bad mood."

Ken swore and sat down again. He put his elbows on his knees and stared at Cal. The younger man looked dead serious.

Cal held the holster and gun out to Ken. In silence, Ken shook his head. Cal drew his hand back, but kept tight hold of the holster.

"Look," Cal said, a muscle twitching in his cheek. "Bubba Gibson came to see Daddy today. Said he wanted to talk about buyin' horses. But that ain't what he wanted to talk about. Not really."

Ken nodded, but he didn't understand. What did Bubba Gibson have to do with this?

Cal cocked his head, as if looking for the right words. "This is hard to explain." He shrugged in concern and puzzlement. "Daddy says Bubba wasn't—himself—you know? There was something botherin' him."

Ken nodded. His eyes had gone their coldest blue.

"Well," Cal said, stroking the holster absently, "Bubba finally says Gordon Jones is threatenin' to come back for Nora. And he's talkin' crazy. *Mighty* mean and crazy."

Ken's eyes narrowed.

Cal's mouth drew down at the corner. "Daddy didn't get it at first. For a long time he said Bubba talked in circles. But he was nervous. Real nervous."

He bent forward, more intent, his gaze as implacable as Ken's. "He finally spit it out—Gordon thinks it's Bubba after Nora. Because of what happened in the Longhorn. Gordon's been goin' for Bubba, harassin' him—by long distance. Threatenin' him."

"Threatenin'," Ken repeated tonelessly. He didn't welcome threats, nor did he back away from them.

"See," Cal said earnestly, "Gordon must not know about you yet. He thinks it's Bubba after Nora. And Daddy sure didn't tell Bubba about you—he just gave him a mighty hellacious lecture for gettin' into such a fix. Then Bubba went off, sulled up like a possum."

"Gordon's threatenin' Bubba," Ken said, his lip curled.

"So far. But when he finds out it's you Nora's interested in, he might just go nasty loco. You're the one he's gonna go loco *on*."

Ken lowered his head and swore through clenched teeth. "But Nora ain't heard from him. Not a word. She would have said."

Cal put his hand on his friend's shoulder. "Who knows what goes on in his head? That boy ain't *right,* hoss. And it sounds like he's gettin' less right all the time."

Ken raked his hand through his hair and stared at the floor. He said nothing.

"You ought to take the gun," Cal said.

Ken raised his head, a stubborn slant to his mouth. A pulse ticked in his temple. "I don't like guns. I don't want a gun."

"Slats, *he's* got guns. He's always had 'em. He thinks they make him a man or something."

Ken's mouth curled more contemptuously. "He's wrong."

"Yeah? Well, he's wrong, but he's got a gun. What good's it gonna do you to be right if he starts sprayin' bullets?"

"Oh, *hell*," Ken said bitterly and pushed his hand through his hair again.

"Take it," Cal insisted, holding out the gun to him again. "If you won't do it for yourself, do it for me. Daddy said Bubba was spooked. I think it spooked Daddy himself. He told me to come talk to you."

Ken shook his head, his expression obstinate.

"Then take it for Nora and Rory," Cal almost pleaded. "Look, they could get hurt, too."

Ken frowned harder. "There's better ways. Let me talk to Bubba myself. And then Wayne Jackson. Let the sheriff handle this."

Cal sighed in exasperation. "How do you know when this damn fool might show up? The sheriff might not be around. What is it with you and guns, anyway? You never say. You got a major problem or something?"

Ken's head snapped up, his eyes blazing. "Yeah. I got a problem. But it's private, all right?"

"Yeah?" Cal said cynically. "I hope you can *keep* it private. I know you got your principles and all, but don't get too damn noble. It could get you dead."

"I can take care of me, and I can take care of mine," Ken said, his eyes like chips of ice.

Cal's face was as somber as Ken's. "I guess we'll see," he muttered. "Won't we?"

BY THE TIME Gordon reached Monterrey, his nerves gave him such pain he felt like a man on fire. He left the stockyards and headed for the nearest bar, letting Luis and his henchman unload whatever needed to be unloaded—hogs, guns, ammunition—Gordon no longer cared. He drank Dos Equis, and found, like a man under a spell, he couldn't get the prayer out of his head:

Matthew, Mark, Luke and John,
Bless the bed that I lie on.

It ran through his mind, repeating like a broken record. It no longer made sense to him, but nothing made sense at this point. It was as if someone had pulled out the linchpin of reality, and reality was coming apart.

He knew he should stay in Monterrey and rest, but he could not rest. He wanted back across the border so badly he almost cried again.

In the bar, he took enough amphetamines to give him energy to get back to Val Verde on the Texas side. Then he had to pop more pills—downers this time—to stop his hands and knees and voice from shaking.

On the way back to the stockyards, he thought people on the streets were looking at him strangely. When he picked up his truck, he thought Luis looked at him strangely. When he crossed the border, he *knew* the guards looked at him strangely.

He prayed, Bless the bed that I lie on.

He went through the border check as if moving through a terrible dream. When he finally was safe on the American side again, he once more had to pull the truck off the road and weep. He had never been so frightened in his life, and the fear wouldn't go away. It was as if it had poisoned him.

All he wanted was to be home in Crystal Creek. He wanted his mother and his old room and his old bed. He wanted to hang on to Nora so he could convince himself he was still real. He wanted to possess her so violently that all his own fears of violence were snuffed out.

It occurred to him that there was someone he was supposed to hate for trying to take Nora from him. At the moment, he could no longer remember whom he was supposed to hate or how much. It seemed he should be phoning somebody and talking about killing.

It seemed there was somebody he was supposed to kill.

Vaguely it occurred to him that maybe Nora wouldn't be happy to see him again. The thought angered him so much he was nearly sick.

But then he remembered he had a plan for that scenario, too. He'd just knock her up and get her pregnant again. Pregnant again. Keep them pregnant and barefoot. That was how it was supposed to be done. That was how.

Rest. He had to get rest.

He steeled himself and took a combination of pills to calm and strengthen himself, and when he could drive again, he checked into the first motel he could find.

It was a fleabag, but he didn't mind. He took two sleeping pills, and fell into the bed fully clothed and slept for the first time in thirty-six hours.

He dreamed he was a little boy in Crystal Creek again, and almost everyone loved him. Those who didn't, he killed with his shiny little gun.

Bang. Bang.

CHAPTER THIRTEEN

KEN CAME LATE to pick up Nora and Rory, which was unlike him. When he finally arrived, he was quieter than usual.

Maybe he's decided he really doesn't care about us, Nora worried. *Maybe he wishes he'd never gotten involved.*

But Ken, even though he seemed distracted, was attentive to Rory. During the movie, he put his arm around Nora and held her hand. There was such intensity in the simple touch that she knew he cared for her, cared so much it gave her a strange, swooping feeling that shook her.

But something's wrong, she thought. *Something's bothering him.* She herself was still deeply troubled by what Rory had said about Gordon, about the pills and the threats of violence. But she and Ken couldn't talk until they had taken Rory home and tucked him into bed.

What complicated charades adults went through for the sake of children, Nora thought sadly; how many times had she pretended to be brave and all-knowing for Rory when in truth she was frightened and didn't know what to do?

She was grateful when the boy was finally in bed, and Ken took her by the hand, leading her to the front porch. He sat on the same wide railing again, leaning against the wall.

He drew her down next to him, so that she was safe in his arms, her back against his chest. She let her head rest against the comforting solidity of his shoulder and snuggled closer to him. His arms tightened around her more securely.

"What's wrong, sugar?" he said. His warm breath tickled her ear and stirred tendrils of her hair.

"What's wrong with *you?*" she asked, looking up at the stars. The dark sky was hot and cloudless. "Something's bothering you. I can tell."

He was silent. He kissed the nape of her neck, a long, tingling kiss that made her shudder with pleasure. "I'm sorry," he said at last. "It's Gordon."

Pleasure fled. She stiffened. "Gordon?"

His embrace grew almost fierce. "I'm going to take care of you. I promise that."

She knew he meant what he said, but she was still alarmed. She twisted so that she could peer up at his stern, shadowy face. "What's he done? Gordon?"

"He's threatenin' Bubba Gibson. To stay away from you. I talked to Wayne. To the sheriff."

"Bubba?" Nora put her hand on Ken's shoulder in concern. "But *why?* It makes no sense."

His muscles flexed beneath her touch. "Because of what happened Saturday at the Longhorn. Gordon's got it into his head that Bubba wants you."

Nora made a sound that was half laugh, half gasp. "Bubba Gibson and me?"

"Look, sugar, I talked to Bubba. He didn't like talkin'—not at all. But, yeah, Gordon's been callin', hasslin' him."

Her fingers tightened on his shoulder. "But—what about you? What if he—when he finds out about you?"

Ken's hands fell to her waist, holding her possessively. "The last thing you have to worry about is me. I can take care of myself."

"But—"

"I mean it," he said almost savagely. "Don't worry about me. You worry about yourself and Rory. Wayne Jackson knows the problem. If Gordon shows up, the sheriff's department'll have its eye out for him. If he comes near you and I'm not here, you call them—immediately—you understand?"

She nodded numbly.

"Bubba won't file a formal complaint against him," Ken said. "I don't know what his problem is—Mary, maybe. He says he doesn't want his name dragged into it. Still, Wayne says he'll do everything he can. You're going to be taken care of, Nora. And the McKinneys will help. Cal said he and Tyler will watch out for you, too. Nobody's going to hurt you. Nobody."

She was frightened, not for herself, but for him. "But you—when he finds out about you—"

"He's not going to hurt me. I told you. I can take care of myself."

"But he's—so unpredictable. Oh, Ken—you should stay away from me. I'm just getting you in trouble."

His hands tightened on her waist, almost hurting her. "Stay away from you?" he said with disbelief. "No way. No way. Ever."

The passion in his voice made her put her arms around his neck and hug him, her face pressed against his chest. He held her as tightly as she held him. He kissed her hair.

"This is terrible," she said, closing her eyes. His starchy shirtfront scraped her cheek, but she couldn't bring herself to break from the embrace. Haltingly, she told him what Rory had said about the pills and the threats of hitting.

"I'm going to see Martin Avery," she said. "I've made an appointment."

"I'm goin' with you," he said. "We'll take care of this together."

"You don't have to—"

"Together," he repeated from between his teeth. "From now on—from here on out—everything is *together*."

He raised her face and kissed her so fervently that she clung to him helplessly, dizzied by how impassioned, how ardent he was.

Her lips opened beneath his, and with a surge of joy, she suddenly understood she no longer feared the coming weekend. She loved this man and she wanted him. She wanted him as wholly and completely and intently as he wanted her.

FRIDAY DAWNED hot and humid, but wisps of cloud sulked on the far horizon. A strange electricity seemed to shimmer in the air, as if a storm were struggling into being, but had not yet focused and gathered itself.

Nora drove Dottie to the Austin airport, Rory hanging over the seat between them, chattering about what he would learn at camp. "Bird study," Rory said, enjoying his own list. "Canoeing. Orienteering.

Wood carving. I'm gonna be an Eagle Scout some-day.''

She and Rory kissed Dottie goodbye and watched her board her plane to Dallas. Then they drove back to Crystal Creek, and Nora helped Rory pack his duffel bag and roll his bedroll. He put on his official Cub Scout shirt and his official Cub Scout shorts and fastened his official Cub Scout knife to his official Cub Scout belt. He put on his official Cub Scout hat, and gave himself an official Cub Scout salute in the mirror.

Nora watched him, hiding a fond smile. Then she drove him to the church where the vans would pick the boys up and take them to camp. She waved goodbye to him, knowing better than to try to kiss him in front of his friends.

He looked so happy and excited that it gave her a stab of complex emotion. He was her baby and he was leaving. Then she drove to Martin Avery's law office. Ken was waiting outside, parked in his white truck.

She stepped out of her car, and he was there, on the sidewalk, holding out his hand to her. Gratefully she took it. He looked so tall and handsome that she felt another pang, this time of pride. He gave her his slow, one-sided smile. Hand in hand they walked into the attorney's office to see what they could do to keep Gordon away.

BILLIE JO DUMONT was in a bad mood. She showed Ken and Nora into Martin's office, saying he would be with them in a minute. Before she shut the door, she gave Nora a glance of undisguised jealousy.

Billie Jo didn't know what Nora Jones, of all people, had done to deserve Ken Slattery. Billie Jo had pursued him herself several years ago with all her considerable persistence. All she'd gotten for her pains was the surprising discovery that he was the best kisser in Claro County. But she'd had few kisses to enjoy. He'd been polite, but firm. He was not interested in Billie Jo.

Nobody was interested in Billie Jo this week. She was as lonely as if stranded in the center of the Sahara. Her emotions swung erratically between anger and depression.

She hadn't seen Bubba since Monday night. She hadn't even talked to him. He left messages on her answering machine, but kept saying he couldn't come see her; he wasn't feeling well.

Was he lying? (She would kill him if he was lying.)

Was he telling the truth? (She would die if he was really sick and she couldn't go to him.)

Billie Jo fretted—*what* was going on? Was Bubba finally going to leave his wife for good? Or was he about to reconcile with the little frump, shutting Billie Jo out of his life forever?

She wanted to call him up and demand answers, but she could not. She had no rights—none—and that was the poisonously bitter thing about being the Other Woman. She could make no demands at all. She was at Bubba's mercy, and although she loved him in her way, she hated him, too, for keeping her so powerless.

Oh, she thought unhappily, what was *wrong* with her? She was pretty enough; she'd always known that. Billie Jo was a cuddly, affectionate person who liked sex and who loved men—why couldn't she get one of her own that she could *keep?*

She glanced at Martin as he opened the door and entered the office where Nora and Ken waited. Martin treated Billie Jo as casually as if she were part of the office furniture. She might be a big, enormous zero as far as Martin was concerned. The air-conditioning was fixed now, and he pulled the door shut behind him, shutting Billie Jo off from the sanctity of his office and from any sight or sound of Ken and Nora.

Oh, there was no question that a wedding was in the air, Billie Jo thought enviously. Martin had had her pull the file on Nora's divorce and the custody agreement regarding Rory.

Yes, Ken Slattery was going to the altar, sure thing, and it didn't even bother him that Nora had a half-grown *child.* Imagine! Picking a woman with a child! How could you make whoopee with a child always underfoot?

Oh, it wasn't *fair,* fumed Billie Jo. How could a quiet, brown-haired little waitress like Nora Jones get herself two husbands, when Billie Jo couldn't even get one? It wasn't right, wasn't right, wasn't right.

Today Billie Jo just hated Nora Jones. She hated Ken Slattery, too, just on general principle.

And she hated Bubba, as well, and loved him and hated and loved him in such a dizzying circle of emotions she wanted to rage and weep. She felt as explosive as an atomic bomb.

"DO YOU FEEL BETTER?" Ken asked Nora, after they'd left Avery's office.

She nodded, even though she was disappointed. Martin said the custody business should be easy enough if Gordon would cooperate, but the protective order would be more difficult, especially if Bubba Gibson refused to be brought into the case. He was, after all, the one Gordon had repeatedly threatened.

"Billie Jo gave me an absolutely hostile look," Nora said worriedly. "Do you suppose she knows about this business with Gordon? That she blames me?"

"Don't worry about Billie Jo, sugar," Ken said, putting an arm around her shoulder. "She don't—doesn't have a thing to do with you or me."

Nora tried to give a philosophical shrug and an equally philosophical smile. Both failed.

"Hey," he said, giving her an encouraging squeeze, "cheer up. If you don't, I'll have to go kissin' on you right in the middle of Main Street."

This time her smile was shy, but real.

He looked down at her, his own face growing serious. She knew it was the thought of kissing—and more than kissing—that brought the familiar look of quiet intensity to his face.

"Nora," he said hesitantly, "about this weekend—at the lake. You haven't changed your mind? Because if you have, I under—"

"I haven't changed my mind," she said. She rose on tiptoes and gave him a quick, demure kiss on the cheek. "I just have to go home and get ready. To get my things. Will you pick me up at six? Like you said?"

He stared down at her with such a mixture of hunger and affection that she went warm and shivery at the same time.

"I'll be there," he said, not taking his eyes from hers.

THE VACATION HOUSE, owned jointly by the Mc-Kinneys and Carolyn Townsend, overlooked Austin's Lake Travis, a blue jewellike body of water that was Texas-large and Texas-spectacular. In some places its shoreline was rolling and verdant, in others cliffs of pale limestone rose like towers.

J.T.'s house was on a grassy slope that led to a dock, but directly across the lake was a view of cliffs, great layered slabs of stone so impressive they made Nora think of castles and kingdoms.

The two-story house was beautiful, a yellow clapboard in Victorian style. A broad, roofless porch ran around three sides, ornamented with white railings.

"It's beautiful," Nora breathed, half intimidated. She felt as if she were a country mouse about to enter a palace.

Ken swung open the door and picked up her overnight case. Nora gave it a quick, furtive glance. Once more shyness and guilt flooded her. The overnight case seemed a symbol that she was about to become a fallen woman. Maybe she couldn't even fall successfully. Maybe she really was still frightened of sex. That old worry had resurrected itself, too, now that she and Ken were actually here, actually alone.

He must have sensed her rising nervousness, for he took her by the hand and drew her into the living room. His hand felt so warm that she knew hers must be snow-cold. She swallowed and laced her fingers more tightly through his.

Then she gave a little gasp of awe. Dominating the center of the room was the biggest fireplace she had ever seen, a two-sided one. Of rose-colored stone, it towered the whole two stories, for the house had a cathedral ceiling, and instead of a true second floor, a loft arrangement ran about the upper level.

The wall of the lake side of the room was all glass, large windows that framed the sliding door leading to the porch. A couch upholstered in nubby blue-gray fabric and matching easy chairs formed a cozy group on one side of the fireplace.

On the other side were an antique round oak dining table and pressed oak chairs. Paintings and family photos filled the walls.

"I've never been in a house like this," she said in a small voice.

"Well, it ain't—it's not like mine," Ken said wryly. "Mine is just an empty old house."

Nora's fingers tightened around his. "It doesn't seem empty when you're in it."

"This one doesn't seem so pretty when you're in it. You put it to shame."

She smiled and her shyness evaporated as he bent to kiss her. But no sooner had his lips brushed hers than his own shyness, or at least some sort of fierce restraint, seemed to reassert itself.

"I don't mean to rush things," he muttered. He set her suitcase beside the fireplace and went back to the truck for his own things.

He returned with a battered duffel bag that was like a well-used version of Rory's and set it beside her case. He stuck his thumbs in the hip pockets of his jeans and stared at the high ceiling. He cleared his throat. "Cal said not to worry about supper. He and Serena'd fix something up. He said just to look in the kitchen."

He shrugged and nodded to himself, not looking at her.

Why, he really is having a fit of shyness, Nora thought, touched. *And he wants to do everything exactly right. Oh, I love him. How could I help it?*

"I told 'em not to bother," Ken said, his tone almost grumbling, "but Cal said I can't cook nothin' but water, and Lord knows that's right. Let's see what mischief they've done."

Slowly, almost tentatively, Nora linked her arm through his. He looked down at her and slowly smiled. She understood and he understood. They loved each other, it was their first time together, and they were both nervous about the newness of it all. The sweetness filled Nora with a tremulous warmth.

"Yes," she said, squeezing his arm. "Let's look."

The kitchen gleamed, all polished oak, blue and white tile, and copper. There was a brace of roasted pheasants in the refrigerator, a casserole of wild rice and two bottles of white wine from the vineyards of Tyler McKinney's fiancée. A bowl of salad sat on one shelf, mixed greens sprinkled with halves of cherry tomatoes.

There was a note propped against the salad bowl.

Slats:
Put two teaspoons of water in the rice and nuke it at medium for 3½. Do the bird-guys at me-

dium for 7 minutes. Don't nuke the salad. Or do even you know that?

                              King of the Cowboys.

Nora laughed and Ken looked wry. "The smart aleck thinks he's at home even on the kitchen range," he said. "Serena told him that stuff. It's all he can do to unwrap his own moon pie."

A large wrought-iron table stood on the porch, and they ate there, watching the evening sun tinge the water gold and gild the cliffs across the way. The sky had filled with clouds for the first time in days, and mounds of them banked the wide sky, slowly changing colors.

Nora watched how the light gleamed in Ken's hair and bronzed his high cheekbones. "You and Cal McKinney," she said, twirling her wineglass stem, "you're such good friends. But you don't seem alike."

Ken raised his eyebrow ruefully. "We aren't alike. There's times I wanted to whomp the tar out of him. But he's the most generous son of a gun alive. When he was a kid he used to tag after me, wantin' to learn to rope and such. And Miss Pauline—well, she asked me to look out for him, kinda."

Nora smiled with admiration. "Because he looked up to you, didn't he?"

Ken gave an embarrassed shrug. "He'd listen to me. Don't ask me why."

"And Miss Pauline," Nora said, "you admired her, didn't you?"

"She was a lady."

"I know. I thought she was wonderful. She used to loan me books. Most people never even knew I was there or what I was like. But she did. I cried when she died.''

Ken nodded solemnly. He set down his glass and stared at the sunset. "She was a good woman. You remind me of her. In ways.''

"Me?" Nora said, her eyes widening. "I remind you of *Miss Pauline?*''

He nodded again.

"But—she was a great lady. A strong lady. And so educated—''

"Yeah. You remind me of all that." He turned to face her again. "Don't you know that, Nora? That you're a lady? And strong? And bright? And—educated, too?''

"But—but I hardly know anything. I'm just starting. I don't want you to see me as something I'm not.''

"I don't. You know who else you remind me of?''

She shook her head. "No.''

"You'll think it's dumb.''

"No. I wouldn't.''

He set his jaw and pushed his empty wineglass away. "All right. I'll tell you the truth. You remind me of me.''

She blinked in surprise.

He went on with the sober, pained expression of a man who didn't like speaking of his past. "You didn't have much of a childhood. Me, either. You sorta—got kicked out of the nest early. Me, too. You had to make your own way. You had to kind of make yourself up as you went along. You had to find what you wanted and make it happen. I did, too.''

He paused, a muscle in his jaw working. "That probably sounds real conceited like. Like I think I'm something—or something."

Emotion swelled in her chest, fluttered in her throat. Impulsively she reached across the table and put her hand over his. "You *are* something. You're something wonderful. You never talk about yourself. Do you know that people think you're a little mysterious?"

He gave an embarrassed laugh, but he took her hand and held it firmly.

"They do," Nora insisted, smiling. "You seemed to come out of nowhere and make yourself absolutely indispensable to the McKinneys. You're the best foreman in Central Texas, and everybody knows it."

"Oh, now hell, Nora, I'm *not* the best—"

"You are," she said with conviction and loyalty. "J. T. McKinney always says it. I've heard him say it myself. Everybody respects you and always has."

He shot her a sharply questioning look. She understood.

"Yes," she admitted. "Even me. All these years. I—thought a lot of you."

He was silent a moment. His thumb stroked her palm. "Then why wouldn't you look at me?"

She bit at her lower lip. "I suppose I was frightened. And I thought I was—was through with that kind of thing."

A low rumble of thunder startled her. His hand tensed around hers. The thunder sounded again, louder and more insistent. Nora glanced in confusion at the sky. The cloud castles, which had been muted shades of pastel, had suddenly turned gray and seemed to be growing darker still.

A breeze had sprung up, but neither of them had noticed. Somehow, lower, blacker clouds had scudded in from the west and were weaving angry wreathes in the sky.

A drop of water hit the tabletop. Then another. One fell into Nora's half-empty wineglass. Still another glanced against the edge of her eye and began to run down her cheek like a tear.

"Rain," she said in wonder. "It's going to rain."

Almost at her words, the breeze turned into a wind. The changing light on the lake danced as ripples rose. More drops began to pelt down, making dark spots on the porch's painted yellow floor.

"I'd better take you in," Ken said, rising and drawing her to her feet. But they both stood motionless, watching the mounting power of the coming storm.

"The rain feels wonderful," Nora said, raising her face to it. "I love storms. Let's stay out—can't we? Oh, rain—it's been so long."

"You'll get soaked. Don't you care?"

"I want to. It feels so good. Doesn't it?"

He was standing behind her. He put his arms around her, drawing her close. "It feels good."

Nora nestled more closely against him. The next time it thundered, she saw lightning across the lake, a bright chain of it. The rain kept pouring down in great warm drops.

Ken laughed and held her more tightly. His arms glistened with rain, and her hair, her blouse, her cotton skirt were quickly growing sodden with it.

She opened her mouth to taste it, then laughed, too, and had to shake her head to toss the rain from her eyes.

"Come here," Ken said in a low growl. "You've done gone and blinded yourself."

He turned her around, drew his shirt from the confines of his belt and wiped her eyes with its edge. She blinked up at him through rain-starred lashes.

His blond hair was darkened by the wetness and fell in a damp wave over his forehead. She reached up to wipe it back into place. "Your hair's all wet—"

"Your face is all wet. Your mouth is all wet—"

He lowered his face to hers and took her lips, his tongue tasting the rain on them, then growing more intimate. Nora's mouth parted eagerly for him, and she, too, could taste rain on his flesh.

The warmth of his long body made the wind seem chill by contrast. Lightning flashed again, closer this time, making patterns of colored stars dance behind Nora's closed eyelids. The thunder rolled so loudly that she could feel it in her chest, shaking her heart.

Ken's hands moved up and down her back, feeling its planes beneath the sculpted wetness of her clothing. His lips traveled to her jawline, then her throat, then her breasts. Through the wet cloth, his mouth warmed first one hardened nipple, then the other, then returned to the first.

Breathless, she rested her cheek against his soaked hair, holding tight to his shoulders for support. His touch was making her so dizzy with desire that she let her eyes flutter open, trying to orient herself.

The lake was almost disappearing beneath gray, lashing veils of rain. The wind made the water seethe

like surf, turning the scene even more mistily vague.
All light seemed to be escaping from the world.

No one can see us here, Nora thought, closing her
eyes again. *There are no other houses near. The rain
is like a curtain. The rain is like a room of our own.*

He kissed her mouth again, a kiss as wild and deep
as the storm around them. Her hands slid up beneath
his loose shirt, caressing the hard, wet surface of his
back. The thunder gave another of its heart-quaking
rumbles, and he pulled her closer to him, one hand
beginning to unfasten her blouse.

Then her breasts were bared to the rain, and he was
kissing them again, his hands tight around her waist.
Nora made a little sound deep in her throat, unlike any
sound she had ever made before.

He straightened, staring down at her, breathing
hard. The rain ran down his face, but he no longer
seemed to notice. He paused from touching her just
long enough to unbutton his own shirt and strip it off.

It fell soundlessly to the floor of the porch, and he
pulled her against him again, so that his hard chest
was warm against her nipples. He turned her face up
to him, and let his lips take hers again.

"Nora," he breathed against her lips. "I put this
belt buckle on for you. Would you take it off for me?"

Trembling, she drew back from him. She shook the
water from her hair so that it wouldn't drip into her
eyes. Her fingers fumbled as she tried to undo the silver buckle, but he didn't help her. He stood watching
her, his hands taut on her upper arms. Her fingers
shook harder.

At last the buckle came undone, and she drew the
belt from its loops. She stared up at him, still holding
it.

"Now, Nora," he said, taking a deep breath, "I'd like to take you in."

She shook her head, still trembling. "We're—all wet. We'll track up the house."

He gripped her arms tighter. "It's a lake house. It's designed to be tracked up. Will you let me take you in?"

Something seemed to be melting inside her, turning her as liquid as the rain. She nodded numbly, loving the desire she saw in his face.

He took the belt from her hand. He scooped up his shirt, then lifted Nora effortlessly in his arms. Somehow he managed to open the door.

He stepped inside and when the door eased shut behind him, he tightened his hold, carrying her cradled even more closely to his chest.

"We're going to need towels," she whispered, hiding her face against his throat. "To wipe off all this rain."

"No, we won't," he said fiercely. "I'm going to kiss it off you. Every drop."

He carried her into the bedroom.

CHAPTER FOURTEEN

WHEN NORA AWOKE, her body tingled with a sense of sheer aliveness. She stretched, and the crisp sheets crackled with her movements. She remembered falling asleep in Ken's arms and smiled, then blushed.

Had that couple making such wild yet tender love really been *them*—bookish Nora Jones and quiet Ken Slattery?

And now she understood why people called it "making love." Gordon had always called it something different and ugly.

With Gordon it had been a different and ugly thing, but Gordon now seemed like a distant nightmare, growing vaguer and less real each hour she spent with Ken.

She stretched again, wondering where Ken was. His place beside her was empty. She touched the rumpled sheets where he had lain, wondering how she could miss him so much after only one night. The universe seemed lonesome and incomplete without him. Where was he?

As if in answer to her question, he came through the door, carrying a tray. The tray had a wrapped gift on it, a dish of strawberries, a plate of toast, a cup of coffee, and a small vase containing three clover blossoms. Under his arm was another gift-wrapped box, a much larger one.

Nora rose on one elbow, pushing her tumbled hair from her eyes. She smiled shyly at him and pulled the sheet up higher. She was naked beneath it.

He was fully dressed, his usual low-slung jeans, his belt with the silver buckle, a shirt of ice blue that matched his eyes.

He set the tray on her lap, put the large present beside her, then reached into the closet and drew out another of his shirts. "Here," he said gruffly, and held it so that she could slip into it. He understood that she was still shy.

"What is this?" Nora asked, buttoning two buttons of the shirt and staring down at the tray.

"Breakfast. It's the best I can do. Sorry."

"You shouldn't do this. I should be up, making you ham and eggs."

"Don't want 'em. Rather do this."

"And flowers even?" Nora shook her head in happy disbelief. "You brought me flowers? Nobody ever gave me flowers before."

He shrugged and sat beside her on the bed. "They're nothin' but clovers. But clovers make me think of you."

She touched them and smiled. At his house, she had seen the struggling little clover in the oversize flowerpot. She had recognized the plant as the one she'd accidentally uprooted, and had been touched. She was coming to realize that under Ken's stoic surface was a sentimental streak no one had ever suspected.

She began to eat. The toast was already cold, the coffee too strong and the strawberries too sugary, but she wouldn't have hurt his feelings for the world.

A self-critical expression crossed her face. "I shouldn't be doing this. I should get up and change the sheets downstairs." She blushed again. "We got them damp last night."

She took a bite of toast so that she wouldn't have to meet his gaze. Last night, soaked with rain, they had made love in the downstairs bedroom. Then, once again, he'd taken her into his arms and carried her upstairs, to the largest of the loft bedrooms, to sleep in a dry bed. Once there, they'd found themselves making love again.

"The sheets are washed and in the dryer," he said. "The bed's airing."

"You shouldn't do that—and I should be up. There's other work. We left a mess on the porch last night—"

"It's cleaned. The dishes are in the dishwasher."

She looked at him with fond exasperation. "Why are you *doing* this? You're spoiling me."

"It took me so long to get you, I don't want to chance losin' you."

She looked at him, and the naked hunger in his face shook her. Instinctively she reached for his hand. His fingers tightened around hers possessively, and a muscle flickered in his cheek.

She wanted to be in his arms again, to make love to him again. He wanted it, too; she could tell. Her heart seemed to take a long, tumbling fall.

"Open your presents," he said. He released her hand, as if he didn't trust himself to touch her any longer, as if the temptation was too great and the time was still too soon.

"You shouldn't bring me presents," Nora said helplessly.

"I wanted to. Besides—it's our anniversary. Sorta. A week today."

He took the tray and set it on the bedside table. Then he put the large box in her lap. It was gift-wrapped with a huge golden ribbon and a gold sticker that said Neiman-Marcus, one of Texas's most exclusive stores.

"Our anniversary? You *are* sentimental. I never would have guessed this about you—ever. And Neiman-Marcus... what on earth—?"

"Open it."

"I don't deserve all this," she said, but began unwrapping the box. The paper was so lovely she hated to tear it, so she untaped everything carefully and detached the ribbon as gently as possible. "Why, I never had anything from Neiman-Marcus in my life. What have you gone and done?"

He said nothing, only watched as she opened the box.

When she peeked beneath the tissue paper, her heart contracted with a pleased surprise so intense that it hurt. Inside the box was the most beautiful woman's suit she had ever seen, a tailored blue-gray tweed. Beside it nestled a pair of matching blue-gray leather shoes. She gasped.

"A suit? With matching shoes? It's the most beautiful—" She was too overcome to finish the sentence. She picked up the suit jacket and pressed it against her breast, stroking its rich texture. With her other hand she touched one of the shoes, assuring herself it was real.

Ken looked self-conscious, a loner not used to indulging in loving gestures, but wanting to please now that he had done so. His voice was brusque. "You said you used to want to be like Miss McDuff when you taught. You said you liked her suits and matching shoes and all—this is for when you start practice teaching."

She looked at him, tears rising in her eyes. She hugged the jacket more tightly. "You remember me saying that?"

"It's nothin'," he said, more gruffly than before. "Dottie helped me pick and get the size." He handed her the smaller package. "You've got one more. Happy anniversary."

Gently, almost reverently, she laid the jacket back in the box. He took the box and set it on the floor.

"This feels like a book," Nora said, unwrapping the second package as carefully as she had the first.

Ken, unsmiling, nodded.

She drew off the paper and stared at the book, bewildered. It was a well-used volume, with a green leather cover and gilt-edged leaves. It looked familiar, its heft and texture somehow even *felt* familiar. The title sent a pang of nostalgia through her—*Great Poems of the English Language*.

She looked at Ken, who was still not smiling. "This looks just like the book Miss Pauline loaned me when I was a girl," she breathed. "Just exactly."

"It is the book."

Memories surged back to Nora. Pauline McKinney pressing the green book into her hands. "Now you read this," Miss Pauline had said, smiling. "You'll like it. It's a special book. I know you'll take good care of it."

She had kept the book for an entire, blissful week, reading and rereading. She had been thirteen years old, and it had seemed the most wonderful book in the world to her. To own it would have been very heaven.

"But it can't be—" she shook her head in disbelief "—it can't—"

She opened it to the title page and saw an inscription in fading ink: To Pauline, with love from J.T. The date beneath J.T.'s signature was twenty-five years old.

Under the first inscription was a newer one, in straight, spare letters, its black ink fresh: To Nora because she is a poem herself—all my love, Ken.

She gazed down at the book and shook her head, tears once more stinging her eyes. "But how—? I shouldn't— How did you—?"

He shrugged and kept his expression stolid. "I didn't do anything. It was Cal. He thought you should have it."

She closed the book and held it to her chest, even more tightly than she had hugged the jacket. "But— the rest of the family— I'm the last person who should..." The sentence trailed off because her voice grew choked.

The more emotional she became, the more impassive Ken grew. "No. Cal asked the others. They ain't— they aren't poetry readers, the McKinneys. He says you should have it."

"Me? Why me?"

"He says, things like that there—that book—" Ken muttered, "should belong to who loves them most."

Nora stroked the leather cover, unable to speak. She was aware of Ken's eyes on her, but didn't want to look at him, for fear she would lose her struggle to keep from crying.

"You like it?" he asked, concern in his voice.

Mutely she nodded.

"Now, Nora, don't go and cry on me."

She shook her head, furiously denying that she was fighting back tears, but he seemed to know better.

He put his arm around her and squeezed her tightly. With his free hand, he took the book and set it on the bedside table.

"Come here," he said, drawing her into his embrace. "I want you happy, not sad."

"I am happy," Nora managed to say, pressing her cheek against the wonderful strength of his shoulder. "I've never been so happy."

He hugged her more tightly. "Last night—it wasn't—too bad for you?"

His touch woke strong, new fires in her, fires that had never burned until he had touched her the first time. She put her arms around his neck and lifted her face to his. Her vision was blurry with unshed tears, but his strong-boned, solemn face seemed beautiful to her.

"Last night," she said, "was like nothing that ever happened to me before. I didn't think I'd ever care for a man. Not that way. But you taught me." Her voice shook. "You taught me."

A low rumble of thunder grumbled from across the lake. Nora remembered the thunder shaking her heart as Ken had kissed her in the storm. She remembered the feel of his body, warm in the cool of the wind, his shirt wet beneath her fingers, and the taste of rain on his lips.

"Teach me more," she whispered, the tears still trembling in her eyes.

He gazed down at her, his expression guarded, as if unsure she could mean what she said.

"Please," she said. She raised her face to his, asking for his kiss.

In the distance, a new storm rumbled again. Ken's mouth swept down to capture hers, and something between a growl and a moan vibrated softly, deep in his throat, mingling with the sound of the thunder.

As he kissed her, he lowered her so that they lay together in the bed, each trying to draw the other nearer. The sheet fell away from Nora, and Ken wound a lean leg around Nora's bare one. She sighed with pleasure, twining her legs against his as intimately as she could, her body arching to curve against his.

His fingers brushed her breasts as he undid the buttons of the shirt. Then, gently, he raised her to a sitting position again and drew the shirt from her. It dropped away, fell silently to the floor.

To be seen naked in full daylight made her suddenly timid. She reached for the sheet, wanting to cover herself again, but his hand closed firmly over her wrist.

"No," he said, his eyes intense with desire. "You're beautiful. I want to see every part of you, touch every part of you, kiss every part."

Sharply, she took in her breath. She let the edge of the sheet fall from her hand.

He bent and kissed her on one breast. "You're beautiful," he murmured, then kissed her other breast. "All over," he said.

She quivered. She bent to kiss him on the hair. She reached for his belt buckle, but he caught her hand softly.

"Not yet," he said, kissing her between her breasts. "Not yet. We have all day. We'll take our time."

He lowered her to a lying position again and bent over her. He kissed her bare shoulder, then her mouth again.

"We won't hurry this," he breathed against her lips. "We'll take our own sweet time."

He made the time go slowly, and he made it sweet, so sweet she thought she might die of it.

GORDON HAD RETURNED to Lubbock. Dirty and unshaved, he had not showered for three days.

His head felt odd, and it frightened him. He sensed, vaguely, that something had happened to him, something he didn't understand.

When he'd awakened in Val Verde, he'd felt less nervous, less desperate, but he'd also felt distinctly *strange*. He had the unsettling sensation that some part of his brain had broken off and drifted away.

It wasn't an important part, Gordon was sure, because he was still functioning perfectly. He'd done what he was supposed to, and done it exactly right. He'd picked up the load of goats in Val Verde and hauled them to Fort Worth. (He'd hated the goats. They all had weird, yellow eyes that were satanic.)

Now he was back in Lubbock, safe in his apartment. He would get his money from Charlie, tell him he was selling his share in the trucking rig, and that he was heading for Crystal Creek. He would make Nora and his mother take him back, and if Bubba Gibson got in his way, he would kill him.

Safely locked and bolted inside his apartment, Gordon drank two beers to fight the amphetamines that had kept him trucking the long haul from Fort Worth. His head began to buzz pleasantly.

Then he got into the shower, and he stayed there for almost half an hour. He emerged and took a pill to steady his hands. He shaved, nicking himself only once, and combed his wet hair into place.

He looked at himself critically. His skin was gray, his eyes bloodshot, and his muscles were going slack. *This* was what Charlie's crazy schemes had reduced him to, this pasty-faced stranger with circles under his eyes.

He needed to lift weights again, go back to the gym. He needed to get out of Lubbock and back to where people knew and loved and protected him. Maybe he would become adviser to Dottie—tell her how to run the coffee shop and invest her money—and she would pay him.

Gordon wouldn't actually work in the coffee shop. That kind of job was demeaning and repulsed him. But a management position—that would be good. That he could tolerate.

Yes, he would go back and tell the women how things should be done, and they would be grateful and they would obey and see to his comforts. Yes, everything would be perfect.

This time he'd prove he was the boss—especially to Nora. She'd follow his orders in his coffee shop and in his house—he'd decided to move into Dottie's house and make it his own—and she'd obey him in bed, too.

This time he'd teach her to do things his way—or else. He'd been too easy on her before. This time he'd keep her in *submission,* the way she was supposed to be.

He pulled on a clean pair of jeans and a black T-shirt, then padded barefoot to the phone to call Charlie. All the way back from Fort Worth, he'd rehearsed what he was going to say to Charlie: "I want my money. I'm going to pay off Steponovich, then blow. No more of this Mexican tripping for me—I'm out of it. Put my share of the truck up for sale and send the money to Crystal Creek. I gotta go home. The women need me, and I got business opportunities there."

He carried his vials and bottles of pills to the phone table with him because he no longer felt secure when they were out of his sight. He opened a fresh beer, drank half of it, then sat down and pushed the buttons of Charlie's number.

"Charlie? It's me, Gordo. I'm back. Listen, I got some news for you. I want—"

Charlie's growling voice interrupted him. "You damn fool. You damn near blew it at the border both ways—coming and going. I got word. You were so wired you were nearly fried. You're *out*. You haven't got the guts for it."

Gordon's stomach lurched, and his face began to burn. Charlie was insulting his courage? Charlie was insulting his manhood? If Charlie wasn't such a scary

dude, Gordon would...would what? Kill him. He
would kill him, that was what.

Gordon tried to make his voice steely. "I got too
much brains for it. No more of this Mexican tripping
for me—fine. I'm out of it."

Gordon paused. He was supposed to say something else, but Charlie had gotten him all mixed up. He
took a long swallow of beer.

Charlie laughed sarcastically. "Brains? You, boy,
are seriously deficient in that department. But you got
one thing right. No more Mexican trippin' for you."

By this time Gordon was so upset, he hardly noticed the additional insult. But he remembered what
he was supposed to say, and he said it. "I want my
money. I'm going to pay off Steponovich, then blow.
Put my share of the truck up for sale and send the
money to Crystal Creek. I gotta go home. The women
need me, and I got business opportunities there."

Nothing answered him except an ominous silence.
He could picture Charlie in his mind's eye: the
cropped head, the black mustache, the bulging muscles. And his killer's black eyes. *That was why he
couldn't kill Charlie. Charlie had killer's eyes because he was a killer himself. Gordon would have to
practice before he took on Charlie.*

Gordon tried to swallow, but a knot seemed lodged
in his throat. "Listen," he said, and began to repeat
himself, "I want my money. I'm going to pay off Steponovich, then—"

"You listen," Charlie said. "Steponovich's already got the money. But you owe him more. Fifteen
hundred more."

What? Gordon's mind rocked numbly. "But how—how did he—? Fifteen hundred more? I can't—"

"Steponovich's lookin' for you, Gordon. He ain't happy with you. I give him the money to keep you safe—but you forgot interest. Steponovich wants interest on his money. He wants it *now*."

Gordon took a drink of his beer and fumbled with a bottle, trying to get a tablet. His hands were shaking again. "Now? Now? Fifteen hundred? How can I—"

"Look, Gordo," Charlie said in a patronizing voice. "You're trouble. It's no longer a pleasure doin' business with you. I'll buy your share of the rig for fifteen hundred, pay it directly to Steponovich, then you *vamoose, savvy?* You get outta my life, outta Steponovich's. You go back to Crystal Creek, and you take care of your *women*."

Charlie put such an ironic spin on the word *women,* that Gordon felt as if he'd been struck.

"Fifteen hundred?" he managed to say. "Fifteen hundred? I got three thousand invested in that rig—"

"Fifteen hundred," Charlie said with finality. "Steponovich wants his money tomorrow. What other choice you got, Gordo?"

Gordon couldn't get the cap off the pill bottle, and tears of frustration filled his eyes. "You're *robbin'* me," he almost sobbed. The cap flew off the bottle with such violence that the pills jumped out and scattered across the floor. "You're *robbin'* me."

"Wrong. I'm savin' your sorry ass, Gordo, but I am purely tired of you, boy."

Gordon swore. He desperately searched for something to say that would save his dignity, but could think of nothing. He blinked back tears and put a hand on his aching stomach.

"Consider it a done deal," Charlie said and hung up.

The line buzzed in Gordon's ear, almost the same high pitch as the buzz in his head. He slammed down the receiver. Still fighting tears, he got down on his hands and knees and, with his shaking hands, tried to collect his scattered pills.

He picked up two and stuffed them into his mouth, washing them down with the last of his beer. He tasted lint and wiry carpet fibers, but he swallowed anyway. Then he sat on the floor and stared into space.

Had Charlie sold him out? Or saved him? He didn't know. He had set out on his dangerous mission to Mexico in hopes of paying off his debts, getting ahead at last.

Now, after nearly killing himself with nerves making the damned run, he had less than he'd had when he started. And Charlie didn't want him for a partner anymore. Charlie had laughed at him, said he had no guts. Go home to your *women,* Charlie had said.

Gordon's mouth twisted. He was angry, but confused. He would pay Charlie back—someday. But not now. Charlie would expect it now. Charlie was the kind you had to take by surprise. You had to hit him before he knew he was hit.

But the other people in his life Gordon could handle. Right now, the thing to do was just go *home.*

And nobody at home was ever going to hassle him again. Or they'd pay for it. They'd pay in blood, and it'd be a rehearsal for killing Charlie—if he decided Charlie deserved it.

"Nobody messes with me," Gordon vowed in a slurred voice. Still sitting on the floor, he reached for the phone. He punched out Bubba Gibson's number. He had it memorized by now. All the things he was afraid to say to Charlie, he would say to Bubba.

If he took some more amphetamines and started out now, he could be in Crystal Creek by twilight. He'd have Nora back in his bed. He'd make her pay for the hell she'd put him through. And she'd never cross him again if she knew what was good for her.

Oh, she would pay, she would pay.

"WHAT'S WRONG?" Ken said, tracing the pensive line of Nora's mouth. "You look like you're a million miles away."

It was afternoon. They lay in each other's arms on the daybed on the front porch. They were watching yet another storm approach from across the lake. He nuzzled her ear, trying to make her smile. He loved making her smile. But this time, he failed. Her face stayed somber.

"I'm so happy here," Nora said softly, "until I think of Gordon. What's he going to do when he finds out? I—worry."

"Come here," Ken muttered, drawing her closer. "Haven't I told you not to worry? Don't think of him, sugar. That part of your life's done with."

She looked into his eyes, her own troubled. "He's so unpredictable lately."

"Then don't try to make predictions about him. He may not do anything at all."

"But he—"

"Shhh," he soothed her, "this is our time, yours and mine. No ghosts from the past. Don't make me jealous."

At last she gave him the smallest of smiles. "You? Jealous?"

"Me. Jealous. I've wanted you too long. And now that I've got you to myself, I don't want to share."

She drew back slightly, her hands on his shoulders. "You always say that. That you wanted me for a long time. How long? Or are you just teasing?"

He remembered how long and felt his own face grow sober. "Longer than was fittin', I reckon."

"How long? Tell me."

He searched her face. He could still see traces of the serious little girl she had been. Too often he could also see the aura of hurt that Gordon had created.

He touched her face, laying the back of his hand against her cheek. "Since you were about nineteen, I guess. When you and Gordon came back to live with Dottie. One day I saw you walkin' down the street. It was winter. You were bundled up in an old green coat. You didn't have gloves or a hat. You were carryin' Rory."

"That green coat," Nora whispered, touching her finger to his lips, "you remember that? It was Dottie's. I didn't have a winter coat of my own when we came back. You can remember me in that coat—really?"

"It took me a minute to recognize you. You'd changed. You'd grown up. And it was bitter cold, but you didn't seem to notice. You just kept talkin' to Rory, talkin' and laughin', like you didn't have a care in the world."

He put his hands on either side of her face, lacing his fingers through her hair. "But I knew you had troubles. Anybody who knew Gordon, knew you had to have troubles."

"Dottie was good to me, though," Nora said in a voice so soft it was nearly a whisper. "She was always kind. For Christmas that year, she bought me a coat of my own."

He kept staring into her eyes, wanting to make the pain he could see there go away.

"I remember," he said. "It was red—with a black collar. But I always remember you in the green one on that day. God, it was cold. And Rory was big—he must have been heavy to carry. But you just kept on smilin' and talkin'. Then you carried him up the stairs and into the library. And I thought, *My God, she's still crazy about those books of hers.* I guess it happened then."

She smiled again, making his chest hurt. The only way to ease the pain was to draw her closer, so he did.

"You fell in love with me because I walked into the library?" she asked, snuggling against him, burying her face against his shoulder.

He held her more tightly. "Yes. No. Maybe. I fell in love *when* you walked into the library. That's all I know."

"But that was—almost six years ago."

"I know. Believe me, I know. And then you went to work in the Longhorn. You always had a book by the cash register. You'd read when business got slow. Sometimes, I'd make my coffee last a long time. Just so's I could sit and watch you read."

She nestled more closely against him, and he ran his hands up and down her back, feeling the softness, the femininity of her.

"But you never said anything," she said, her voice almost dreamy. "You never gave a sign."

"It wouldn't have been right. Not then. And even after the divorce, you weren't lookin' at any men. I knew I had to bide my time."

Nora wound her arms around his waist and squeezed him. "I love you." She raised her face and kissed the point of his jaw. Desire, which had been banked and glowing in him, suddenly flared into flame again.

"My God, Nora," he said, his voice ragged. "I keep wanting you so much. I want you again. Now."

He kissed her so deeply and so passionately that both of them forgot about the pain of the past and about Gordon Jones.

All they thought about was love and how lucky they were, at last, to have found each other.

GORDON'S TEMPER smoldered when Mary Gibson answered the phone. Was Bubba such a coward that he didn't even dare lift the phone receiver any longer?

"Where's your stinking husband?" Gordon demanded. "Where is he? If he's with my wife, I'll kill him. You give him that message, hear me?"

"I suggest you give him the message yourself." Mary Gibson's voice was eerily calm. "He's not with your wife. He's where he usually is on a Saturday afternoon, on his way to see *Miss* Billie Jo Dumont. If you want to talk to him, why don't you call him there—for a change?"

Gordon blinked in confusion. The buzzing in his head made him wonder if Mary had said what he thought she'd said. "He's at Billie Jo Dumont's?" he asked, trying not to slur his words.

"Yes." Mary made the word one long, bitter hiss. "Where else?" Then she hung up, so loudly that Gordon winced.

He sat staring at the receiver resentfully. Had Bubba gone back to Billie Jo? Or was he really off chasing after Nora? These conflicting thoughts were painfully difficult for Gordon to sort out.

Well, he'd find out. He would call Billie Jo's. Then, if he found Bubba there, he would take out all his frustrations on the old fool.

If Bubba wasn't there, Gordon would tell Billie Jo she'd better watch out; Bubba was lying to her, too. He almost smiled. If Billie Jo suspected Bubba of double-dealing, she'd kill him. Gordon wouldn't have to.

He called information and got Billie Jo's number. She answered on the second ring.

"Hello?" she said in that syrupy voice of hers.

Gordon sneered. "I hear tell that *Mr.* Bubba Gibson's there. Put him on the line. I wanna talk to him."

"He's not here—yet. Who is this? I don't like your tone."

"I don't like your tone," mocked Gordon. He disliked Billie Jo intensely. She always acted as if he wasn't good enough for her.

"Maybe he's not gonna see you. But he better not be gonna see my wife, 'cause I have told him repeatedly that I aim to make him into dog meat if I find him near her."

Billie Jo was not as stunned by Gordon's announcement as he would have liked. Anger and suspicion mingled in her voice. "Gordon Jones," she accused, "this is *you,* isn't it? You have repeatedly told Bubba *what?* How long has this been going on? Since when?"

Gordon disliked her snotty tone. "Since the old fool forgot he had you on the string and took after my wife, that's since when. You tell him that Gordon Jones will blast him to kingdom come if—"

"Do you mean that sorry business last Saturday?" Billie Jo demanded. "Have you been hounding Bubba since last *Saturday?* Nothing happened, dammit. Bubba was trying to make me jealous, is all. You let Bubba alone, or I'll crawl right through this telephone wire and strangle you with my bare hands."

"Don't you threaten me," Gordon shot back, insulted. "I said tell him that I'll blast him to—"

"Oh, shut up, you fool," Billie Jo snapped. "He doesn't want your wife. If you have to threaten somebody, get the right person. Ken Slattery. He's the one that's got your wife—right now. They're up at the lake together this very weekend. In the McKinney family's lake house. Everybody knows about it. Bubba—the idea!"

Ken Slattery? Slattery? Gordon had the sensation that somebody had hit him hard, knocking his brain askew. "Ken Slattery? What you talkin' about, woman?"

"I'm talking," Billie Jo retorted, "about Ken and Nora in their love nest. Ken Slattery's all she can see. She doesn't give an old fig for *you.* She's going to marry him, everybody's betting dollars to donuts. So *there.*"

Gordon's stomach pitched. "You're makin' this up. You tell Bubba—"

"I'll tell Bubba you're so stupid you don't know when your own ex-wife is absolutely through with you, you dumbbell. And your mother, too. Everybody's *sick* of you, Gordon. They're fixing to dump you for good. Your mother was even in Martin's office the other day, writing you out of her will. She's *disowning* you, Gordon. Not that I blame her."

Billie Jo sounded so sure of herself that Gordon couldn't get his bearings. The woman had to be lying. But if she was lying, how could she sound so bitterly truthful?

"You're makin' this up," he repeated. "You tell Bubba—"

"Gordon, you jackass, the other day, your own mama asked Martin for a will that leaves you *out.* And she asked about taking away your custody privileges and getting an order to keep you away from Nora and Rory. She even asked about *adoption.* She wants Ken Slattery to adopt your son. That's what she thinks of *you.* He wants to do it, too."

"You're lyin'," Gordon insisted, but the buzz in his head had grown so loud it made him want to weep with rage and frustration. He swore. "You're lyin'!" he almost screamed. "And you tell Bubba—"

"Bubba's got nothing to do with this," Billie Jo countered, acid in her voice. "I've told you more than you need to know, but you get one thing straight—you leave Bubba alone. I mean it."

"My wife wouldn't be in no love nest—my mother wouldn't—there's a kid to take care of, you lyin'—"

"Your mother and kid are out of town. Forget that other stuff. And forget about Bubba. What's important is that Nora's probably in bed with Ken this minute— *I'd* be, if I was her."

Gordon's thoughts swam drunkenly. What was the date? The middle of July or something. That really was the time Dottie usually went to visit her sister. And Rory had said something about Scout camp. And Slattery had been in the restaurant that day, too. Slattery had stood up for Nora.

Slattery. Everybody had conspired to fool him. All this time it had been Slattery!

"You tell Slattery—" he began, his voice ragged with warning.

Billie Jo cut him off. She sounded angry and as if she were about to cry. "Tell him yourself, you cowardly worm. You're just a great big *nothing,* Gordon Jones, and you always have been." She slammed down the receiver.

Gordon sat, stunned, still holding the phone in his hand.

He felt things falling into place. Click, click, click.

They had all lied to him and deceived him. Bubba wasn't after Nora. It had been Ken Slattery the whole time. They'd used Bubba to throw him off the trail. Bubba had covered for Slattery. *Click.*

They had all turned against him: his mother, Nora, even Rory, his own son. They had betrayed him. In treachery and secret they were working against him, as cold-bloodedly and poisonously as if they were a nest of vipers. *Click.*

While he was crossing the Mexican border, risking his life and freedom to get home to them, they had played him the double cross. By fraud and hypocrisy, they were cheating him of everything and handing it to another man. *Click.*

Of course. It made sense. Nora wouldn't be attracted to a fat old toad like Bubba. But Slattery—he was another matter. Oh, those quiet men, those silent men—they were the ones you couldn't trust. Slattery had knifed him in the back so neatly that Gordon was only now feeling the sting.

Charlie's contempt for Gordon had wounded him, but the contempt in Billie Jo's voice had enraged him. And their disdain was only the tip of the iceberg. Back in Crystal Creek, he was despised and an outcast. Even his own mother, sneaking and underhanded, was trying to victimize him and make him play the fool. He knew Billie Jo was telling the truth—she'd blurted it out, then regretted it, he could tell. *His own mother.*

So they thought he was nothing, did they? So they thought they could walk all over him, did they? Did they think he was too cowardly to strike back? What kind of fools were they? He'd show them. He'd show them all.

He was filled with a rage so immense it seemed to have turned him into ice, inside and out. When he rose from the floor, he was no longer shaking.

With a motion so deliberate it seemed calm, he tore the phone cord from the wall and tossed the phone aside. Then, swaying slightly, he went into his bedroom, where he kept his guns.

CHAPTER FIFTEEN

IN THE HOUSE by Lake Travis, Nora sighed and laid her head against Ken's naked chest. She closed her eyes, sated with love and happiness. Here, with him, held in his strong arms, she felt secure and safe, for the first time in her life.

"Are you awake?" he murmured against her hair.

"Yes."

Thunder rolled in the distance, deep and echoing.

"It's goin' to rain again," Ken said.

"I know."

He smiled. "It happens every time we go to bed. Do you think we cause it?"

She laughed softly. "Maybe."

"We've invented something better'n the rain dance."

"Much better."

"All of Central Texas should be grateful."

"Eternally grateful."

He shifted in the bed so that they lay facing each other. He kissed her forehead. She ran her fingers over the gold hair that covered his chest like a breastplate. His hands moved languidly over her naked body.

"Trouble is," he said, "I don't want to get out of this bed. Every time I do, I just want to get back in."

His touch caressed her into a dreamy, sensuous state. She wound her arms around his neck and nuzzled his throat. "Then let's not get out. Let's stay here."

"Do you want to?"

"Yes."

"Really?"

"Yes."

They stretched together like a pair of cats, then twined their legs together more intimately. Nora smiled at him. "Nobody would ever have imagined *me* being like this." She kissed his chest, then his collarbone, then his chest again.

His hands cupped her hips. "I did. I imagined it all the time."

"What do they call it, being like this?" Nora asked, nibbling and kissing the sharp curve of his jaw. "Is this *wanton?*"

He drew her closer and shook his head. "No, sugar. This is just called being in love." Then his lips took hers.

"YOU CALL THIS being in love?" Billie Jo Dumont shrieked. She picked up a brass vase of artificial flowers and flung it at Bubba's head.

Bubba ducked, and the vase clanged against the wall, bounced, then rolled across the carpet spilling silk blossoms and plastic bittersweet. For the life of him, he couldn't comprehend why she was so furious.

"Now, love woozle—" Bubba said.

"Don't you 'love woozle' me," Billie Jo fumed, putting her hands on her hips. "After the way I've compromised myself, the least you can do is tell me the truth."

Bubba had no idea what she was talking about. "Sweet thing," he said, "I done told you the truth. The heartburn had me, that's all."

"Heartburn." Billie Jo sniffed in indignation. "That's all?"

Bubba straightened and hitched up his pants. He thrust his thumbs belligerently into his belt. He didn't know what had gotten into Billie Jo. She was getting downright possessive. Possessive women made him uneasy.

"If I say I had the heartburn, then that's what I say," Bubba stated with as much dignity as he could. "And I don't see how no heartburn can *compromise* you."

"Oh!" Billie Jo cried. She fought against tears, lost the fight, then hid her eyes behind her hand, angry that Bubba was seeing her cry. "All I ask for is the *truth,*" she said in a choked voice. "Do you know what I went through this week? Do you know what terrible thoughts I had? After I have suffered the tortures of the damned, the very least you could do is *confide* in me. Then on top of everything, you let me get caught off guard and break a professional confidence. Oh!"

Bubba's face grew redder. He hated seeing Billie Jo cry. She was supposed to be happy and accepting, otherwise, how was he supposed to have fun with her? Back home he had one woman making him feel guilty as hell. Why on earth would he need two? Maybe he should have listened to J. T. McKinney's lecture.

J.T. had made Bubba feel so guilty that the only cure was a fresh dose of sin. Bubba had dared Mary's disapproval to make this journey into town to see Billie Jo. He was finally in the mood for—indeed he badly needed—a happy, snuggly woman, eager to please. Instead he'd found Billie Jo in the strangest mood he'd ever seen.

On the phone, she'd seemed fine, her old, accommodating, affectionate self. But when she'd opened the door, all had changed. What could have happened?

She'd fallen into his arms, collapsing against his chest. "Oh, Bubba," she'd said, "I'm so glad to see you. Are you all right? Tell me everything."

Bubba had held her tightly, but her words surprised him, putting him ill at ease. *What* was she talking about? What was he supposed to tell her? That for a week Gordon Jones had intimidated and terrorized him half-sick? That was not the sort of thing a man admitted to his mistress.

"Tell you what?" Bubba had asked innocently, patting her bottom. "My digestion was kickin' up, is all. You know Mary. That woman is tryin' to kill me with rich food. Lawsy, it's been a long week. Let's make whoopee now and conversation later. Come on, love buns. Daddy wants to go to Mattressville."

Bubba had meant the invitation to sound flattering. But instead, Billie Jo was offended. She kept demanding the *truth*, whatever she meant by that. And she kept making angry, mysterious statements about having compromised herself because of him. What had *he* done?

Bubba refused to be bullied by any woman, and he most adamantly refused to discuss Gordon Jones, because he considered the subject humiliating. J.T. had given him no sympathy. He had been so contemptuous that Bubba was even more mortified than before.

Now, instead of visiting Mattressville, Bubba had had a vase chucked at his head, and Billie Jo was dissolving into angry, accusing tears. *What good was a mistress in a bad mood?* he asked himself helplessly.

"Billie Jo," he said, trying to placate her, "don't go and get yourself in a state. What you need is lovin'—"

"Is that *all* you think of?" Billie Jo demanded. "I can go without hearing from you for days and days—I can think every horrible sort of thought—I can jeopardize my own professional integrity—but you want to shrug it off and hide things from me, you want to use me like an object—"

"Now, sweet thing," Bubba pleaded, "why would I lie to you? Come back to your daddy's arms."

"You're *not* keeping anything from me?" Billie Jo asked, wiping her eyes and glaring at him.

"Not one tiny thing, woozle," Bubba said as sincerely as he could.

"Nothing's been bothering you but a bad case of heartburn?"

"Not a thing, except not bein' able to see you."

"You haven't had one other teeny, tiny problem to contend with? Something you ought to share with a person you love? So she might be prepared for it?"

"Not one," Bubba lied. "I tell you everything, sweetie. May God strike me dead if I've kept one little secret from you."

Billie Jo gave him a long, suspicious look. Bubba inhaled and held his breath, so that his chest stuck out farther than his stomach. He lifted his chin, trying to look strong, loving and noble.

Billie Jo kept staring at him, her look growing as flat-eyed as a snake's.

"Get out of here," she said with surprising force.

Bubba looked at her in amazement.

"*Get out,*" she repeated. "Gordon called here. I know everything. How dare you lie to me?" She groped for another weapon and picked up a wooden banana from the fruit bowl on the table.

"Now, Billie Jo," Bubba said, but he found himself backing toward the front door. "Now angel baby darlin'—"

"I will *not* be lied to."

"Now, baby—"

"You will *not* lock me away from the rest of your life."

"Billie Jo—"

She narrowed her eyes. "I have faithfully loved you and sacrificed for you, Bubba Gibson. I have all but ruined my reputation for your sake. Now I've even gone and violated Martin's confidence. You say you love me—but you treat me like—like your bimbo. When things happen, you should share them, so we can face them together. You will *not* hold out on me."

"Billie Jo, I swear that I haven't held back on one blessed thing—"

She pitched the wooden banana at him. He raised his arms to defend himself, and the banana hit him in the left elbow, hit him surprisingly hard.

"Out!" screamed Billie Jo. "Out! Out! Out!" She reached for a bunch of carved wooden grapes and threw them at him with all her might. Then she reached for an apple and an orange.

Bubba fled. As he darted out the door, the wooden apple caught him between the shoulder blades. He ran all the way to his pickup truck, expecting any moment to be assassinated by an oak pineapple or the fruit bowl itself.

Billie Jo slammed the door and dissolved into tears. All the week's frustrations clamored within her. It would have been one thing for Bubba to come to her, at last, to take her hands in his and to confess what he had been going through this week. She would have told him that she knew, she understood, that she would stand by him, that she would be his prop and his support during this trauma.

She would confess all about Gordon's call and that she had, in her fervor to protect Bubba from his enemy, perhaps said more than she should have. Bubba would have comforted her and been impressed by her passion on his behalf.

Then, perfectly open and trusting and honest and mutually comforting, they would have gone to bed and made love, no secrets between them.

Instead, Bubba had pranced in the door with a gleam in his eye and a glib lie on his lips, and Billie Jo just couldn't take it after her hellacious week. She erupted.

Everything about her life pained her, and all she wanted to do was escape. She went to the bathroom, shook two sleeping pills out of her prescription bottle and washed them down with a cold swallow of water.

Then, all the fight gone out of her, she shuffled into her bedroom and changed her clothes. She took off the cute pink and white shorts set she'd put on just for Bubba. She slipped into her frumpiest nightgown, and got into bed.

Once in bed, she rolled over on her stomach, hugged her pillow and began to cry again. She wanted so much from Bubba, but he was willing to give so little. Had she been wrong to ask for more? Had she driven him away for good now?

When she wasn't sobbing over Bubba, she thought of how she'd blurted out office secrets, and how appalled Martin would be if he ever found out, and she wept harder. At last the pills took effect and she slipped into troubled sleep.

It had never crossed her mind that all of Gordon Jones's wrath might now be directed at Nora and Ken Slattery. She had been too involved in her own problems even to think of warning them.

But even as Billie Jo drifted through her uneasy dreams, Gordon Jones was rolling home, vengeance on his mind.

THE EMOTION that dominated Gordon was implacable rage. Billie Jo's revelations had shaken his life like an earthquake. He was no longer the hero going home for his just rewards. He was the victim in a tragedy of staggering betrayals. He could not get over it: *everyone* had betrayed him. *Everyone.*

It was past belief. Treason and treachery past bearing.

A man who suffered such violence had no choice except to resort to violence himself. It was the only justice. It was the only right.

Gordon had taken a handful of amphetamines back in Lubbock, not bothering to count them. Now his head buzzed like a hive of enraged bees, and the word it kept buzzing was *vengeance, vengeance, vengeance.*

Slattery would be the first to feel his fury. Slattery, that coward hiding behind the smoke screen that he and Bubba Gibson had conspired to create. Slattery, who at this moment was defiling Gordon's wife. Slattery, who schemed to rob Gordon not only of his woman, but even his son—even his mother.

Of all the things Billie Jo had said, none cut so deeply as her statement that *Dottie* had gone to Martin Avery. She wanted another man to adopt Gordon's child. She was cutting Gordon himself out of her will and her love.

Who could have made Dottie act in such a way? Slattery, Gordon thought with wild conviction, it had to be Slattery.

Slattery had probably been working behind Gordon's back to rob him of everything, spreading every sort of lie and slander.

Well, Gordon thought, clenching his teeth, Slattery would pay. He'd pay in blood. Gordon had spent most of the trip planning the coming confrontation with Slattery, savoring it.

He knew Slattery didn't carry a gun, never touched one. Gordon remembered. Slattery was a distant man and a bit mysterious, and part of his mystery was his disdain for guns. That disdain had always puzzled Gordon, but now it pleased him.

Slattery probably didn't have the stomach for guns, that was his problem. He only had the guts to sneak around stealing another man's wife, his son, even his very mother. Gordon would face him and show the world what a coward Slattery was.

Gordon had brought several guns, including his semiautomatic assault rifle. If he chose, he could pick Slattery off like a bird from a telephone wire. And any number of other people as well.

But Gordon was too much a man to do that. He would approach Slattery and throw him a gun. "Take it," Gordon would order. "Take it and fight like a man."

Slattery, knowing he had no choice, would reach for the gun, but Gordon would be quicker. He would shoot Slattery down and watch with pleasure while he bled to death.

All that Gordon hoped was that Nora would be there to see who was the real man. Then she would realize that Gordon was her proper master. And no jury in the country would convict him. Not for killing a wife stealer.

Nora. When Gordon thought of Nora, all possible scenes beyond Slattery's death grew vague. Perhaps she would sink to her knees, begging for mercy.

Perhaps she would even be grateful he had saved her from a man as conniving as Slattery. He could punish her, punish her as badly as she deserved. He'd take her back at his leisure, after she'd suffered properly.

But what if Nora didn't fall to her knees? What if she wasn't grateful? He supposed he'd kill her, too. Perhaps he'd have to kill everyone who had once pretended to love him.

KEN AND NORA had risen from bed to rummage in the kitchen for an impromptu supper. Evening was fast falling, and a light rain drummed against the windows.

The lamplight in the kitchen gave everything a golden cast. Nora listened to the low grumble of the thunder and felt protected and cozy.

She sat on a stool by the counter, her chin propped on her hand. Rather dreamily she watched Ken constructing a pair of enormous sandwiches.

"I should be doing that," she said.

"You do it all week long. It's my turn."

She sighed, happy simply to have him in her sight. He'd pulled on his jeans and boots, and although he'd donned his shirt, he hadn't buttoned it. His straight hair was tousled and hung over his forehead, glinting in the lamplight.

Nora was barefoot, her toes curling on the stool's rungs. She wore her jeans and the shirt Ken had given her that morning. It was pleasantly large, and she liked the intimate feel of his clothing next to her bare skin.

She tossed a strand of hair from her eyes. "I should brush my hair," she said.

He looked up, gave her a slow crooked smile, and shook his head.

She smiled back. "No?"

"No. I like you rumpled. It reminds me of how you got rumpled. Makes me want to rumple you again."

He opened a bag of potato chips, poured a heap on each sandwich plate and carried the plates to the table. "Let's eat. I've got to keep my strength up."

"I don't want you to get rumpled out."

"You're gettin' bold."

"Yes. I am."

She rose and went to the counter. He had opened a bottle of red wine, and she poured two glasses. She followed him to the table and set them down.

"Oh," she said, "just a minute. I forgot place mats and napkins. Let me get them."

Playfully he blocked her way, taking her in his arms. "Let's rough it. Sit. We don't have to be formal."

As he started to kiss her, a loud squeal of brakes in the drive ripped across the quiet sound of the rain. A car or truck door slammed, and half a moment later, booted feet hit the porch running. Someone jerked at the locked door, then began a loud, frantic knocking.

"Slats! Open up!" It was Cal McKinney's voice.

Ken's grip tightened on Nora's arms. He frowned in the direction of the door. "What in hell—"

"Slats! It's me—Cal—" The knocking banged so violently that it almost drowned out a roll of thunder.

Cal's voice alarmed Nora. She stared at the drapes that hid the sliding glass door. They quivered from the impact of Cal's blows on the metal doorframe.

Ken, too, looked worried. "What's he want?" he muttered. Quickly, he released Nora and moved to the door.

He yanked the drapes partly open, and almost simultaneously unsnapped the lock. He slid the heavy glass door open. Cal quickly entered, glanced over his shoulders and banged the door shut behind him.

His pale blue shirt was spotted with rain, and his hair curled with dampness. He carried the black leather holster, and in the holster was the gun. He looked first at Ken, then at Nora, then back at Ken. Something wild flashed in his hazel eyes.

He was breathing hard. "Gordon," he said without introduction. "He's heading this way."

Without realizing it, Nora took a step backward. Fear went through her completely, as if someone had impaled her with a spear.

Ken's shoulders tensed. *"What?"*

Cal glanced out at the drive, then reached for the cord of the drapes and jerked them shut. "Don't ask me why, man. He's right on my tail," he said. "Get away from the windows."

Ken shook off Cal's hand. He stepped away from the glass, but his eyes went cold. "Gordon?"

Cal nodded, glancing at Nora again, his face taut. "I was in town, putting gas in the truck. I saw him, thought I should follow him. He saw me, too. We started havin' a little race. By the time we hit the lake turnoff, he was drivin' *crazy*, man—and he was heading here. I ran him off the road, but he got right back on. I said, don't ask me how—"

Another scream of brakes filled the air. Metal crunched against metal, as if Gordon's car had clipped Cal's truck. There were three long seconds of silence. Then a car door slammed.

"Take this," Cal said, thrusting the holstered gun toward Ken.

The thunder rolled. "No," Ken said, his jaw rigid. He nodded toward Nora. "Get her out of here. Take her out the back way."

Footsteps echoed on the porch. They drew nearer.

Cal spun on his boot heel and stared at Nora. "Call the sheriff," he ordered. He shoved the gun at Ken again.

Ken shook his head.

Cal swore. "Jesus! What am I gonna have to do? Kill him for you?"

"Nobody's killin' anybody. Nora, get out of here. Take her out of here. Did you hear me?"

Nora stood frozen, unable to move.

"Slattery?" She recognized Gordon's voice. It had an odd sound, as if he wasn't completely sober. Terror gripped her. "I know you're in there, Slattery. Come out and face me—like a man. Stop sneaking like a snake behind my back and face me."

"Get her *out*," Ken said between his teeth. "I'm going to talk to him, is all."

Cal swore again. "*You* get her out. I'll talk to him."

"Slattery? You comin' out? Or do I kick this door out? People that live in glass houses shouldn't steal wives. Nora, get yourself out here. You get yourself to my side—where you should be. Then maybe I won't kill him. Maybe. I'm gonna count to three. Then if this door doesn't open, I kick it open."

Nora's stomach churned. An old fear she hadn't felt for years filled her, and she found herself moving toward the door, anxious to appease Gordon, anxious to do whatever it took to calm his rage.

"No," Ken said fiercely, seizing her by the shoulders. "No." He stared into her eyes, his own blazing implacably.

"One," said Gordon, menace in his voice.

"Son of a *bitch*," Cal snarled through clenched teeth. He yanked the drapes half-apart, and with almost the same motion, threw the door open. He stepped onto the porch, still holding the holster, but holding it far out, as if he didn't want to use the gun. "Now, Gordon," he said placatingly, "don't go talkin' about kickin' my daddy's door down. This is gettin' out of hand. Why don't you and I sit down and have a drink?"

Gordon stepped back to the edge of the porch. He shook his head. His figure was shadowy in the rain and thickening darkness. Then a long shimmer of lightning lit the sky. Nora caught a flickering glimpse of Gordon's features. The expression on his face appalled her. It was not the expression of a sane man.

Worse, he was wearing a gun on his right hip, and he held another, still holstered, in his left hand. Unlike Cal, he held it close, almost lovingly. Then the glare of the lightning faded, making Gordon into an indistinct silhouette again.

"Butt out, McKinney," Gordon said. "I'll take care of you later. You ran me off the road, you bastard."

"Well, hell, Gordon," Cal said, a smile in his voice, "I didn't mean to. It was all in fun. But let's talk—"

"I want my wife, and I want Slattery," Gordon said. "Nora! Get out here! Slattery? Slattery?" Gordon began to cluck like a chicken, mocking what he thought of as Ken's cowardice. The sound had a deranged ring. Then he stopped as suddenly as he had begun. The only noise was the soft, steady patter of the rain.

"Let me go to him," Nora said in a shaking voice. "I'm the one he's really mad at. I know how to handle him—"

"No!" Ken retorted, almost pushing her toward the back door. "Leave. Get out."

"Now, Gordon," soothed Cal, "wouldn't you like to have a shot of whiskey, buddy? My daddy's got a fifth of Wild Turkey under the counter. I'll tell you what—let's have a few drinks and—"

"McKinney, get out of that doorway," Gordon said viciously. "If Slattery isn't out here in thirty seconds, I'll start on you."

A breeze rose, making the drapes flutter. Nora watched numbly as Ken stepped into the night. He stationed himself in front of Cal, his thumbs hooked into the front of his belt. Perhaps ten feet separated him from Gordon, who stood near the steps, poised like the gunfighter he wanted to be.

"You got a problem, Gordon?" Ken said in his quietest voice.

Lightning flared weakly again, silvering Ken's hair, casting a brief, will-o'-the-wisp illumination over Gordon's face. His face seemed empty, his eyes dark and wasted.

My God, thought Nora, *he looks ten years older than he did last week. What's he done to himself?*

Mercifully the light died, and all she could see of Gordon was his dark shape.

He squared his shoulders. "I've got a problem, all right. You're the problem, Slattery. You're after my wife. Nora? Nora? Get out here."

Nora's muscles tensed. She would have obeyed his call, but she saw Ken hold up his hand, a gesture telling her not to come. She held her breath and didn't move.

"She's not your wife anymore, Gordon," Ken said in the same quiet voice. "She hasn't been for two years."

"She made her vows to me forever," Gordon answered. "What man put together, let no God put in thunder. Let no God put in sunder."

He doesn't even know what he's saying, Nora thought with a fresh surge of panic.

Ken stood his ground, keeping his hand half-raised in a gesture of peace. "She's her own woman, Gordon. And I want no trouble with you. I'm not a fightin' man."

"No! You're a sneakin' man—you're after my wife. You're after my child. You're after my mother."

Ken shook his head dubiously. "Gordon, this has nothin' to do with your mother."

"Don't you mention her name," Gordon almost screamed. "Don't mention my mama's name. I want Nora. Nora? Nora! Get out here—I want you to come kneel at my feet, Nora. Nora, you come here and kneel, dammit—"

"Slats, this boy's out of control," Cal said in a low voice. He tried to step to Ken's side, but Ken made a tense motion signaling him to stay back.

"Nora, if you don't come out here and kneel, I'll shoot this dog down and come in and *make* you kneel. I'll do worse'n that."

He's going to kill us all, Nora thought. Her knees shaking, she stepped to the door. If it would help to kneel, she would kneel. He had done worse to her in his time.

"Stay back," hissed Cal, and once again she halted.

"Don't talk to her like that," Ken warned Gordon. "She doesn't have to take it from you anymore."

Gordon was silent for a moment. It was as if he was trying to remember something. When he spoke, he sounded as if he was making a speech that he'd rehearsed. "Slattery, you're a sneak and a thief. I come to settle this man-to-man. The old way. I got a gun."

"I see that," Ken said without emotion.

"I brought you one, too." Gordon paused, as if for dramatic effect. He threw the holstered gun at Ken's feet. "Take it," he ordered. "Take it and fight like a man."

"No."

"Take it and fight like a man."

"No."

"Jeez, what a stinking coward you are. You want Nora?"

There was a beat of silence, broken only by the hushed sound of the rain.

"Yes," Ken said. "I want her."

"Then," said Gordon, his right hand hovering near his gun, "fight for her, you son of a bitch."

In the distance lightning flickered, followed by a dull mumble of thunder.

"Not with guns," Ken said, weariness in his voice. "You want to fight, I'll fight you. But no guns. Drop the gun belt, Gordon. Then I'll fight you if you have to fight."

Gordon laughed. "Take it, Slattery. I'll give you to the count of three again. If you haven't picked it up by then, I draw. And I'll shoot you apart. A piece at a time."

"I don't like guns."

"Then you ain't no man," Gordon mocked. "One."

"For God's sake," said Cal, "the man doesn't like guns. Fight fair, you little—"

"Shut up. I'll kill you both. Nora? I seen you in the doorway. You gonna watch me kill 'em both? I'm gettin' ready. I'm countin'. Two. Get ready to die, cowboy."

Suddenly Ken went into a crouch, reaching for the gun.

"Jesus, you fool—*don't*" Cal said, suddenly throwing himself between Ken and Gordon. His stance was menacing and he was drawing the Smith & Wesson from its holster.

Gordon was faster. His hand snapped to his hip and then almost straight out in front of him. A blaze of light spurted and a roar filled the air.

Cal's body gave a violent jerk forward. Then, staggering, he lurched backward. The gun fell from his hands, clattering to the boards of the porch.

Nora screamed.

"Cal!" Ken's cry tore the rainy darkness.

Cal's back hit the plate glass so hard that it shook, and his legs buckled. He caught at the drapes that fluttered in the damp breeze. Clutching them, he fell, crumpling at Nora's feet. She couldn't see his face anymore. It was covered with blood.

"He drew on me!" Gordon shouted. "He had a gun all the time—you two drew on me first. Die! Die!"

He aimed his gun at Ken's head, and a second shot rocked the night.

CHAPTER SIXTEEN

THE LIGHTNING PLAYED behind Gordon, an eerie blue flicker that outlined him. To Nora, his dark shape seemed to swell, grow larger, overwhelming her vision like some monster in a dream.

From the corner of her eye she could see Ken lying on the floor of the porch. He still held up his head, she could tell, but he didn't move. She was afraid to look more closely; the sight would rip her heart in half. No, it was already ripped in half, and she was stunned sick.

She knew that Gordon was looking at her; even in the darkness she could feel it. The lightning shone again, from another direction. Shadows played across his face. He seemed to smile malevolently.

Ken lay helpless, wounded, and Gordon, smiling, was going to shoot him again.

You'll have to kill me, too, Gordon, she thought in defiance. *You'll to have to kill me before you can kill him.*

She ran to Ken, trying to throw herself down, to shield his body with hers. But Ken rose on his knees, catching her. She flung her arms around his neck, her eyes squeezed shut, waiting for Gordon to fire a third time. She hugged Ken as tightly as she could, her body tensed for the coming blow.

If I die, she thought, clinging to Ken, *I'll die loving you.*

Behind her, Cal groaned.

"It's all right, it's all right," Ken said, holding her so close that her ribs almost cracked. "Baby, it's all right."

Cal groaned again, louder. "Je-hosh-a-*phat!*" he said. "This smarts like hell."

"It's all right, it's all right," Ken repeated in Nora's ear. "Honey, get up. I've got to see to Cal, baby. Help me see to Cal."

He got to his feet, drawing her with him. She didn't think her knees would support her. He held her to him with one arm. His other hand held a gun, and it was aimed at Gordon.

"Fall down, you son of a bitch," he snarled at Gordon, "or I'll shoot you again. Calvin? Are you alive, boy?"

"Ouf," Cal muttered. "He grazed me, is all."

Nora's eyes fluttered open. She clutched Ken, staring up at him without comprehension. She began to shake.

Ken hugged her to him more securely, but kept the gun trained on Gordon. "Calvin! I said, are you alive?"

"And I said, 'Yes,' dammit," Cal said in a pained voice. "This is as bad as gettin' kicked in the head by a horse."

"How bad are you hurt?"

"Not bad, dammit—chill out."

Nora forced herself to look at Cal. He'd raised himself to sit, slumping against the plate glass. He was wiping the blood from his face with the hem of the drapes.

"My mama would switch me if she saw me bloody her good drapes like this," he grumbled.

He's alive. And Ken's standing. Ken's got a gun, Nora thought numbly. *And that must mean that Gordon is—Gordon is—Gordon is—*

She made herself turn in Ken's arms so that she could see Gordon. The inconstant lightning flared again. Ken was standing, but Gordon was sinking to his knees.

At first, Nora thought that he was smiling grotesquely at her. Then, with a shock, she realized why his mouth twisted so strangely. Gordon was crying.

His knees struck the porch floor with a thud. He held his hands in front of him in almost a prayerful attitude, cradling his right in his left. His shoulders shook with muted sobs.

"You shot me," he said. "You *shot* me in the hand."

"Shoulda put it between his eyes," muttered Cal, wiping his forehead.

Nora looked at Ken again. "You shot him? He didn't shoot you?"

Ken nodded without emotion.

Nora turned to Gordon again. His holster was empty, his gun nowhere to be seen. His shoulders heaved harder.

"It hurts," Gordon wept. "It *hurts*."

"Tell me about it." Cal's voice was sarcastic. "Lawsy, could somebody get me a towel?"

Ken gave Nora an encouraging hug. "How about it, sugar? Can you get him a towel? And make sure he's all right?"

She nodded, although she kept gazing with fascination at Gordon's hands. When the lightning flared, she saw blood oozing between the fingers that he clamped protectively around his right hand. It dripped to the porch floor to mingle with the rain. The thunder gave a tired rumble.

"You opened up the whole back of my hand," Gordon whined. "I can't move it." He hunched over, as if protecting himself from further pain.

"Call 911, too," Ken told Nora. "Say there's been a shooting at the McKinney lake house." Keeping his gun on Gordon, he kicked the second gun, the one Cal had dropped, behind him, far from Gordon.

Nora tried to gather her wits and regain control of her emotions. She walked back inside the house, but her movements did not seem real; they seemed to take place deep inside some dream.

Mechanically, she dialed 911 and said that there'd been a shooting at the McKinney lake house and two men were hurt. Just as mechanically she went to the linen closet and took down a pair of towels. She thought of Gordon, sobbing and holding his hand, and took a third.

She wet the towels under the faucet, filled a basin with ice and water, and carried the towels and basin back to the porch. She willed her hands not to shake, and they did not.

She walked up to Gordon and handed him a wet towel. "Here," was all she said.

He sniveled, but made no other reply. He collapsed to a sitting position and leaned against the porch railings. His legs stuck straight out in front of him. He wrapped the towel around his injured hand. "I think I'm gonna be sick," he said. "Help me, Nora. Hold me. I'm cold."

She ignored him and went to Cal instead, sinking to her knees beside him. She wiped his face and dabbed at the shallow wound that creased his scalp at the hairline.

"You're sure you're all right?"

He grunted assent. "Head wounds always bleed like the devil."

She made a makeshift ice pack and pressed it against the crease.

Ken glanced at Cal, his eyebrow cocked cynically. "Why didn't you *say* it was your head? I wouldn't have worried."

"Slattery," Gordon said in a shaking voice, "you set me up. You said you couldn't use a gun. You led me on. You lied."

Ken shook his head. "I said I didn't *like* a gun. I never said I couldn't use one."

Gordon bowed his head and wept with even more abject misery. The lightning played, and the thunder rolled, growing more distant. Mingling with its sound was the shrill keen of sirens, faint but rising, coming nearer.

Gordon's head shot up. His body stiffened. He swore. "Cops?" he said in disbelief. "Cops?"

No one answered him for a long moment.

It was finally Cal who spoke, his tone contemptuous. "They won't be surprised it's you, Gordon.

They've been asking about you. Federal boys, too. They're going to have a lot of questions for you.''

"Cops?'' Gordon repeated, panic rising in his voice. "Federal? *Federal?* Questions? Oh, God, oh, God. I can't go to jail—I won't go. If I don't talk, the cops'll throw the book at me. If I do talk, somebody'll *kill* me. Charlie—Chessman, they'd have somebody kill me. You can't do this.''

Nora, still kneeling beside Cal, didn't understand. What did Cal mean, that federal authorities had asked about Gordon? This was the first she'd heard of it. What was Gordon mixed up with?

And what was he babbling about? What did his crazy friend Charlie have to do with this? Who was Chessman? What did Gordon know, and how could it put him in danger?

"Cops *lean* on you,'' Gordon said. "They'll say if I talk, I'll walk. But I *can't* talk. They'll lock me up a hundred years. And Charlie and Chessman—they'd get me killed anyhow—to make sure I stayed quiet. The Mexican guns are heavy stuff—you're *dooming* me. Don't do this to me. Please. Let me go.''

Shakily, Gordon rose to his feet. Ken tensed, but kept the gun trained on him. Nora, frightened, also rose. She put her hand on Ken's arm.

"Please,'' Gordon begged. "Let me go. Please.''

Ken shook his head. "I can't, Gordon.''

Gordon inched toward the porch steps. The lightning glimmered dully, and Nora saw that his face, although streaked with tears, had gone stony. She thought she understood that look, and she feared it. It meant that Gordon was desperate enough to do anything, no matter how foolish.

Even as the apprehension flooded through her, Gordon acted. He turned and fled across the yard. She felt the muscles in Ken's arm tauten.

Cal tried to rise. "Shoot him!" he cried. "Dammit—shoot!"

"No!" Nora breathed, clutching Ken's arm more tightly. The sirens, close now, rent the night with their shrillness.

"Stop him!" Cal yelled, then crumpled again, swearing in frustration and pain.

Nora could barely see Gordon's figure, disappearing into the darkness. He headed toward a stand of trees, hesitated, then suddenly zagged in the other direction, toward the road that led to the highway. His path was as erratic as that of a frightened rabbit.

"Gordon, don't be crazy," Ken shouted, but he didn't shoot.

"Gordon—" The approaching sirens swallowed Nora's cry. She gripped Ken's arm harder.

She could no longer see Gordon. Blue lights flashed, coming down the road, as the cars from the sheriff's department raced nearer. A spinning red light in the darkness announced the ambulance.

Again Ken's voice ripped across the night. "Gordon, for God's sake, don't—"

Then above the siren's scream, a sudden shriek of brakes rose, so piercing and torturous that Nora hid her face against Ken's sleeve. She heard a thud of an impact, powerful, yet muffled by the shriller sounds. She heard a man's cry.

The sirens stopped. For a moment the night was quiet again, except for the rain and the sound of metal doors slamming.

"Where'd he come from?" a voice demanded. "All of a sudden, he was in front of me. I *tried* to stop—"

"Stand back. Is he alive?"

"I *tried* to stop—"

"He wasn't there, then all of a sudden, he was—and we were right on top of him. Bobby tried—"

"I tried—"

"He tried—"

"Stand back. Shorty, turn him over. Who is it? Oh, God, is it Gordon Jones? It is. It is. Is he alive?"

"Barely."

"Bobby couldn't help hitting him—"

"I tried—"

"Don't try to move him. I think his back is broken."

"It's Gordon, all right. Oh, Lord. Who's gonna tell Dottie?"

Cal sagged against the plate-glass door, his hand to his head. "What the hell happened?"

Ken had both arms around Nora, and her face was still hidden against his sleeve. "Gordon," Ken breathed. "I think he got hit. Nora, stay here with Cal. I'd better go see."

"No," she said from between her teeth. "I'll go, too. It's my place. I have to—for Dottie."

Ken didn't protest. He nudged Cal with his boot. "Hey, kid. Stay put. Don't try to get up again. Hear me? Come on, Nora."

The short walk through the rain seemed endless to Nora, endless and nightmarish. Even more nightmarish was the string of vehicles parked in a haphazard line where the road met the drive, their colored roof-lights whirling, casting mad shadows on the trees that edged the road.

A cluster of men gathered around a motionless shape, shining flashlights on it. The roof lights colored them with shifting reds and blues, and the shadows danced just as wildly on the men as on the trees. To Nora, it was a scene from hell.

Gordon lay unmoving in the wet dirt of the road. His eyes were blinking in the assault of light, but he didn't seem to see anything. His face was drenched with rain. A drop of blood shone at the corner of his mouth. He lay at an odd angle, an unnatural angle.

Shakily, she walked to Gordon's side, then had to lean against Ken as she stared down.

Gordon's expression was dazed, frightened. He looked strangely young and innocent to Nora, almost like the boy she'd known all those years ago.

"Oh, Gordon," she whispered brokenly, "what have you done to yourself?"

She sank down, weakly sliding from Ken's embrace to kneel beside Gordon. She took his left hand in both of hers. His was stained with blood and mud. "Gordon?"

He blinked up into the changing whirligig of lights. His pupils were as tiny as pinpoints. "I want my mother," he said, his voice so weak that it was like a child's.

"It's all right," Nora said, squeezing his hand between hers. "You're not alone."

Oh, Gordon, Gordon, she thought, *thank God Dottie doesn't have to see this.*

His mouth quivered. He was trying to speak again. Nora bent closer. "Tell my mama," he said, "that— I'm sorry. From now on—I'll be good."

"She'll understand, Gordon."

His mouth worked more spasmodically. "Tell her—" he stopped and grimaced with pain " —Chessman and Charlie were—bad. I should have told on them. They were bad. I don't want to be. I wasn't gonna go to Mexico again. Tell her. Tell her I'll—be good."

His hand began to shake uncontrollably and she gripped it tighter. His eyes grew more dazed. Another drop of blood welled at the corner of his mouth, and then another.

"Gordon?"

"I want Brolly. Where's Brolly?"

Nora went cold at his words. Brolly had been Gordon's childhood dog. He had been dead since Gordon was nine.

Nora reached out and tried to wipe away the rain from Gordon's face. She kept her other hand clenched around his. "Brolly's at your feet, Gordon. He's asleep. At your feet."

Gordon's head made a tiny, convulsive motion, something like a nod. "Mama," he said, his words growing less distinct. "I been prayin' a lot. Really, Mama. Matthew, Mark—Mark—Mark—Luke..."

His chest sank as his voice quivered off into a sigh. His lips quivered, then went still. The hand in hers became heavy with limpness. The madhouse lights played over his face, danced across his eyes, but he did not blink.

She stared at him in numbed disbelief. She felt Ken's hands on her shoulders. A man reached down and shut Gordon's unseeing eyes.

"He's gone," somebody said in a voice devoid of emotion.

Someone else muttered in agreement.

"Oh," Nora said, watching the rain strike his still face. "Oh."

"Come on," Ken said quietly.

He drew her to her feet. She released the dead man's hand and took Ken's, then collapsed against him. The lights spun, the rain fell, and Nora felt as if the world would have slipped away into darkness and nothingness if there had been nothing to support her, to keep her anchored to reality.

Ken held her fast.

THE SHERIFF'S DEPARTMENT kept them separated for hours, while each of them—Nora, Ken and Cal—was questioned. Nora, shaken, wanted nothing more than to rejoin Ken. Vaguely she understood that they all *must* be questioned separately to see if their stories corroborated one another. The knowledge did not soothe her. She wanted the questions to end. She wanted Ken.

Then a man from the Bureau of Alcohol, Tobacco and Firearms appeared. He, too, had questions. Everyone seemed especially interested in Gordon's statements about Charlie, the man named Chessman and the guns in Mexico.

They repeatedly asked Nora the same questions, to see if she would change her story. She never did.

At last she was ushered into the sheriff's office. Ken and Cal were there, Cal with a bruised forehead and a patch of white adhesive at his hairline. Ken rose and went to her, wordlessly putting his arm around her.

He led her to a seat beside his and kept his arm around her shoulders. The sheriff, Wayne Jackson, sat behind his metal desk, his lips clamped tight. Sitting in a straight-backed chair next to Jackson was the ATF man, whose name was Husby. He looked as somber as Jackson.

Wayne Jackson was a huge man with a weather-beaten face and dark eyes. He shook his head, then trained his gaze on Nora.

"Nora?" he asked with some concern.

"I'm fine," she lied, fearing her voice betrayed her. In truth she was exhausted, both emotionally and physically.

Wayne, unsmiling, shrugged, as if he knew she lied, but he could do nothing about it. He looked down at a yellow legal pad with penciled scribblings, then back at them. "I've got something to say to all of you. I know it's late. I know you're tired. But listen. This is important."

Nora nodded but felt like an automaton.

"Just get the show on the road, Wayne," Cal McKinney said. "Serena's gonna be worried sick about me."

"Gordon's dead," Wayne said.

Nora flinched, and Ken tightened his embrace.

"The coroner's calling it an accidental death," Wayne said without emotion. "There were at least four witnesses who saw it clearly. He came out of those trees and dodged right in front of a sheriff's department car. Lord knows why. There was no way it could have kept from hitting him.''

"I—didn't see it happen," Nora said. Images of Gordon lying in the rain haunted her.

"I know," Wayne said with surprising gentleness. "I just want you to know that this isn't a cover-up. The actual cause of death was accidental." He paused. "Dottie's been informed. She's been told what happened, but only in general terms."

Nora stiffened. "How did she—how did—?"

Wayne's face stayed impassive. "She took it hard. Her sister wanted her to rest and to come back here tomorrow as scheduled. That's what'll be done."

Ken frowned. "What about Rory? Surely to God you're not sending some officer to Scout camp to tell the kid his father's dead?"

"No. Nora can tell him. Or Nora and Dottie. However they think best. There'll be no public statement until Rory's notified."

"Notified," Ken said, clearly disgusted with the coldness of the term.

Wayne gave him a mild glance, then looked down at the notes on the yellow pad.

"Now, according to all three of you, Gordon said several things that were of—how shall we say?—a sensitive nature."

Husby, the ATF man, nodded in sober agreement. He was a large man, portly, without an ounce of humor in his face. "Yes. A sensitive nature."

"People with the ATF," Wayne said, nodding toward Husby, "have been asking about Gordon. Because of this Charlie friend of his. Charlie's been suspected for a long time of running contraband to

Mexico. Small-time stuff. But lately, there's a possibility of—bigger things."

"We've suspected certain drivers," Husby said, "because of certain patterns, certain connections. The problem is connecting upward."

Nora looked at the two sober-faced men, not quite seeing them. Gordon's face kept floating wraithlike before her. She shook her head. "I'm sorry. I don't understand."

"We don't know who's in charge of this smuggling," said Husby. "Who's supplying the goods. Who makes the contracts. We've got no names. We've got lateral connections. We've got nothing that connects upward. To higher echelons. Until, maybe, tonight."

Nora felt Ken's arm tighten around her shoulder. *Chessman,* she thought. *Gordon said something about Chessman. Is that the name they've been looking for?*

"What you're saying," Ken said, lowering his brows, "is Gordon was involved with smuggling. That what he said may give you a lead to solve it. Is that it?"

Husby kept his face blank and his voice without emotion. "I never actually said that, Slattery. Assume what you like—as long as you say nothing. The investigation is still under way. If we're lucky—and we may be—you may never be called to testify. We'll have plenty of proof without you. Gordon had a few interesting phone numbers in his wallet. Also a couple of Mexican names. There may be more of interest in his apartment."

"I see," Ken said, his tone deliberate. "You pursue the case. But what we heard, we don't make public."

"Correct." Husby bit off the word with authority.

"Now what this means," Wayne said, scratching on his tablet with a pencil, "is this. Tonight Gordon came to the lake house to settle a personal score. He was belligerent. There was a scuffle. Authorities were called. Gordon tried to flee the scene. There was an accident."

"Mr. McKinney, here, was slightly hurt," Husby added smoothly. "Nothing else of import occurred."

"Slightly yourself, buddy." Cal glowered. "It ain't *your* head."

"Steady, Cal," Wayne said, warning in his voice. "It's in the best interests of ATF to downplay this thing for the time being. It's also in the best interests of Nora. And Dottie. And Rory."

Cal didn't look any happier, but he tossed a glance at Wayne that said he understood.

Wayne gave a curt nod. "Normally, we wouldn't tell you *this* much. We'd tell you to keep quiet, and that'd be it. But because it's—well, frankly, Nora, because it's Dottie, and because Gordon's made such hell of her life, I think she should know that at the end, he finally might have done some good.

"You can't give her details, of course. Maybe someday. And of course, she's not to say anything. Again, maybe someday. But it might be some consolation to her. To know he did some good at the end."

Nora bowed her head again, blinking hard. "Thank you, Wayne."

A painful look crossed Wayne's face. "As for Rory, Nora, I have to leave that to your discretion. He's only a child. You know better than I do how much he needs to know. And how far he can be trusted to keep quiet.''

A choking lump had formed in her throat, but she forced herself to speak. ''Thank you again, Wayne. I—''

She couldn't finish. She collapsed against Ken, and he held her tight. ''Let me take her home, Wayne,'' he said. ''For God's sake.''

''Right,'' Wayne said with a tired sigh. ''Take her home.''

WHEN THE OFFICERS let them go, a deputy took them back to the lake house. Cal insisted he could drive, said good-night and headed straight for the Double C. Ken got their belongings, then drove Nora to his place. He feared both the lake house and Dottie's home would hold too many memories of Gordon for her.

When they reached his house and went inside, Nora felt as if she'd finally found sanctuary. She sighed with relief.

''Tired?'' Ken asked, looking down at her. They stood in his living room, their arms around each other's waists.

She nodded. She was tired and worried and felt a little foolish besides; she had never put on her shoes. She had sat all those long hours at the sheriff's department barefoot, clad in rolled-up jeans and Ken's oversize shirt.

''Hungry?'' he asked. ''We never did eat.''

She shook her head. She had no appetite.

''Then let's go to bed,'' he said gently. ''And I'll hold you. Just hold you. All night long. I think that's what you need.''

She sighed and laid her cheek against his chest. "Yes. Hold me. All night long."

She kept on his big shirt. He kept on his jeans. He turned out the light, then opened the bedroom door slightly, so the light from the hall kept the room from total darkness. He climbed into bed beside her and took her in his arms.

She started to cry, now that it was all over.

"It's all right," he said. "Get it out of your system. I love you. I've got you."

At last, her tears spent, she lay in his arms, too exhausted to sleep. "Ken?"

"Yes, sugar?"

She took a deep breath. It hurt, because her chest still ached from crying. "Are you—will you tell me about the guns? About you and guns? I couldn't believe he hadn't shot you. I still can't."

She laid her face against the hardness of his bare shoulder. He was silent a moment, then expelled his breath in a long, harsh sigh.

"It's not—" he paused for words "—real nice. But I should tell you. You should know."

She waited for him to begin. She put her hand on his chest to feel the comforting rhythm of his heart. He turned his head to kiss her on the hair, then lay staring up at the darkness.

"I grew up in West Texas. I had me a daddy about like Gordon. He was a ranch hand. He used to—misuse my mama. And us kids. I was the oldest. I'd catch it worst."

He paused again. Nora could feel the reluctance in him, the cost it took for him to speak. "I got to hate him. And—my mother puzzled me—I didn't understand why she never tried to make him stop. She didn't defend us. She didn't defend herself. Never. I resented it.''

He fell silent for another moment. Nora felt his heartbeat speed, grow harder. ''Now, I was big for my age and good at most ranch work, which was good, because I could earn money. But the thing I was best at was shootin'.

''When I was fourteen, we moved again. We were always movin'. He lied about my age so I could quit school and work. Well, he'd always drunk a lot, but he started gettin' particular bad.

''One night, I just had a bellyful of it. He came home and started layin' into my mother. I told him to stop, and he slammed me clear across the room and into a wall. I thought for a minute he'd killed me. Then he started after her again.

''So I got up, I went in my room, and I came out with a gun. And I said, 'If you don't stop, I'll shoot you.' He laughed. He said, 'You don't got the guts, boy.' ''

Nora rose slightly in bed and stared down at his shadowed face. Even in the darkness she could see the pain etched into it. She touched his cheek and a muscle leaped beneath her fingertips.

''So I shot,'' he said matter-of-factly. ''I didn't shoot to kill him, just to stop him. I shot his ear off, is what. He fell down, screamin' I'd made him deaf.''

He swallowed. ''My mother came over to me, and she looked at me like she hated me. I said, 'All I wanted was for him to stop. For once, I wanted him to stop.' ''

"She just stood there, and she looked at me. He was still on the floor, yellin'. And then she said to me, 'He is my *husband*. And your *daddy*.' She slapped me as hard as she could. 'Get out,' she said. 'And don't ever come back.' I did, and I didn't. I got out. I never went back. I never had much stomach for guns since, though."

She shook her head. "Ken," she said softly. "Oh, Ken." She touched his cheek again.

He reached up and took her hand in his, letting both rest on the pillow, lacing his fingers through hers. "It was a long time ago," he said. "It don't—bother me no more. Anymore."

She bit her lip and tears stung her eyes. He squeezed her hand.

"I'm sorry," she whispered. "I'm so sorry."

"No," he said, squeezing her hand again. He put his other hand to her hair and stroked it. "I don't want you feelin' sorry. I'm lucky. I found this ranch, I found the McKinneys. Most important, I found you and Rory. I aim to take care of you. I don't want the old mistakes made again. And they won't be."

"No," she said, laying her hand on his heart again. "They won't be."

He gave her a searching look. "I've heard tell that some men fall in love with a woman 'cause she reminds 'em of their mother. Not me. What I liked about you is you weren't like her at all. You have fight in you. Independence. The courage to leave a bad situation. You love that boy. And you're strong for him."

"I love you," she said, her throat tight. She bent and kissed him. He folded her in his arms and kissed her back, long and deeply.

Then he held her, cradling her head against his chest. "Nora," he said, "I know you're worried. You're worried about how Rory will take this. This is going to be hard on him. And Dottie. But we're going to get through it. Together. I promise you that. We'll get through."

She rubbed her cheek against the crisp hair of his chest. She kissed him over his heart. "Yes," she whispered. "We will. Together. We will."

His fingers touched the top button on the shirt she wore. There was questioning in his touch.

"Yes," she said, her lips against the beat of his heart. "Yes."

They made love, slowly, passionately, intently. It was a way of promising each other that they would indeed survive and endure together, that they would triumph over the past, and that they would create a future as strong and good as love itself.

THE TOWN WONDERED and supposed and gossiped. Then it wondered and supposed and gossiped even more.

It wondered how Dottie faced her son's death with such strength and even something that approached serenity. Nora never told Dottie the uglier details of the night that Gordon died. Ken and Cal vowed never to tell her, either.

Instead, Nora told Dottie only that there had been an altercation, and that fortunately nobody was seriously hurt. But when the police came, Gordon, frightened, tried to run away and was hit.

She told her, as well, what the sheriff had said. That Gordon, dying, might have told the police things that would do great good. He might have given them the information they needed to erase something genuinely evil from the world.

And finally Nora told Dottie that Gordon had spoken repeatedly of his mother at the end. He had wanted her to know he was sorry and that he had been praying a lot.

"He died praying, Dottie," Nora said, her arm around the other woman. "That's how he died, with a prayer on his lips."

Dottie did cry, but the town never saw her do so. She cried in private. Then she dried her tears. Dottie was not the sort to indulge in tears for long.

She stood straight and tall, and she kept her chin high. She told Nora she must do it for Gordon, out of respect for the good he had done in his life. After all, she said, he had been her joy when he was a baby. He had brought Nora into her life, and he had been part of Rory's creation.

Somewhere, Dottie believed, the good part of Gordon still lived and would always live, at peace at last. For the sake of that goodness, she would go on. From the strength of that goodness, she would draw strength.

THE TOWN SUPPOSED that Rory took Gordon's death so much in stride because he was young, and he had not lived with his father for some time—Gordon was probably a peripheral figure in his life.

In truth, Nora and Ken and Dottie, all three, worked as hard as they could with the child, trying to make him understand that there had been good in his father, and that Gordon's death was an unfortunate accident.

Ken took Rory fishing again, alone this time, and told him about the complex feelings he'd had about his own father. Rory listened intently, understanding that sometimes other children had parents that they feared. He began to understand, as well, that when children see too much violence, their own feelings can become violent.

"You just try to work with those feelings," Ken told him. "You try to make something good out of it all, instead of something bad."

Rory nodded. He even talked a bit to Ken about his feelings, feelings he'd never discussed with Nora and Dottie.

Although Dottie was dubious, Nora insisted on taking Rory to talk to a psychologist, to make sure that the boy wouldn't be too confused by too many emotions. After all, he had to deal not only with his father's death, but also with the prospect of a stepfather.

The psychologist said he'd like to talk to Rory once a week for the next few months, but smiled and said to Ken and Nora, "You've very lucky. That little guy's got his head screwed on pretty straight. I think he'll handle things."

Nora had been so happy, she'd kissed Ken on the cheek, right there in the doctor's office.

TOWN GOSSIP FLOURISHED. What had really happened at the lake house that night? Nora, Ken and Cal all remained tight-lipped, and the police refused to release anything except the barest information.

New vistas of gossip opened when, near the end of July, authorities broke up a large gunrunning ring, including several men from Lubbock—one of them Gordon's old partner, Charlie Foss, another a wealthy liquor store owner named Eduardo Chessman.

Was it true that Gordon Jones, with virtually his dying breath, had given police the information to crack the case? Dottie held her head a bit higher. Rory smiled more often than he used to. But none of them—Dottie, Rory, Nora, Ken, Cal—ever said for sure.

So that gossip, too, had its day and died. Other topics captured the town's interest. Bubba Gibson and Billie Jo Dumont were together again—even though there was something haunted in Billie Jo's eyes that hadn't been there before.

Bubba would walk down the street in broad daylight with his arm around Billie Jo, calling her his love woozle. How long would Bubba play the aging Casanova? How long would Billie Jo settle for being the Other Woman? How long would Mary Gibson put up with the scandal of it all?

And was the sheriff, Wayne Jackson, developing a gleam in his dark eye for a certain musically talented young lady of Crystal Creek? Had Shirley Jean Ditmars had her thighs liposuctioned? It certainly seemed that *something* unnatural had happened to them.

Oh, yes, even in a town as small as Crystal Creek, the opportunites for gossip went on forever.

KEN HAD Nora, Rory and Dottie to his house for supper. He was always careful these days to include Rory and Dottie as much as possible. It often made romance awkward, but Nora loved him so much for doing it that it sometimes brought tears to her eyes.

Serena had made another of her famous pizzas, and Cal had saddled up Grumpy, so that Rory could ride a real rodeo horse.

The meal over, dessert finished, Rory went back outside to contemplate this most fabulous beast.

Dottie sighed and pushed her chair away from the table. "It was wonderful." She smiled, patting her stomach with her freckled hand. "Just wonderful."

She looked from Nora to Ken, then back to Nora again. "And I want to tell you something."

Ken and Nora, still lingering over their coffee, looked at her expectantly.

"The two of *you* are wonderful," Dottie said. "Nora, I've told you more than once about how I feel about you. That I love you as much as if you were my own daughter. There's nobody better than my Nora."

Nora colored slightly at the praise. Ken flashed her a private look that said, *That's right. There's nobody better than my Nora.* There was love in his eyes and pride in the curve of his half smile.

Dottie turned to Ken. Her face grew more serious. "But I've never told you, Ken." She paused and clenched her hands together in her lap, but her eyes did not leave his. "I've lost a son. Nothing can replace him. But you've been so good to Nora and to Rory— and bless you, even to me—that I feel like God has given me a second son. You."

Tears rose in Dottie's eyes, but she blinked them back.

"I—I have to say again that—that I don't think of you as replacing Gordon. No one can. But I think of you as a son because I think of Nora as a daughter, and you are as much a part of her—the two of you are as much a part of each other—as heaven intended man and woman to be."

She swallowed, then lifted her head higher, still keeping her gaze trained on his. "There are people in this town," she said, her voice tight, "that will say, 'Dottie Jones is an unfortunate woman. Look at what life's given her.'"

She tossed her head, a rebellious gesture. "I'm here to tell you that's not so. I'm a lucky woman. Much has been taken from me. But look what's been given to me. Nora—Rory—and now you, who love them so much."

The tears shone afresh in her eyes, this time in spite of her blinking. "You love them so," she said, nodding, "that I know they're always safe with you. Safe and cherished and blessed. I could die happy this moment, knowing that they've found you. And for that, I love you."

She ducked her head and angrily brushed away her tears. "There," she muttered. "I've said it. I've been meaning to say it. And after I've gone and said all that, the least you could do is come give me a kiss, you big galoot."

She dug into her pocket, drew out a handkerchief and blew her nose, making a comic *toot* that broke the tension. She stuffed the handkerchief back into her pocket, then stared at Ken. "Well?" she demanded.

He looked thunderstruck, a man unaccustomed to emotions suddenly confronted by unexpected hordes of them. Yet he looked touched, as well. Wordlessly he rose and went to Dottie. He took her hands and drew her up to stand. He gazed down at her, tenderness in his eyes, but something troubled playing on his lips.

"No," Dottie said tartly, as if reading his mind. "I don't expect you to say 'I love you' back to me. It took you five years to work up the nerve to say it to *her*."

She gave Nora a short, ironic nod. "So," Dottie said, staring up at Ken, "just give me a little kiss. And a hug, if you're feeling generous."

Ken bent and kissed her cheek. Dottie smiled shakily, then kissed him back soundly on the sharp line of his jaw.

He put his arms around her, and hugged her. Nora saw the emotion passing over both their faces and bit her lip to keep it from quivering. She, too, blinked back tears.

Instead of breaking his embrace, Ken hugged Dottie to him more tightly. She put her arms around his neck and hugged him back.

"Let's put the pain behind us," Dottie whispered in a husky voice. "Because there's joy ahead. My Nora's going to be happy. My Rory, too. Take care of them always."

"Always," Ken assured her, hugging her again.

"Grandma!" Rory called from the porch, "Come out here—Cal's gonna let me ride with him, and we're gonna rope a calf! Tell Mom and Ken to come, too."

Dottie sighed, a long, shivering exhalation. Then she drew back from Ken. "Now we're all going to have to look at that fool horse again. As if I never saw a horse before! That boy's so taken, I'm afraid he'll turn into a horse himself. Well, let me go first. The two of you take a minute for yourselves.''

She gestured for Nora to rise and come to her. Nora did, and Dottie reached for her hand and put it into Ken's.

"Another thing," she said with false sternness. "The two of you have got to take more time alone. I'm going to insist on it. But for now—" she looked up at Ken and gave him a conspiratorial pat on the arm "—you'd better at least steal a kiss from her. I know you want to. You've been eating her up with your eyes every time you look at her."

"Grandma!" Rory's voice was taut with excitement and impatience. "Come *on!* And get Ken and Mom, too."

"I'm coming," Dottie called, and she started for the door. "But give Ken and your mother a few minutes. They're busy. All right?"

"All right," Rory said with a shade of disgust. "But you come, okay?"

Dottie smiled, almost to herself, opened the door and went outside, leaving Ken and Nora alone.

He put his arm around her shoulders.

She wound her arm around his waist and looked up at him happily.

He smiled. She smiled back.

Neither said anything because they had reached the stage where things didn't always have to be said to be understood.

He bent and kissed her, just as he'd been aching to do all evening. He kissed her so long and so deeply, they both grew dizzy and desirous with it. They could not get enough of kissing.

But then there was a clattering on the porch steps, and they knew too much time had passed, and Rory was impatient for them to come watch him. They broke away and looked at each other, almost shyly, almost guiltily.

Rory burst through the door. "Mom—Ken—come on—come see."

"We're on our way," Ken said with a rueful sigh. One arm around Nora, he started for the door.

But Rory stood still, blocking their path and gazing past them. "Hey, Ken?" he said, his voice quizzical.

"What?"

Rory squinted at the dining room table. At its center, in the midst of the clutter of dishes, stood an oversize pot with a single clover plant growing in it, large and thriving and ready to blossom. Its leaves were verdant, and its buds were parting to show lavender petals.

Rory frowned. "I meant to ask you. How come you got an old clover on your table? Does it mean something or something?"

Ken looked at Nora, then smiled. Keeping one arm around her, he put his other hand on Rory's shoulder and started to guide the boy back outside.

"That clover? It's a long story . . . son."

If you enjoyed
THE THUNDER ROLLS

don't miss

GUITARS, CADILLACS

by Cara West

the next installment of the
Crystal Creek series
coming to you in November

COUNTRY MUSIC—TEXAS STYLE

Jessica Reynolds should be on top of the world. Fans love her music and she is about to embark on a national concert tour. So why isn't her heart singing as loudly as her voice? Could it have something to do with Crystal Creek's own sheriff? Wayne Jackson seems determined to protect Jessie from the advances of overzealous fans...and big-time gamblers. Jessie can't help hoping his reason for hanging out at Zack's during her gigs is more personal than professional.

Watch for it next month wherever Harlequin books are sold.